Eve made her escape out the French doors down to an unlit garden.

A full moon and the sheen of satin nullified her intentions to blend into the greenery. Julian moved as stealthily as he could.

"What are you up to, Miss Reynolds?"

"Me? I'm not the one chasing down ladies in dark gardens! Too much punch, Lord Westleigh?"

Julian's fingers closed around her arm, and he smiled at the dawning comprehension that the minx was truly a worthy opponent.

"I haven't touched a drop. And I am sure of at least one thing." He leaned in, close enough for his breath to move the curls that rested against her ear and send a shiver down her spine. "You . . . are . . . not . . . an . . . innocent."

He leaned close, so ready to taste her, so hungry to have her, but she leaned away from him, pressing her hand against his chest. "Beware, Lord Westleigh, perhaps you are right. . . ." And then he heard her slow, sweet exhale as he covered her mouth with his own. Her lips were soft, yielding reluctantly at first and then responding to his need, fueling it until he was sure he'd forgotten why he'd thought to teach her anything.

Turn the page for rave reviews of sizzling romance by Renee Bernard!

Praise for the first two books in the steamy Mistress trilogy

MADAME'S DECEPTION

"Bernard hits the mark for sizzling-hot romance, developing a well-crafted story around the classic erotic fantasy of the student and her teacher, and spinning an element of suspense into the plotline."

—*Romantic Times*

A LADY'S PLEASURE

Winner of the* Romantic Times *Reviewer's Choice Award for Best First Historical Romance

"I savored every word!"

—Sherrilyn Kenyon,
New York Times bestselling author

"Wonderful. . . . Hot and blatantly sexy, with a wonderful plot that keeps the reader on edge with its many twists and turns. The dynamic, achingly tender ending will gain Ms. Bernard many fans."

—*Winter Haven News Chief* (FL)

"An erotic romance that delivers not only a high degree of sensuality, but a strong plotline and a cast of memorable characters."

—*Romantic Times*

"A great read with many explicit, steamy love scenes and well-developed characters. Highly recommended."

—*Romance Reviews Today*

"Bernard writes like a seasoned star, crafting a hot and passionate romance sizzling with heat and passion. . . . A great read with intriguing twists of fate and scintillating erotic action!"

—FreshFiction.com

and for
Renee Bernard

"Renee Bernard dazzles readers."

—*Booklist*

"Renee Bernard is an author to watch. . . . Her characters are terrifically winning."

—CompuServe Books Forum

Also by Renee Bernard

Madame's Deception

A Lady's Pleasure

"Mischief's Holiday"
in *The School for Heiresses*

A Rogue's Game

RENEE BERNARD

POCKET BOOKS
New York London Toronto Sydney

Pocket Books
A Division of Simon & Schuster, Inc.
1230 Avenue of the Americas
New York, NY 10020

First Pocket Books paperback edition May 2008

For information about special discounts for bulk purchases, please contact Simon & Schuster Special Sales at 1-800-456-6798 or business@simonandschuster.com

Cover illustration by Alan Ayers; hand-lettering by Iskra Johnson

Manufactured in the United States of America

10 9 8 7 6 5 4 3 2 1

ISBN-13: 978-1-4165-2422-9
ISBN-10: 1-4165-2422-3

To Cindy, who will sputter in protest, but Julian owes her his life and this book would never have happened without her. You are the friend who seems to love me no matter what . . . and when we are elderly widows living together to pool our pension checks, I will count on you to make my life interesting by hiding my medications, by insisting that Drambuie has nutritional value, and by making me laugh until I cry.

And to Geoffrey, for always keeping a straight face when I tell him what I'm writing, and for never getting jealous when I fall in love with my heroes—only because I suppose he knows they could never really take him in a fair fight.

And to the Elf, you are my fairy child and you make me believe in magic—every day.

"If you could give up tricks and cleverness, that would be the cleverest trick!"

—Rumi

A Rogue's Game

Chapter One

"Your luck hasn't changed, young man." Lord Shelbrook spread out his winning cards with a gleeful flourish, which Julian Clay, the Earl of Westleigh, deliberately ignored. He was too experienced a player to betray his chagrin at having spent another evening having his pockets picked by his host.

You're a heartless witch, Lady Luck, to save a man's life only to leave him mired in poverty.

"Barnaby, if that were true, I would not be sitting here tonight in your elegant home." Julian tossed his own cards facedown on the table, conceding defeat with a graceful flick of his wrists before stretching his long legs. "But perhaps a change of pace . . ." His words trailed into an artful yawn, demonstrating a show of fatigue and boredom at the game, and effectively ending his self-inflicted torture for the evening.

Shelbrook began to count his small windfall, too distracted to note that his guest's attention had shifted to the large portrait of Lady Shelbrook over the mantel.

Julian studied the icy blue eyes and aristocratic angles of the woman's face, aware that the painter had barely masked the subject's haughty nature. With her golden curls and strawberry complexion, his hostess was exactly the sort of woman who had once held great appeal for him. She was beautiful, sexually voracious, and married.

So why does my stomach churn every time the delectable harpy bats her eyelashes in my direction?

Julian shrugged and stood as Barnaby swept his winnings into his pockets. *God knows I could use the release,* he lectured himself silently—and Beatrice was more than willing when it came to a clandestine romp with one of her husband's acquaintances. Julian's old reputation had preceded him, and his hostess had made it clear that her hospitality came with certain expectations—namely, that he would make her unwitting husband a cuckold on command. He'd naturally obliged her, an easy enough concession to make in light of the lady's enthusiasm, but his own interest had waned after the first less-than-stellar tumble. Hers, on the other hand, had grown. The woman was becoming a pest. But it hardly seemed courteous to complain to a man about his wife's lovemaking when he was getting a fashionable address at which to hang his hat while he was in town, and all in exchange for the "pleasure" of his company. It was the kind of rent he could afford, at least.

He forced himself not to sigh. "I believe I'll head out, Barnaby."

"Care for company?" Lord Shelbrook looked up eagerly, like a child ready for sport.

Julian shook his head. "And have you pick my pockets out in public as well?" He smiled to soften the blow, unwilling to insult his current host by declaring that he couldn't bear to hear more of Lord Shelbrook's insipid stories of his "wild young days." Shelbrook's hospitality, though occasionally irksome, was posh and well timed.

And timing was everything.

Barnaby's happy countenance dimmed a bit, but he recovered quickly. "Very well. Off with you, then! I wouldn't expect a young man like you to linger in a dusty house with an old married man when London's entertainments await you."

"You aren't decrepit just yet, friend." Julian clapped him on the shoulder, soothing Shelbrook's pride. "Another night?"

"By all means!" Barnaby rang for a carriage, and within moments, Julian had made good his escape.

Before leaning back against the cushions to

gather his wayward thoughts, he instructed the driver to head toward a fashionably dangerous part of town. His return to London had been just as he'd envisioned it, but nothing felt the same. He'd expected to simply return to his life and resume enjoying the delights of each moment as he had before. In the past, Julian had made no effort to account for the productivity of his days. Instead, he'd savored the thrill of good cards in his hands, or an eager woman at his side. He'd cared for nothing but the pursuit of pleasure and his next social engagement.

Until now.

The carriage lurched, and Julian winced at the twinge in his side, shifting his weight to relieve the dull, familiar ache. He'd spent too many idle hours this evening trying to wheedle a few winning hands from Shelbrook, and his recently healed wound wouldn't let him forget it. Julian wasn't the kind of man to dawdle over his recovery, and after months on his back and limping around the countryside chafing at the restrictions of his injury like a chained bear, he'd been only too happy to make his escape from his doctor's endless coddling. London beckoned, and he wasn't going to let the vague discomfort that lingered in his side stand in his way. *Hell, it probably rankles Drake more than my ribs pain me to think that I, his worst enemy, saved his beloved Merriam's life . . . and he's in my debt to this day.*

A bittersweet victory, at best. The scars he carried would always remind him of the fateful night he'd stepped in front of a bullet intended for the Duchess of Sussex.

It could have been worse, though, Julian thought as he subtly moved again to protect his right side. His archnemesis and former friend, Drake Sotherton, the Duke of Sussex, had planned to bury Julian with debt but had relented in light of those recent events. The slate had been wiped clean, and Julian's complete financial ruin had been narrowly avoided, but neither man had had any desire to take their reconciliation any further. Too many years had passed and they'd inflicted too much pain on each other to repair their friendship; besides, Julian acknowledged that he was altogether the guiltier party in the matter, and he wasn't foolish enough to seek forgiveness from Drake for cuckolding him with his first wife, Lily.

Ah, Lily! You'd have deliberately made a villain out of a monk to win a wager for a shilling, and you'd still have looked innocent to the world.

She'd brought out the worst in him, and he'd wanted her for all the wrong reasons. Only after facing his own death could he admit that what he had shared with Lily had never even remotely resembled love. The tangle of the tragedy still amazed him, but he dismissed the sordid affair with Lily from his mind. The past was long gone. There was nothing to do but face the present and the future. Julian had been touted as a hero for fending off the duke's murderous servant after she'd confessed to killing Lily, and he had returned to London to discover a mountain of invitations from eager members of the Ton. The Earl of Westleigh was now a much-sought-after commodity for the social season, and he marveled at the strange twists and turns of fate that guarded his reputation. He was hardly angelic, but no one seemed to recall this fact when guest lists were drafted. Julian's notoriety only added to his appeal, while Drake was still practically persona non grata for scandalously seducing a shy little widow, openly keeping her as his mistress and then marrying the poor creature.

Julian shook his head. All sins were relative, and he'd been extremely lucky that the worst of his own shortcomings had missed public notice. Still, he'd survived only to find his pockets empty despite Sotherton's generosity. Years at the gaming tables had won him little, and now reality loomed. He had a title and lands, but no substantial income.

Luckily, the Ton remained ignorant of the dire extremes of his financial situation. Being relatively broke wasn't uncommon amongst the Peerage, but his opportunities would be limited if the meager state of his credit became a topic of public banter. The invitations on his morning trays would evaporate and his circumstances would disintegrate rapidly.

No one in the Ton knew (though a few friends might have guessed that his "cupboards were bare"), but Julian wasn't the kind of man to waste sleep or time worrying over the specters of scandal and bankruptcy that haunted his steps. Nothing was going to keep him from the Season ahead.

I'll make the best of it and laugh in the face of disaster. After all, isn't that what heroes do?

He would have to take his cache of goodwill from playing the hero and use it to create opportunities to recover his fortune. Either Lady Luck would start to smile a bit more sweetly in his direction—or he might have to consider the unthinkable. Julian shuddered. *A marriage of convenience to some dull, wealthy dove and God help me. I think I'd rather the bullet hadn't missed its mark.*

Not that he wasn't aptly suited to the role of fortune hunter, but he found the very thought of it nauseating. It was one thing to seduce the lovely women of the Ton for the sheer thrill of the hunt—and another game entirely to track down a rich prize for his survival. Light pockets didn't mean a man couldn't afford a touch of pride. He'd never wasted time in the past considering his personal honor, but apparently even the Earl of Westleigh had his limits.

Better to risk ruin in games of chance, he intoned silently, than the ruin a wife could wreak.

Matrimony seemed an encumbrance at best, and at worst . . . An image of Beatrice in his dressing room just yesterday afternoon, on her hands and knees begging for his cock, flitted past his mind's eye. He'd experienced firsthand how easily a married woman could be "led astray," and he'd wickedly encouraged more indiscretions than he wanted to admit to. He'd never wasted any pity on the husbands, feeling certain that any fool blind enough to while away hours in brothels and clubs without realizing that his wife wouldn't wish to enjoy her own adventures deserved what he got. Julian knew full well that a woman's capacity for pleasure matched a man's—no matter what the crusty pillars of society touted.

And now that he was a "selfless hero," he didn't think there was a bedroom door in London he couldn't breach.

As the carriage moved through the streets, Julian felt unsettled. A restless mood undermined his usual confidence. Courtesans with soft hands awaited him on silk sheets, ready to soothe the fire in his blood, but a new reluctance overtook him. Those same soft hands would be outstretched for payment, and he'd tossed the last of his coins onto Shelbrook's table that evening. He could request more credit, but his appetite waned at the thought of owing money for sexual favors.

The impulse to visit his old haunts passed, and

Julian called to the driver to redirect him to a different address—one engraved on an invitation he'd received earlier in the week and had almost tossed away. His mood lifted as the carriage turned around. Julian took a deep, slow breath. It was time to venture out into the respectable world and see what entertainments his peers had to offer.

After all, a man could only lose for so long.

"What a dear little thing you are!" Lady Morrington repeated again, her blue-gray curls bobbing sympathetically as she led her newest young friend toward a table near the windows. "To put up with such tiresome company!"

"Not at all," Eve Reynolds lied sweetly. "You are too kind to allow me to impose on your game." She gave each of the aging biddies at the small table a look of awe and admiration, as if she'd felt honored to be in their glorious presence. It was a performance too subtle for the theater but well suited to the intimate stage of an evening with the Peerage. The three women preened in response, openly pleased to find a young, respectful lady so aware of her place and with so much apparently to learn about their card games.

"It is no imposition," Mrs. Cuthbert pronounced as she reached up to pat Eve's slender hand. "I only wish we'd a few more younger guests to keep you better entertained. I cannot think that Sophie,

Margaret, and I are lively enough company for you."

It was true that Mrs. Margaret Wickett's card party wasn't a great draw for the younger set, but Eve's uncle had chosen it for exactly that reason. The small, fashionable gathering was tailor-made for their purposes. A dozen card tables were spaced throughout the gold and green salon, allowing guests to play or mingle about to watch the different groups. Unlike the rowdier gambling venues of the city, these elegant private parties were more comfortable and intimate, so few guests really worried about their purses. They were more likely to relax and wager without fear of the consequences, confident in the knowledge that the games were strictly for fun. So while her uncle, Mr. Warren Reynolds, made an overt show of bonding with the men just two tables away, loudly winning and losing in equal measure, she'd been quietly left to play the role of an inexperienced and naïve young lady with the older women, laying the trap once again.

"You are the very best of company, Mrs. Cuthbert, and I only hope I can follow your lead." Eve lowered her eyes to her hands, wishing for a brief moment that she'd been a thousand leagues away, far from Mrs. Wickett's grand salon, the card parties, and the endless games her uncle expected her to play.

"Isn't she a dear little thing?" Lady Morrington

intoned. The ladies nodded in agreement, and Mrs. Cuthbert waved another invitation to the open chair next to her.

The matter settled unanimously, Eve demurely took her place to complete the foursome. The cards were dealt, and she retrieved her cards only after the others had collected theirs. The feel of the cards in her hands reassured her, and an odd calm settled over her as she began the ritual of play. Through her lashes, she noted the ladies' telling expressions and mannerisms as they studied their cards and anticipated either victory or defeat. After only a few rounds, Eve had a complete command of her opponents. She knew when they would yield and when they would increase their wagers, when they thought they had a hand of great strength and when a show of finesse might have served them better as the opportunities of good leads came and went. They were not without skill, and Lady Morrington, despite her propensity to prattle about her extreme "shy and delicate nature," was a potential tiger when it came to her tricks.

But she was also the wealthiest woman at the party and Eve's primary quarry.

Time passed quickly, and Eve did her best to win sparingly and lose with notable grace, letting her partner garner the glory. It was not as simple a task as it appeared on the surface, but she wasn't new to the nuances of "nearly" winning—and the women seemed amused and touched by her sincere efforts to keep up with their lively pace of play.

A few more hands, dear ladies, and then we shall see if this was money well spent or—

"Is that the Earl of Westleigh?" Mrs. Cuthbert said in a whisper that could have carried across a battlefield. Eve lost the thread of her thoughts as she watched the women titter and blush like schoolgirls, gaping at the man in question, who, Eve guessed from the direction of their stares over her own head, was still in the doorway. A rustle of similar exclamations swept through the room, and Eve bit her lower lip to hide her frustration as Mrs. Cuthbert continued, "Margaret! However did you manage it?"

Mrs. Wickett blushed before putting her cards down. "Whatever do you mean? Now, if you'll excuse me, I'll make sure Mr. Wickett doesn't get a chance to make the earl regret his decision to come."

Eve deliberately refused to turn and look behind her at the fascinating paragon that could make Mrs. Wickett rush from her chair. She was sure that the man wouldn't appreciate another person openly staring at him.

"What luck! I've never known the earl to bother with a gathering such as this, but then again . . . perhaps his brush with death has taught him to appreciate the finer things in life." Lady Morrington set her own cards down to await her friend's return.

Eve's eyes widened at Lady Morrington's strange pronouncement. She was positive that she'd missed a critical step. *Brush with death?* "Why would any gentleman avoid good company such as this?"

Mrs. Cuthbert answered without taking her eyes off the scene unfolding across the room behind Eve. "It's quite a saga, but let us just say summarily that we were too staid and boring for the vibrant young Lord Westleigh. But it seems he has had a change of heart."

Lady Morrington nodded. "I overheard Lady Shelbrook say he's been the consummate gentleman and guest since his return from the country. I understand he is staying in their townhome while hunting for a new house of his own in London. But she seemed quite taken with the man."

"What woman wouldn't be?" Mrs. Cuthbert noted sagely, shocking Eve a little with her open appreciation of the mysterious Earl of Westleigh. A dozen questions rattled forward in her mind, but she knew better than to voice them. Her interest could easily be misinterpreted, and she had no desire to have these women think her overeager on the subject of death-defying noblemen who interrupted a perfectly good evening's work. But the urge to turn in her seat was almost more than she could bear.

Damn it. Whoever he is, he needs to sit down somewhere and let Mrs. Wickett return to the table so that we can finish this hand! I was so close!

At last their hostess returned and took her place, her cheeks decidedly rosier. "I invited him to sit at the colonel's table, though he said he wished to observe a while before settling in."

"He's *observing* our young friend, it seems," Lady Morrington said with great enthusiasm. "What a delightful turn!"

Eve knew it was her own imagination that sent a shiver down her spine, as if his gaze had actually been touching her skin and making her body react. A flush crept across her cheeks, but she resolutely ignored it and studied her cards. To turn now would only fuel the women's gossip and spark a humiliating conversation about fated meetings and the fanciful attachments of youth. He was still behind her and out of view, but she decided at that moment that if he'd been Adonis himself, he wouldn't have gotten a single glance from this earthbound female. Eve Reynolds had far more important things on her mind.

"Speaking of turns, was it not your lead, Mrs. Wickett?" Eve asked with her best show of shy manners. "I confess, I've almost forgotten which suit is trump for this hand!"

While looks were exchanged, the ladies apparently decided to forfeit the chance to tease her any further, though none of them failed to indicate to Eve at every moment where the earl was standing in the room as he observed the players. Like groundhogs watching a hawk overhead, their gazes were continually drawn to the latest arrival to the party. Eve struggled to keep them on task.

"Shall we re-deal and begin again?" Eve asked.

"No need, dear thing," Lady Morrington replied. "Margaret, it's your lead, and this time do try and read Mrs. Cuthbert's mind."

The women laughed at the jest, and Mrs. Cuthbert nodded. "I am staring at my cards as pointedly as I can. Ah, the elusive rapport of a good partner!"

Play resumed, but Eve couldn't shake the sensation that she was being studied from afar. She managed her cards by rote skill and finally gave in to the gnawing need to see for herself this paragon of a rogue who had avoided good company until the specter of death had driven him to Mrs. Wickett's salon.

If only so that I can set this foolish curiosity aside and concentrate!

Male laughter at her uncle's table gave her the perfect excuse to shift back and steal a subtle look at the room's other occupants. She'd expected to pick him out after a quick search, but she almost gasped out loud at the shock of finding him instantly—for there was no mistaking the "vibrant young earl," and his gaze was most decidedly locked on her.

He was the most unnervingly handsome man she had ever seen. He was a study in gold, with his tawny blond hair and eyes the color of molten amber. Even his skin betrayed an unfashionable tan that added to her impression of vibrant power. Tall and well formed, he looked like a Thoroughbred stallion straining at the slips, trapped in a room full of dodgy ponies—so completely out of place that she immediately forgave the older women for acting like blushing schoolgirls. After all, she'd turned to peek at him, and, like a dunce, she'd gotten caught in the act.

All pretenses evaporated under the intensity of his study, and Eve didn't think the Earl of Westleigh was the sort of man to miss even a casual observer's glances. His eyes never wavered from hers, and she felt a shiver at the danger. Long seconds strung together, and Eve was aware that with each tick of the clock, the threat was growing. Still, she felt unable to look away. The Earl of Westleigh was the most breathtakingly gorgeous man she'd ever seen. His look was an inquiry so pure and primal that every fiber in her ached to answer him. She lifted her chin defiantly, challenging him to be the first to end it. *A gentleman would cease this scandalous study and let a girl gather her wits!*

But *this* gentleman had other ideas.

His golden brown eyes telegraphed amusement

at her dilemma, as if he'd been enjoying her discomfort, and a new wave of restless heat danced over her skin.

"Oh, my!" Mrs. Cuthbert's exclamation finally broke through, and Eve turned back in her chair, facing the ladies with a genuine sense of embarrassment.

"I-I see that the . . . I hope I haven't held up the game," she finished weakly, fighting off the sensation that she had just been floating a few inches above the floor.

The ladies laughed. "Aren't you a dear little thing!" Lady Morrington said with a gleam in her eye. "I believe I can speak for all of us when I say that our group will seem all the duller for lack of your company."

Oh, God. She's dismissing me, and Uncle Warren will have a hysterical fit when he realizes I've failed to—

Mrs. Cuthbert chimed in merrily, "I know you speak for me! I'm not one for gossip, but I should hate to miss a firsthand account of Miss Reynolds's social season—especially now."

Lady Morrington nodded decisively, her scheme confirmed. "I realize that cards are a dreadful waste of your youthful hours, but I insist that you join us for our Tuesday afternoon gatherings. It is a bit of whist, or whatever game suits us, but we would love to include you. It is nothing so grand as this, but perhaps if your uncle will allow it—"

"Yes, thank you. I will ask him," Eve said.

Victory.

Relief pushed away the panic that had choked her at the thought of her uncle's reaction at her botching this first critical step in his ambitious plans. It was more than she'd hoped for—a standing invitation to a weekly game of cards and an entrée into their small wealthy circle. The earl's presence had probably been the deciding factor in Lady Morrington's spontaneous proposal. The gossiping old birds were hoping to have a front seat at the handsome earl's pursuit of her, apparently mistaking his lustful looks for gentlemanly interest. They were going to be disappointed, but Eve wasn't about to be the one to spoil her victory by telling them. She made sure her expression revealed none of her emotions. Normally, she was a master of the art of disguising her true feelings, but now . . .

He was still there.

It was easy to recall the look in his eyes and to feel that heat uncoil within her again at the thought of the wicked invitation she'd read in his gaze. The older women's reactions were no mystery. It seemed the Earl of Westleigh was not a man any woman could effortlessly ignore. But Eve was not about to melt into a puddle and yield an evening's victory to a distracting rogue with golden eyes and smoldering good looks. She had waited too long for this Season and a chance for freedom.

Look your fill, sir. I'm no simpering debutante to faint when you smile.

Julian deliberately chose a table in proximity to the dark-haired young woman who had sparked his curiosity. He'd almost missed her at first, but something about the way she held herself . . . Truly, she wasn't his type—he favored the more classically lovely English roses, with their golden curls and pink, creamy curves, but there was something about her that compelled a thorough study. With pale skin and coal black hair, she had a vague, exotic air about her. Julian decided that while she was no stunning beauty, with her unfashionably wide, albeit lush mouth and high cheekbones, she was lovely nonetheless. She lacked the delicate features and heart-shaped face that seemed to be in vogue, but her eyes were undeniably stunning. Fringed with long, black eyelashes, they were a sapphire blue he hadn't expected. This was no porcelain doll. She was far too vibrant and unique, despite the demure cut and dark blue color of her gown. Her figure seemed sleek, though he could only guess at her height. The more he stared, the more she seemed like a gypsy queen sitting there so calmly among the colorless people of the Ton. She was young, but she didn't appear to be frivolous or naïve. She'd fearlessly stared him down, and by the look of her play, she was equally fearless when it came to the turns of a game.

As he'd strolled the salon, it had been her play that had held his rapt attention. She was graceful and controlled. And now, as he covertly continued to study the dove, he was amazed at the subtle workings of her strategies.

Or I'm reading too much into the lamb's cards because somehow the sight of her lips is making my mouth water—so ready to taste . . . He wondered how long the façade of polite civility would last if they were alone, if she would tremble coyly before giving in to a sensual nature she attempted to hide from the world. Or would she ignite at the first stroke of his tongue, the first sweep of his hands?

He shook his head and glanced at the dismal cards in his hand, swallowing a grimace as he barely managed to break even. A change of venue had done little for his luck, but by God, the mystery woman was worth a few more miserable hands.

His opponents chattered mindlessly and all too readily offered to share the information he sought about the exotic young bird in their midst. Over each spread of cards, another tantalizing detail was revealed. She was a debutante. Her uncle, a Mr. Warren Reynolds, was a man of means, though no one at the table was sure of his industry or the source of his vast fortune. Mr. Reynolds had lofty connections and had been introduced by enough of the Ton that he and his niece were welcome amidst the bluest bloods of London—if not by right of birth, then by invitation. Her uncle sat three tables away, and Julian noted that the man kept a better eye on his niece than he did on his cards.

Miss Eve Reynolds. What a puzzle you are . . .

As if he'd spoken her name aloud, he watched the subtle stiffening of her back—as if she thought to play the prude and ward off his attentions. From a loose gathering on her head, long sausage curls trailed down her neck to hang down between her shoulder blades, each lustrous black spiral begging to be touched. He speculated about the length of her hair, if he was to remove all the pins and combs. A fleeting image of fingering the smallest wisps back from her delicate ear, or raking his hands through the soft silk of her hair so that he could bury his face in the fragrance, sent his blood pulsing into the pit of his stomach. Julian knew he was on the brink of an arousal that would trap him at the table no matter how bad the cards.

An inconvenient moment to be distracted, sadly. So much for the advantage of a clear head! But for the first time in his life, he felt disconnected from the game. The thrill of the chance to win a fortune was hollow, and the cards at his fingertips felt cold.

His brow furrowed at the sensation. Julian tried to remember another occasion when he'd felt indifferent to chance. Even earlier in the dull quiet of Barnaby's study, he'd experienced the sweet hope of winning and the dance of the cards across green velvet had commanded his attention.

Now all he could think of was the debutante nearby and wonder if Lady Luck wasn't toying with him after all.

"Another hand, Lord Westleigh?" the gentleman dealing asked politely.

His gaze flickered back to her profile, and his smile was pure sin. "At the very least."

Chapter Two

"Who was he? Does he know you from somewhere?"

Eve kept her hands tucked inside her wrap to hide the defensive clenching of her fingers against the satin. She and her uncle were just a few steps inside the luxurious foyer of the town house they'd leased for the Season, and she wished for the thousandth time that her uncle was a less observant man. "Mrs. Cuthbert said his name is Julian Clay, the Earl of something-or-other. Westleigh, I believe. And no, Uncle Warren, I can't imagine we've crossed paths before tonight."

He shook his head, unconvinced. "He seemed to be looking at you quite intently, as if he recognized you."

"Oh, please! He was clearly out of his element

and I was the only woman in the room without dust in my hair. The man was just surveying the scene and hoping for a bit of flirtation to enliven his evening." She held out her wrap to their elderly butler as he came forward to greet them. "Good evening, Barnett. I hope we didn't keep you up too late tonight."

"Not at all, Miss Reynolds." He smiled as he took her things. "A pleasant night for you, I hope."

Warren Reynolds brusquely waved him away, dismissing him before unbuttoning his coat. Only when the servant's steps had faded to silence did he continue. "Well, I can't blame the earl for hoping. I'd forgotten how dull these evenings can get. But you played it rightly. Better to continue to mind your manners, girl, and keep any notions of flirting well in hand. These people get one whiff of impropriety from a lady and I swear they puff up like parrots and we'll be deaf from the squawking."

He didn't need to voice the threat. Eve kept her eyes level with his, aware that any sign of nerves could be misread as guilt—and Uncle Warren wasn't the kind of man to miss much. "Lord Westleigh is nothing to me, and frankly, I think you'd say that he served his purpose tonight."

"Did he?"

"Bless him, yes." The phrase was Warren's own, and it made him smile. Eve felt a weight shift off her chest. His mood was bound to improve with her good news. "He distracted the ladies, and while they were entertained, I managed to get a good handle on their habits and tells. So you see," she went on playfully, "even an earl has his uses now and again."

Warren laughed. "On the rare occasion! Good girl!" He sobered, and she could guess at each turn of his thoughts, so familiar was she with her uncle's thinking after five years of his guardianship and "mentoring." "There could be an opportunity here. I'll make some inquiries about this Earl of Westleigh and see if there is a bit of low-hanging fruit to harvest along our way."

"Along our way? I thought the low-hanging fruit was the point entirely."

"Not necessarily!" he corrected her cheerfully. "I am wondering if we cannot find you a rich husband this Season. What a coup that would be, eh? And what a joy to see you happily wed!"

"A-a husband?" She quickly swallowed a hundred arguments about why any man deemed a good match by her uncle was likely to be a disastrous choice. It wasn't *her* happiness he meant to secure. Uncle Warren wanted a match wealthy enough to ensure that he could retire in luxury, and her preferences did not weigh in the scheme.

Not that she was foolish enough to think that pleading her feelings would make a difference.

"I know I swore off matchmaking after . . . well,

you know—but leave it to me, my dear. I'll find just the right bird for you, and then you'll have your own luxurious salons where you can pluck wealthy feathers whenever you wish!" He squeezed her fingers affectionately. "What do you say to that?"

"I think I'm allergic to feathers, Uncle Warren, wealthy or otherwise." Eve did her best to redirect his thoughts. "Besides, it was a truly successful night. The ladies have invited me to more of their games."

"Money well spent then, money well spent! A few games to ripen them, and in a few short weeks, we'll have the income we need." He absentmindedly kept hold of her hand. "We're bleeding cash here, but it will all pay off if you do as you're told! I know we've had a few scrapes and bruises along the way, but this time we can't fail. I've planned it all out, Eve, and this time, you'll see—I've thought of everything!"

"I know, Uncle Warren. But it's late. Let's talk tomorrow. It's been a long evening, and I think I'll just head to bed."

He shook his head but finally released her hand to let her go. "Sleep, then. Tomorrow is another day to play, Eve!"

She nodded and watched him cheerfully retreat to his rooms. Then she headed for the stairs, taking up one of the lit oil lamps on the side table. The house was completely modernized with gaslights and even electricity in the front rooms, but Uncle Warren had convinced the skeleton staff they employed that he was merely eccentric and wished those conveniences to be used only on the ground-floor rooms and where necessary below stairs. Only the areas of the house a guest might see were kept lit and comfortable—besides his own private rooms, of course. He'd lectured them all that he didn't want his headstrong niece to be "softened" by city living, citing some foolish doctor's quote on the bracing qualities of old-fashioned hardships. Rubbish, all of it, but Eve knew that he believed there wasn't a shilling to spare for frills where no one else could see them. Besides, her uncle wasn't the kind of man to waste a penny on what he deemed "feminine comforts." So there was no hot water or gas to the upper floors, and Eve did her best to act as if this had been perfectly normal. She had to ring for a maid to help her dress, but otherwise she never bothered the small staff.

It didn't help to point out that the extra wages he paid to bribe the servants to keep them from gossiping about his odd frugality could have been applied to those "comforts." It was no use applying logic to the workings of her uncle's mind, and she was too experienced with his stubborn quirks to waste time complaining about the arrangements.

Pride and fear fueled his unpredictable actions, and Eve understood the specter of terror that waited around every corner for both of them. Their lives were not what they appeared to be, and the strain of constantly performing wore on both of them. Uncle Warren wasn't easy at the best of times. He was as intractable as a badger when it came to his schemes, and she knew better than to openly tug at the loose threads of his elaborate strategies. But now she marveled that his good mood had held this long, with a decade of hoarded and hard-won money on the line in this "greater game." He'd decided to put every pence they had into one blazing London Season of gambling and forever escape the web of lies and debt he'd left in his wake.

Her uncle wasn't an intentionally cruel man. Charming, yet selfish and blind to anyone's sensibilities but his own, he'd simply decided years ago that his loving niece should be thrilled to help him in any scheme his warped imagination concocted. Especially when he'd realized how handy she could be at games of chance. And now, on this last glorious Season of fleecing London's elite, Eve doubted it would ever occur to him that she wouldn't happily marry his choice of pigeon to keep her only living relative in fine brandy and soft velvets for the rest of his life—no matter what it took.

She sighed at the sweet luxury of being alone and unobserved for the first time in hours. *The curtain falls and I could dance a jig if I wished . . .*

She smiled, carefully making her way up the risers, wishing she hadn't relinquished her wrap to Barnett so quickly. It was a drafty house, and the summer evening was unseasonably cool. The oil lamp's glow was low, but she preferred it that way. The dim light made it easier for her eyes to adjust to the gloom; even in the relative safety of the house she preferred not to have her senses dulled. The upper floors were supposed to be deserted, but Eve was always wary that a curious servant might stray to poke about. Bribes were all well and good, but she understood that the lure of the forbidden could be more of a temptation than any amount of coin. Eve reached the solid wooden door at the back of the hallway and stepped inside her room with a sense of relief. Setting the lamp down, she moved about the room and prepared for bed without noting the room's Spartan shabbiness. She undressed herself with the skills of a woman unused to assistance, brushing out the creases and hanging the gown immediately on her wardrobe to air it out. Layer after layer was carefully removed and tended to without ceremony, until she ended up in her plain white cotton nightgown, stockings, and robe.

The vanity table was empty except for her brush and comb, a small box for hairpins, and a single vial of perfume. She had a few cosmetics in the center drawer, but for once, she'd agreed with her uncle when it had come to his decision to keep things simple. After all, she was supposed to be a shy and unassuming debutante, apparently not suited to the glamour of the ballroom, destined for spinsterhood, poor thing! It was a role she'd successfully managed in the past, but tonight . . .

As Eve sat to take down her long curls, she made a careful study of her reflection and wondered what it was that had caught the Earl of Westleigh's attention. Not her beauty, she decided. She was anything but beautiful, in her opinion, with her full, wide mouth and strong features. She wrinkled her nose, wishing it had been a bit narrower and more pert, before catching her own glance in the mirror and smiling at the useless musings. Her father had always insisted that she had her mother's bewitching looks and coloring. She was attractive enough, and beauty was not necessarily an asset when it came to the role she currently played. It could draw too much attention, and there was a very real danger in the scrutiny that followed.

So what had drawn the earl's golden eyes to hers? What had inspired his hungry gaze?

She retrieved a small bottle of lotion from the drawer and worked some of the cream into her hands as she puzzled over the question. She'd spoken earlier to deflect her uncle's suspicions, but perhaps she'd gotten it right. Youth alone might have accounted for the earl's singling her out. She was often a slight oddity at the older, more staid parties they deliberately chose, but her uncle usually explained that she was a philosophical soul who hated dancing and preferred the company of his friends. The tale opened the door for sympathetic looks or a distracting game of speculation as people tried to determine if she'd once had her heart broken or if they knew someone who might suit her and draw her back into younger society.

In any case, whatever stir she'd caused by staring the man down in public had no doubt been long forgotten by Lord Westleigh. The earl probably made a game of trying to disrupt the composure of young women, no doubt with an arrogant understanding of the impact his looks could have on the faint of heart. She'd run across such men before, though admittedly, none of the previous peacocks had been nearly as handsome as they'd believed themselves to be.

Julian Clay was altogether more handsome than any one man had a right to be. But she was past the encounter now, and no matter how enticing he'd appeared, she doubted she would see him again. After all, the ladies had made it clear that they'd been surprised at his attendance because he usually preferred more manly and lively haunts.

And just as she'd told her uncle, the earl truly had unintentionally done her a service, though it occurred to her that it went beyond giving the ladies a nice excuse to include her in their weekly games—Lord Westleigh had also captured her uncle's attention, and that might prove to be an incredible windfall.

Because for once, she had a scheme of her own that her uncle hadn't the faintest inkling of—and if all went well, this would not only be her first London Season; it would also be her last.

Over the last few years, her uncle's grand schemes had varied only slightly, depending on the European city they'd resided in. Generally, his schemes had meant integrating themselves into the highest social circles they'd been able to manage and engaging in endless games of chance, taking their wealthy friends' money until either their friends' pockets had been emptied or she and her uncle had been discovered. As she'd matured and demonstrated her uncanny skills at the card tables, Eve had found herself more and more entangled in the greedy web her uncle delighted in weaving.

At first, she hadn't seen it. She'd been sixteen when her father had died and hadn't thought much about why they'd moved so frequently and never settled in one place like other people. All her life, she'd just trusted her wonderful, vivacious father to return from his adventures and parties with delightful stories, and never worried about their peripatetic existence. After his death, there had been Uncle Warren, so much like his brother, bon vivant and charming, and in her grief, his carefree manner had been a soothing balm. So little had changed—at first. Hotels and guest houses, trunks and valises, and endless entertainments had been the fabric of their days and nights. But unlike her father, Uncle Warren had included her at the parties, and she'd loved the sensation of being a part of his grown-up world, which had been so enchanting and decadent. He'd encouraged her to play at the tables—a novelty to their hosts—and a lucrative new channel of income had slowly manifested itself over time.

But her uncle was more reckless than her father had ever been—and, ultimately, more ruthless. Time had passed and she'd finally been forced to face the truth.

Nothing was beneath him. Nothing.

Eve sighed. No matter how hard she tried, she couldn't abandon her conscience. No matter how many times her uncle insisted that gambling was simply a means to the divine end of seeing the mighty brought lower, she couldn't shake the guilty sensation that always came after emptying an opponent's pockets. Her one friend in the world, Jane Kingsley, had always warned her about gambling and its hidden dangers, but even Jane didn't understand. The alternative was unthinkable. After all, when your own pockets are already empty, no one is merciful when you lose.

It would have made her existence so much more pleasant if she'd been able to embrace her place in the world, but instead she'd quietly fought her uncle when she'd been able. Once she'd tried to actively guide him toward respectability and a solid marriage of his own. After all, he was the only family she had. But it had been an impossible cause.

Instead, at nineteen, when the chance to escape and seize a life of her own had presented itself in the romantic city of Venice, she'd taken it. She'd stumbled and lost her heart to the worst kind of rogue—the kind of rogue who disguises himself as a gentleman. Promises of marriage and a real home far removed from the wandering circus of life with her uncle had made Eve innocently surrender to passion and "true love." *He* had been so elegant and sophisticated, handsome and kind . . .

At least until Mr. Dante Moore had unkindly left her bedded, unwed, and humiliated.

Uncle Warren had taken her back with solemn words of comfort, swearing himself to silence on the matter and adding another bond between them, confident that she wouldn't slip away from him again now that he was the keeper of her worst secrets.

He'd patted her hand and calmly explained, "You'll have a clearer head for cards if you forget all these romantic illusions and silly philosophies women invent when left to their own devices. Trust me, dearest."

But trusting anyone ever again had seemed impossible to her.

In the two years since the disaster of Venice, their erratic path across Europe had kept Eve busy and distracted as her uncle had tried to secure his elusive fortunes from whatever unlucky host had invited them in. Eve had grown to dislike all of it, but without funds of her own, or allies she could trust, she'd been forced to simply comply and play the roles he'd demanded—naïve schoolgirl, icy harridan, or damsel in distress—and wait for a chance at escape of her own making.

But now, at long last, they were in London, and Uncle Warren had decided to risk on one huge play everything that remained from the fortunes she'd acquired for him in the past few years. He had set himself up as a wealthy industrialist and obtained letters of introduction and invitations from a few of their previous unwitting victims to make sure they would rub just the right elbows. The games would increase in stakes as they worked their way up the social ladder. With Eve's talents, it would be the Season that would set them up for life.

For life . . . or until my uncle spends it all on women and brandy. That should give the man a year or two before he comes up with another plan to drag us off to Spain or France or who knows where yet again. Unless he really can trick someone into a match—and then it's a life of loveless submission for me. She shuddered and set the brush down before pulling her wrap more tightly around her shoulders. *That's* his *plan, not mine!*

After all, this was England, and she still remembered her father's voice and the warm glow in his eyes when he spoke of his native country. She'd adored her father. He was so jolly and sweet that it had been easy to mistake all his vices for virtues. He'd been popular with his rich friends, and no one had seemed to mind his uneven finances, incessant gambling, or his personal quest for the perfect waistcoat. When he'd died, she'd unpacked dozens of waistcoats in every imaginable hue—many he'd never even worn. *Not two coins to press together to bequeath me, but he left behind a wardrobe a prince would have envied.*

If her father had aspired to find a good match for her, he would never have left her heart out of the equation or viewed it as just another scheme. Although her father had taught her how to play cards, he had never intended her to use the knowledge as a stealthy weapon at the tables. But he had always talked about bringing her to London for her debut, so at least this once, Uncle Warren had fulfilled his brother's wishes.

Finally, after five years of nomadic wandering,

she was the closest she could recall to having a real home. And this time, it would happen under her own power and without relying on any man to rescue her and give her the things she desired most. Instead, she'd decided to seize her own opportunity and make her own way in the world. And so her plan had come to life, and Eve knew that this chance might never come again.

If her uncle was distracted and seemed to be considering how an earl might play into his scheme, let him. If he thought Westleigh the bigger pigeon, he wouldn't watch her elderly doves as closely. So much the better for her. Even if he wasted his time pushing suitors in her path, she was confident that she could discreetly discourage any offers.

She smiled at the simplicity of it. Her uncle could dream of coronets and banknotes all he wanted. It wasn't as if their connections would get them into the earl's livelier circles, so she was inherently safe from his unsettling gaze and distracting good looks. All she needed was one good Season. One good Season to leave her uncle's pockets full to assuage her guilt at abandoning him. One good Season to create her own precious nest egg and make her own way in the world to see if she couldn't have a very different life of her own.

She'd already begun, though on a very small scale. Any cash she'd won at the tables she'd dutifully turned over. What her uncle didn't know, however, was that she'd begun to encourage the women to risk their "silly jewels and trifles," and it was these small treasures she'd started to squirrel away. She'd put them in secret pockets she'd sewn into her skirts, confident that no woman would ever mention to a mere acquaintance like Mr. Warren Reynolds that she'd foolishly wagered and lost an item from her jewelry box. Because of the risk and a bad experience in Prague, her uncle had long ago decided to refuse offers of jewelry and family heirlooms when it had come to settling their victims' debts. It had never occurred to him that she would have ignored his edicts. Hard years had taught her the difference between glass and paste and the genuine articles. And so she had decided to avail herself of the opportunities he hadn't, and she hid the fruits of her labors behind two loose tiles in her bathroom.

If she could keep these wagers "on the side," Uncle Warren would never guess that she had a hoard of small treasures. Once she had enough to live on and start a new life, perhaps enough even to buy a small country cottage somewhere far away from London where no one knew anything of graft and games, she would escape her uncle and disappear forever.

It was a simple plan. And simplicity had an elegance all its own.

Freedom beckoned like a siren, and she closed her eyes to savor the sweet taste of hope. Since her father's death, she'd almost forgotten what it felt like to hope for more than a good hand of cards. The brief and disastrous affair in Venice had only reinforced the sensation that it was dangerous to rely on others for an escape. The long years faded when she imagined her little dream cottage with a garden and trees framing it in her mind's eye. And if ultimately there might be marriage to a gentleman farmer in her future, so be it. But card-playing rogues and thieves like her charming uncle need not apply for the position.

She would have to play it just right. After all, she needed more than one weekly game with the same three ladies to finance her escape. But every step from this moment would bring her closer to her goal, and she was finally playing with the wealthier women of the Ton. She was wise and patient enough to know she had to spread out her victories, so that no one commiserated and discovered a common link between their lighter pockets. The glitter of diamonds, sapphires, and rubies spread across her path, but the daydream took an odd turn as a man with golden eyes started laughing behind her, a warm, predatory growl that sent a shiver down her spine. Eve shook herself and pushed the reverie out of her head.

"Good night, Mr. Clay," she whispered, and

blew out the lamp to make her way to the bed. "And good-bye!"

It was relatively early to be returning to Shelbrook's, considering his usual habit of greeting the staff on his way in at dawn as they prepared for their daily duties. The clock in the hall chimed one as Julian climbed the stairs to the first floor and his rooms. He smiled at the strange twists in his first "respectable" outing in months. He would never have dreamt he could be entertained by watching a woman play cards.

But damned if I didn't just spend the better part of an evening trapped in my chair by an embarrassingly hard cock and the world's worst conversationalists.

It was laughable, but he couldn't remember enjoying an outing more. Though getting more than two tables nearer to the girl would have added to his satisfaction, Julian decided he was oddly content at the windfall of her appearance in his path.

I think I'm up for a good healthy distraction, and if—

"You're early." Sounding mildly annoyed, Beatrice was waiting for him in the middle of his four-poster bed.

"Am I?" Julian crossed his arms. "Have I spoiled your plan to sit there for another five hours before I stumbled in at my usual time?"

The lady looked less than pleased at his jest.

"Don't be foolish! I heard you downstairs and just slipped down the hallway to surprise you."

"And won't Barnaby be surprised to find you missing from his bed?" *Damn it.* He just wasn't in the mood to play along. It was one thing to invite a woman into his bed and another to find her amidst his sheets harping at him.

"He's asleep in his chair in the downstairs library. Too much to drink, I imagine." Her voice dripped with contempt before she seemed to recall the circumstances and tried to salvage her seductive plans. "He won't be upstairs tonight, Julian, my sweet. And I couldn't stop thinking about you and how it felt to have a real man between my thighs and—"

"Beatrice." He held up a hand and took a deep breath, praying that whatever diplomatic skills he had left would save him. He gave her what he hoped was the look of a man sorely tempted by the fetching picture she made. "You risk too much, and I think you mean to torment me to death. You are too beautiful and intoxicating. But you know we can't. Not like this and not tonight."

Her expression was a study in confusion. "I know nothing of the sort. Take your pants off, Lord Westleigh."

Well, there's a phrase to warm a man's blood. Julian's jaw clenched. The Earl of Westleigh did not take orders like a valet. She'd dropped the sheet and opened her arms to display her pert bare breasts and smooth skin, clearly expecting his prompt obedience and rapt admiration. His body twitched a bit in response despite his annoyance, but Julian wasn't about to give in. He drew a little closer, but only to lessen the odds of being overheard. "You're a hard woman to resist."

"Then don't try to." Beatrice leaned back, her expression gaining confidence as she let the sheet slide even lower. "Come to bed, Julian."

"If you heard me downstairs, then it's possible the servants have as well." Julian held still, allowing himself to enjoy the view so as not to insult the lady, but he could see the cold reality of his words sobering her up. "I'm not one to flee gossip, but we have to be more discreet. Every footman and maid will know that Barnaby slept in the library tonight and now here you are. I'm not sure my luck will allow me to survive another bullet if your husband hears of our passion through idle talk—much less discovers the evidence of it in his own home."

She picked up the sheet slowly, restoring her modesty with some reluctance. "You didn't protest about discretion in your dressing room yesterday."

"As I said"—Julian smiled, aware that he'd won a temporary stay of execution—"you are a hard woman to resist. I am only human, Beatrice."

She retrieved her silk wrap and abandoned his bed. "Don't lie to me, Julian Clay." She moved past him, making no effort to touch him.

"You doubt your beauty?"

She reached the door and turned to laugh softly. "Not at all! I don't need *you* to tell me how lovely I am."

"No? Then how do I lie?" he asked warily.

Her smile didn't quite reach the icy blue of her eyes. "You said you were human."

She opened the door and left before he could think of a witty reply. Surprisingly, her remark stung. It wouldn't have killed him to accommodate her, but . . . damn! He felt like a trapped animal. Granted, a spoiled one with lovely furnishings. It was time to look for other lodgings or see if any of his friends who lacked wives were in need of company.

He listened for any sounds of Beatrice's return but gradually relaxed and accepted his hard-won privacy. He poured himself a brandy and let out a sigh. For all that Shelbrook's hospitality came with difficulties, he couldn't fault the man's taste in spirits.

Julian's gaze lit on a side tray filled with a sizable pile of envelopes and cards. He crossed the room to scan the various invitations and found himself deliberately choosing ones Miss Eve Reynolds might attend. Into a small stack went all the notes that in his previous life he would have effortlessly disregarded.

This bird was going to try to hide amidst the dullest

blue bloods—and the wealthiest, I'm betting. If her uncle was as concerned about making the right connections as his tablemates had hinted at, then only the most prestigious gatherings would do. He took a slow sip of the brandy, letting its amber fire soothe his tensions away. *God, who would believe for one moment that I'm going to be voluntarily attending these quiet little soirees? And for what? For another glimpse of Miss Eve Reynolds? Next time, Lamb, we'll see what kind of games you truly enjoy.*

Julian undressed, his thoughts already racing toward the hunt ahead. He chuckled at the irony of it all. After a lifetime of notoriety, only now did he see that the best camouflage might be respectability.

Chapter Three

Julian spared only a passing glance at the ballroom in Lord Hutton's Mayfair mansion. It was crowded with glittering couples creating a chaotic, rhythmic rainbow as they moved through the patterns of the quadrille. His instincts told him she wouldn't be there. Instead he made a direct path for an out-of-the-way salon where a few tables were set up for those too infirm to dance or who only heard the siren call of the cards.

And there she was.

After a week of attending the mustiest of social affairs, he'd finally tracked her down. A dark jewel in their midst, Eve Reynolds appeared almost exactly as he remembered her from Wickett's. Instead of the usual debutante's pastels, once again she wore a dark blue, though satin this time, which complemented her dark hair, and, if he recalled correctly, would likely make her eyes even more dazzling. As before, she was the only youthful creature in the room, and he marveled that no one else seemed to find it strange. One glance across the room assured him that her uncle was elsewhere, and if she had a chaperone, Julian knew he or she would appear quickly enough.

Even so, he lingered for just another minute or two to watch her from a distance. The impression she'd made at Wickett's was reinforced, and Julian smiled at the subtle grace and control she displayed as she made the game look effortless without overpowering or intimidating her opponent. Lady Morrington chatted happily across the table, and Julian knew that she was oblivious to everything but her own hand. He shook his head. No time like the present for introductions, he decided.

He crossed the room behind her and was pleased to realize that he'd successfully taken the lovely Miss Reynolds by surprise. *God help me, I'm enjoying this already.*

"Lady Morrington!" Julian kept his focus on the matron, disarming her with a wicked grin that saved him from trying to keep a straight face as his lovely quarry nearly jumped from her chair to escape. "Can it be that the fates are kind enough to let me greet you again and so soon? Though I didn't mean to intrude on your—"

"Lord Westleigh!" Lady Morrington cut him off, the years slipping away as her eyes sparkled with delight. "You handsome devil! I cannot imagine what has drawn you into my dreary company unless . . ." Lady Morrington went on merrily, "Have you been properly introduced to my young friend, my lord?"

"I don't believe I've had the pleasure." Julian waited as innocently as he could while Miss Reynolds's quiet bids for mercy were completely overridden by the older woman. He had to bite the inside of his cheek to keep from laughing outright at the fiery challenge in those incomparable blue eyes when, at last, she looked directly at him.

"Lord Westleigh, may I present Miss Eve Reynolds? She is a dear little thing, is she not? A passable card player, but improving with my guidance, if I may boast a bit," Lady Morrington said.

"Lord Westleigh." Eve inclined her head a fraction of an inch. "An honor."

Passable. There was an understatement.

"May I join you?" he asked, taking the seat Lady Morrington offered while watching a lovely flush of color move across Eve's cheeks. "I think I could stand a bit of improvement myself."

Lady Morrington beamed, openly amused at his

jest. Eve Reynolds, on the other hand, looked less impressed, her eyebrows arching with skepticism before she marshaled her expression when the older woman gave her a wink.

"But these are just parlor games, Lord Westleigh," Eve stated softly, and Julian decided he liked her voice. It was silky but strong—not squeaky or breathless (two qualities he generally associated with girls her age). "Perhaps you'd be better entertained joining the men in the library. My uncle understood there was more exciting play for a gentleman there."

"Not at all." He took up the deck of cards, shuffling them without looking away from her eyes. *The blue satin does set them off, just as I suspected it might. Lovely spitfire, aren't you? But with dear Lady Morrington soaking up every word of this exchange, you're trapped, Miss Reynolds. No choice but to play, so let's see what you are.* "I love parlor games."

"Why don't you play piquet with Lord Westleigh, Miss Reynolds? I find my eyes need a rest." Lady Morrington leaned back in her chair, effectively throwing her young friend directly into his hands.

"Of course, madam." Eve shifted in her chair, straightening her back as if bracing herself for battle. "Shall I keep score then?"

"Allow me!" Lady Morrington offered, causing a slight commotion as she began to search for paper and pencil.

"I have something here you can use," Julian said, pulling a palm-size leatherbound notebook from his coat pocket. "There is a pencil inside."

"How clever!" Lady Morrington settled into the task, happy to referee and keep the tally. Julian took his time culling the unnecessary cards from the deck in his hands, in no hurry to end the preliminaries. "Where is your family from, Miss Reynolds?"

"Originally from the Cotswolds, but my father preferred to travel the world. I confess this is my first visit to England since my earliest years."

"And how do you find it?"

A dozen answers elusively flitted behind her eyes, but at last she answered carefully, "Very entertaining. I never expected to meet such lovely people . . . to feel so welcome." She glanced at Lady Morrington, a new flush on her cheeks. "Everyone seems very kind."

"Isn't she a dear little thing?" Lady Morrington said as she patted the dear thing's shoulder.

He nodded. "Indeed." Over the fan of cards in his hand he openly studied her, forgetting for a moment that there was anyone else in the room. It was easy to dismiss the world at large as he contemplated once more the allure of a young woman who seemed to be going out of her way *not* to attract attention. She'd braided her long black hair into a coil artfully pinned to the crown of her head with only a few tendrils escaping to soften the look. A blue ribbon choker with a single ornate little onyx bead and matching drop earrings set off her coloring perfectly and drew his eyes to the ivory column of her neck and sensuous lines of her face. Here was a gypsy queen in disguise, and Julian allowed his pleasure to show on his face.

She colored like a virgin under his gaze, and even that possibility excited him as she refused to look away. She was a creature of contradictions. Her posture was calm and confident and her hands were folded elegantly on the table awaiting his deal, but her eyes were a storm of emotions as she defied his rakish appraisal. From Lady Morrington's vantage point, it would seem he was a man besotted, and for the first time in his life, Julian didn't give a damn if he looked the fool. *For it makes Lady Morrington my ally, Miss Reynolds. The sentimental old dear will do anything to further the romantic cause . . . so long as she has a good seat to watch.*

"Are you familiar with this game, Miss Reynolds?" he asked.

Her chin rose a fraction. "Somewhat. Though I am curious to see how *you* approach it."

He lazily began to withdraw the lowest number cards and drop them onto the cloth-covered table.

"I have a feeling we have very similar styles. Did you play cards a great deal during your travels?"

She shook her head. "Not really. Lady Morrington has been very understanding when it comes to demonstrating the finer points of your popular games."

Oh, what a beautiful liar you are, Miss Reynolds.

"You are lucky to have such a teacher," he noted, the last of the discards falling away. "Most girls your age worry more about learning their dance steps, yes?"

"I said as much, Lord Westleigh!" Lady Morrington chimed in. "It's just not healthy for a young woman to waste her time in drawing rooms, don't you agree? She'll dull her senses with such company."

"Not at all!" Eve protested. "I hate dancing!"

Julian felt the sudden wild urge to drag her across the table and kiss her until her senses were far from dull. This was a woman who needed to be kissed beyond reason. She must have seen the sudden flare of desire on his face, for she abruptly stood, her chair nearly toppling at the speed of her movement.

"I apologize . . . Lady Morrington, if you'll excuse me." She turned from the table, her eyes snapping with fury, and Julian could only smile at the delightful twists and turns of their first brief conversation.

"Aren't you going to go after her?" Lady Morrington whispered dramatically, holding out his notepad.

"I believe I shall, your ladyship. I can't imagine what I've done to upset her, but I don't think I will be able to sleep tonight if I don't attempt to make amends. Thank you." He tucked the pad back into his waistcoat pocket and stood to bow briefly, relishing her conspiratorial grin, before following Eve out. *Poor Miss Reynolds. Not an ally to be found anywhere.*

He caught a glimpse of her on the other side of the ballroom as she made her escape out the French doors that led onto a stone verandah and down to an unlit garden. He knew where Eve was heading because he'd been to a party in this house two years ago and had had a memorable encounter with not one, but two eager ladies. It wasn't one of his proudest moments, but certainly a moment of debauchery that had left him with a strong memory of the best points of that garden if one wished to avoid being seen from the main house. He shook his head at the delightful possibilities of Eve hiding from him in those very same hedges.

Granted, her darker gown would normally have made the hunt difficult, but a full moon and the sheen of satin kept her from blending into the greenery. She looked like a nymph in the shadows, outlined in silver and black, as she slipped toward a lush topiary near the walls. He moved as stealthily as he could, cornering her with ease when she took refuge on a small stone bench next to a stone statue of Pan.

"What are you up to, Miss Reynolds?"

"Me? I'm not the one chasing down women in dark gardens!"

She stood and moved as if to run from him, but he caught her easily, his fingers grasping her upper arm and drawing her back to him. "I'm not a villain, Miss Reynolds. It seems a simple question for a man to ask, especially after you've fled such a friendly game of piquet."

She stopped pulling away from him. "A *friendly* game?" Her mesmerizing blue eyes gave none of her thoughts away. "I'm sure you are confused, Lord Westleigh. Too much punch?"

Julian smiled at the realization that she was truly a worthy opponent. No show of fluttery nerves, no signs of fear; if she hadn't lost her composure in Lady Morrington's presence, he might have questioned his instincts. But hers was the supreme bluff of a truly gifted player. He loosened his grip to the gentlest restraint. He was rapidly gaining new respect for the lively Miss Reynolds. *The little minx is good at this.*

"I haven't touched a drop." He smiled before he went on. "Miss Reynolds, perhaps no one has explained the rules of *this* particular game, but when a lady flees from a table, a gentleman is obliged to 'chase her down' to ascertain her state of mind and offer whatever amends he can for the slight, imagined or real, he dealt her. And by running into a dark and secluded garden—"

"I'm not—I don't wish to play this game, Lord Westleigh."

"No? Then what game is it you are playing, Miss Reynolds? For I swear you are not what you appear to be, and I have always loved a good mystery."

"Then how disappointing for you that there are no answers to be found here. I'm sure you'll grow bored soon enough, Lord Westleigh." She met his gaze without flinching.

"I am sure of at least one thing, Miss Reynolds. This keen aversion you have to dancing may prove your undoing." He leaned in, close enough for his breath to move the curls that rested against her ear and send a shiver down her spine. "Tell me what you and your uncle are up to, and perhaps I'll even help you."

"You're . . . imagining things, Lord Westleigh," she whispered.

He pulled back only slightly, enjoying the warmth of her body against his. "Am I really? Come, Miss Reynolds, confess all. Are you aspiring to be a beautiful and wealthy little widow by husband hunting amidst the elderly? Or are you just warming up to pick a few pockets?"

"How dare you!" Eve stepped away from him, and Julian knew it was their awkward proximity alone that had spared him from a well-earned slap. "You spot me once in a salon and now you dare to accuse me of such things? If I confess anything, Lord Westleigh, it will be an increasing desire to scratch that smug look off your handsome face and see how you explain it to your host!"

He held up his hands in a gesture of surrender. "I overstepped. I was rude and may deserve a scratch or two. But you must admit that you are a curiosity, Miss Reynolds."

"Why? Because I am not flattered by your attentions?"

"Because you don't belong here."

She bristled defensively, but the flash of emotions in her eyes told him he'd struck a nerve. "I have every right to be here."

"I'm not disputing the lettering on your invitation. Just noting that you are . . . different than any young woman I have ever met."

Now she seemed curious, most of the anger evaporating from her stance. "In what way am I different?"

"You mean besides your delightful preference for parlor games with crumbling dowagers and dark gardens over glittering ballrooms and polite society?"

A ghost of a smile flitted past her control as

her shoulders relaxed, and Julian savored it. "The ladies at Wickett's were under the impression you didn't get out much into good company," she replied. "Perhaps it is all the rage these days for women to avoid the crush of the dance floor and the suffocating heat of overlit rooms."

"I don't think I've been gone *that* long, Miss Reynolds." He shifted his weight, again closing the distance between them, unwilling to remain the focus of their exchange. "But you elude the point of my inquiries. What are you really doing in London, Miss Reynolds?"

"Besides avoiding you?"

"Absolutely besides that."

"I am innocently enjoying the social season."

"Ah!" He smiled, abandoning any pretense of a harmless interview. "But, my dear Miss Reynolds, I suspect that you . . . are . . . not . . . an . . . innocent."

She gasped before regaining her composure. "I wasn't aware that I radiated such an impression, your lordship. I'll have to cut back on games of piquet if it gives men like you permission to be so insulting!"

"I apologize. Again." His look was pure contrition. "I'll have you know that's likely the most repentant I've ever been—and that includes a childhood incident involving bees."

She *almost* smiled but caught herself just in

time. "Then perhaps you should leave off these ridiculous speculations. You—you know nothing of me after so brief an acquaintance."

"That is not entirely true." He shook his head. "I know you favor strong leads, lose only when you stand to gain, and that Lady Morrington has no idea what a little hunter she's invited into her henhouse." The urge to truly touch her was too strong to suppress. The privacy of their position was delectable, the curve of a hedge giving him all the advantage he needed. Her eyes widened as she realized that she'd started a duel for which there would be no one to intervene on her behalf. "I know that your breath quickens and your color changes every time I get close to you."

They were alone.

She opened her mouth to argue or protest, but she seemed to be having trouble rallying her thoughts. At that point Julian knew victory was his. Even so, she put a hand against his chest to slow his progress. "You know *nothing* of me, Lord Westleigh."

"I know that that will change, Miss Reynolds."

He leaned close, so ready to taste her, so hungry to have her, but he balanced his slow encroachment by releasing her arm, giving her the choice to withdraw from him. The fire in his blood demanded that he conquer her, but every fiber of his being wanted her to be willing. He knew from past experience that few kisses were worth a bleeding lip or a scratched face. She was still capable of injuring him, but like any gambler, he preferred to hedge his bets.

He held his breath, anticipating her retreat or even a demonstration of a false, prudish protest. It never came. Instead, there was a slow, sweet exhale, and she tipped her head back, an invitation he readily accepted. Her lips were soft and so much warmer than he'd expected, yielding reluctantly at first and then responding to his need, fueling it and moving with him until he was sure he'd forgotten why he'd thought to teach her anything. Her mouth parted, and he tasted her tongue against his own, the wet friction telegraphing raw primal need to every part of his body, and Julian cradled her face in his hands to hold her there, to make sure she didn't pull away and deprive him of the contact he needed.

He'd meant to kiss her—just that. But then she pressed herself against him, as if she'd been molded and measured for his body alone. The lush lines of her figure beckoned his hands and he moved them, skimming over satin and skin to learn the outlines of the territory he wished to claim. Her waist was trim and indented for his fingers but not in an unnaturally constrained way. She was slender, but not emaciated, and he almost growled at the sting of desire that whipped through him as he discovered her curves. Her shape pleased him, his blood firing as his hands pressed along her firm flesh, holding her closer and savoring her responsiveness to his touch. She kissed him without reserve, but without practiced skills—a wanton who didn't seem to understand the power at her command.

He inhaled her fragrance, an intoxicating hint of honeysuckle and orange blossoms with an undercurrent of feminine sweat and musk. He could smell her arousal, and his core clenched with the lure of it—he wanted to dip his fingers into the slippery silk of her and taste it on his tongue. Her fingers clutched at his collar and became entangled in his hair, and when her teeth gently nipped his lower lip, he lost all control.

That did it. Leverage. A man needs leverage.

His hands deftly ignored the excess material of her skirts and bustle and found the curve of her bottom to lift her against him. It was three long strides and he had the leverage he needed, using the garden wall and Pan's accommodating pedestal. She gasped at the shift, her feet kicking out as she lost contact with the ground. She broke away from his fiery kisses as the reality of his rock-hard cock pressed upward between her thighs, even through layers and layers of fabric, making her realize that this embrace had officially gone far beyond polite flirtation.

Damn. Every heartbeat roared in his ears, but

he knew better than to push his luck. *At least, not tonight. Still . . .* Her eyes were coming back into focus, and he knew that Eve Reynolds was mere seconds away from recalling her name and all the reasons why a lady should protest her current position.

He rocked his hips forward, grasping her waist, and trailed his tongue in a flickering path down her beautiful white neck toward the edge of her bodice. She moaned, shivering involuntarily, and her thighs parted even as her hands stiffened against his chest, her fingers splayed out to push weakly against him.

"You . . . we . . . must not . . . ," she whispered.

Damn. His cock throbbed, chafing at the confines of his clothes, and it took every last ounce of his resolve to relinquish the ground he'd gained. Slowly, deliberately, he held her close so that he could feel her body moving along his, the friction of her breasts searing his skin even through his shirt as he lowered her back to her feet, aware that he'd likely crushed the satin of her dress, leaving evidence of his trespass—but there was nothing to be done, and some part of him was glad for it.

Once she was steady, he stepped back to catch his breath and allow her to compose herself for a moment. It wasn't exactly chivalry, but under the circumstances, Julian was sure it was the best he could manage. *Careful, Miss Reynolds. One single "come hither" look or word and by God, I'll mount you as you kneel on that bench.*

At last she spoke. "Why are you . . ." She took another deep breath. "Are you . . . trying to toy with me, Lord Westleigh?"

He shook his head slowly, savoring the lingering taste of her in his mouth. A thousand smooth lies slipped through his thoughts, but only the truth would do. "No. I do not toy or trifle with you. In fact, I shall tell you honestly—I intend to have you outright and without one thought of convention. I intend to seduce you, Miss Reynolds. Whatever rules there are in polite society, I have no intention of following any of them. I don't think I could lie to you and say otherwise. I *intend* to do every wicked thing that comes into my mind and to see that you enjoy every one of them."

"Oh!" Her response was breathless with shock. "And to think I thought you were being forward earlier."

"How was that for a strong lead?"

And at that, she turned, picked up the front of her skirts, and ran back up the dark garden path toward the house. Julian simply watched her go.

Her panic was total. In a blind scramble, she skirted the main doors and found another smaller, wooden door that led from the garden into a service hallway near the entrance. Eve was desperate to avoid her hosts and as many guests as she could. Aware that no matter what else might or might not have been true in this world, there was no avoiding the fact that she looked very much like a woman who had been thoroughly kissed. Her expression, the state of her dress, and swollen lips were all too revealing. She found a small, deserted sitting room off the foyer and stood with her back to the door to try to gather her wits. The room was dim, lit only by the glow from the streetlamps and the moonlight that streamed through the windows.

She forced herself to calm her breathing and assess the damage.

Do I have "wanton fool" emblazoned on my face?

He suspected her. He'd guessed too close to the truth for any comfort, and like an idiot, she'd probably confirmed his suspicions by giving in to her instinct to run. If he began to talk, the Season was over and they would be lucky to escape the authorities.

But somehow, Julian Clay didn't strike her as a man looking to administer justice in the courts. And she didn't really think he'd talk . . . not yet.

Isn't he exactly the sort of man I swore I would never allow near me again?

That kiss! It had been an earth-shattering kiss. Naturally, she'd been kissed before—but not like this. Even when she'd thought herself dizzy from her lover's kisses in Venice, they had never robbed her of all reason. She'd never forgotten the ground beneath her feet or what she'd been about to say. How was it even possible to want to scratch a man's eyes out one minute and then find yourself blissfully in his arms the next?

When he'd looked at her like that, with raw hunger and wicked desire, it was as if a floodgate inside her had opened and she hadn't been able to think of anything but how warm his lips might be and how very long it had been since she'd felt so wanted . . .

Ever since her heartbreaking experience with Dante in Venice two years ago, she'd deliberately avoided situations that might have led to any romantic misunderstandings. Eve had begun to congratulate herself on overcoming her weak sensual nature, since she hadn't felt so much as a twinge of attraction for anyone since Mr. Moore.

Until he came into that salon. Until tonight, and now look at me . . . I can't trust myself not to give in—not to let go. I've held on so tightly to that control that I thought I was numb. But I've never been so wrong—and it's as if he can sense it. It's as if he knows me better than I know myself. Dratted man!

Eve had no faith in the nature of men, and until she'd met Julian Clay, she had never felt such an overwhelming desire to do anything more than empty their wallets over a few hands of cards. She trusted no one. Her socializing with the civilized elite, with their decadent tastes and selfish natures, was a means to an end. After her father died, she'd begun to understand that she and her uncle walked among the privileged but were not of them. With one wrong step, one misspoken word, she and her uncle could easily be cast aside and forgotten by the elite members of society whose favor her uncle curried.

Julian Clay is no different. Worse, probably! No matter what he says, he's toying with me and drawing too much attention to our presence in London! Whetford's letters will only take us so far, and if this impossible man derails us . . .

He could have any woman he wanted. Why was he tormenting her? Was he truly set on seduction? The fantasy of Lord Westleigh and his wicked intentions blossomed in her mind and Eve had to bite her lip at the wave of dangerous, wanton images that danced in her mind. She shook her head and pushed away from the door. *Oh, no, you don't, Lord Westleigh! Whatever you are up to, there is more to this than there appears to be.* Her cynical nature asserted itself, and she finally felt calm and normality return. *No. No, I've simply piqued his curiosity.*

After all, what did he have to gain by pursuing her? Was he trying to see if he could blackmail her into something?

He was a formidable opponent, and she acknowledged that it was stupid to assume she wouldn't encounter him again. She would be better prepared the next time they met. She went back to the door and out into the foyer, smoothing her skirts. It was still early, and no one was lingering in the hall making farewells, so she seized the opportunity.

"Young man!" she called. The footman came over promptly, betraying no surprise at seeing her outside the empty sitting room. "Would you summon Mr. Warren Reynolds's carriage, please? I'm his niece and wish to leave. And"—she let out a steadying sigh—"if you could let him know discreetly that I have departed due to a headache, I would be grateful."

"I can summon him now to escort you home, miss."

"No! There's no need." She waved her hand, struggling to keep her tone light. "No need to interrupt his evening. I'll just wait for the carriage in here."

"I'll turn up the lamps for you then, miss."

"No, thank you. The dim light . . . is soothing."

The servant left, and she waited inside the sitting room, praying that her retreat would go smoothly. She'd have preferred to hire a hackney, but she'd left the few coins she'd carried on the table in the salon. It was a simple oversight, but a telling one. Never before had she left money on a table unless she'd intended to.

She could hear the sounds of the party through the walls, the music and laughter drifting on the night air, and she closed her eyes to picture the genteel gathering—all its polite rituals and social niceties. Unbidden, the memory of golden eyes glittering with desire broke into her thoughts and sent a new flush of color across her cheeks.

She knew what her uncle would say. *"Dangle him! Dangle him, girl!"*

At least until he'd finished working out the Earl of Westleigh's financial worth and had decided if he was a worthy contender. But this time, she knew that she was dealing with a tiger she wouldn't be able to tease and tame—not without risking life and limb. Whatever Lord Westleigh might be, he wasn't a fool.

She had no desire to dangle him. And if she wanted to taste freedom, she had to avoid his kisses at all costs. She might not be able to elude him for the rest of the Season, so she would have to arm herself as best she could. *Every player has a weakness.* The next time their paths crossed, she was determined to learn his and have the upper hand.

Chapter Four

"Heard you settled into a few innocent hands at Wickett's the other night—and last night, rumor placed you at a party at Hutton's. *Hutton's?*" Lord Andrews remarked to Julian after downing the last of the port in his glass. The men were seated in the library of their gentleman's club, enjoying an evening of conversation and cards, which enabled Julian to get a better feel for what had been going on in society during his enforced absence. "And now I find you here! How interesting!"

Andrews was a notorious gossip but a longstanding and useful acquaintance. A gentleman with a well-worn look after decades of indulgence, Lord Andrews was a spry man in his late fifties with a perpetual air of jovial innocence about him that belied his knack for sniffing out the latest gossip. He appeared to the world like a cheerful and doddering gnome, as harmless as a teacup. His charm had kept him blameless from the havoc his tales wreaked, but Julian knew that if one wanted information, it made sense to keep a man like Lord Andrews close at hand. The man had a gift for gathering information like no one else in England.

Julian shrugged and refilled his friend's glass. "I'm still a member of the Club, Elton. Can't a man stop in to catch up with an old friend without stirring up suspicion?" He'd actually won a few hands for the first time in a long time during the last few nights since Wickett's. But it wasn't the slight shift in his luck that had lifted his spirits. Oh, no. It was that little minx!

Odds were Andrews was already onto the scent, but if—

"So . . . any young lovelies you wish to tell me about, Lord Westleigh?"

Damn, you're good, old man. Julian shook his head. "You disappoint me. It seems I've been exaggerating your skills in my mind during my recuperation in the country. Come now, Andrews. Why don't *you* tell *me* about the lovely in question?"

Andrews laughed. "It's impolite to gossip about young ladies, Lord Westleigh."

"Gossip about her uncle then." Julian stretched

out his long legs, as if to settle in for a nice long tale. "And don't leave anything out."

"You know I generally *trade* stories, Lord Westleigh."

Julian gave him a sardonic look. "Start talking, Elton."

Andrews leaned forward, happily conceding the battle if it meant showing off his knowledge. "Well, from what I gather, Mr. Reynolds only just arrived in England with the express purpose of enjoying a social season with his niece in tow. Word has it he has made quite a fortune in various investments abroad—"

"Has he?"

Elton shrugged his shoulders. "Difficult to argue the point without a look at his bank accounts, and he has certainly gone out of his way to make a show of his pockets. A fashionable rental in the heart of town, a tailor's bill to make even you nervous, and he certainly has interesting friends."

"Interesting in what way?"

"Interesting in that they all seem to have a few things in common. They all seem to be a bit vague when introducing the man, while they all share a penchant for gambling, recent trips abroad, and, of course, titles and pedigrees." He set his glass down for another refill. "Not entirely alarming, Julian. I believe that describes almost everyone we know."

Julian's gaze narrowed as the puzzle pieces

seemed to move in his head. "Yet you mentioned it . . . so there must be more."

"Ah, well! I cannot give all the best bits away up front. Where is the suspense in that?"

Julian refilled his glass, but he was growing impatient. "The suspense is long past. Come on. Let's have it."

"Very well! I have it on good authority that one of the Reynoldses' primary introductions came from a certain Marquess of Whetford. Apparently he has vouched for them and, with letters he provided, guaranteed the wealthy Mr. Reynolds and his niece a lovely first Season."

"Lord Whetford?" The name was vaguely familiar, but Julian couldn't quite place it.

"There are those who have lent Mr. Reynolds an invitation or two and insist on his good character. But Whetford is the most prominent, and I confess even I was mightily impressed when I heard he was backing the man." Andrews signaled a footman for another bottle. "I think even Lord Milbank said that he would be sure to include them on the guest list for his next masque ball."

"My God, Elton! How in the world do you keep all these people in your head? I am pressed to remember the name of my barber." Not entirely true, but flattery was a currency that often paid handsome dividends when it came to Lord Andrews.

"It is a gift, to be sure. I swear, I can still tell

you every person who attended my thirteenth birthday party." He leaned in conspiratorially and continued, sotto voce, "*And* the names of their oh-so-informative servants! Ah, the sweet taste of secrets!"

Julian smiled. For all that Lord Andrews had the look of a jolly and harmless old man, he was undoubtedly a cunning soul, and Julian knew firsthand how dangerous secrets could be. Lord Andrews collected and traded information with a tenacity and joy that other men might have applied to tracking fortunes. "I'm sure I was discovering other vices at that age. But then, that would be another story I shall be sure to guard from you, Elton."

Elton laughed. "Another time?" He set his cup down and sobered briefly. "I'm guessing that as a young man, your pursuits had nothing to do with cards and all to do with chambermaids."

"You're fishing."

"Very well, then. Keep a few secrets, Lord Westleigh." He gave Julian a look full of mischief. "Now, about the marquess—"

"Clay! Clay, you scoundrel!" a hearty voice interrupted, and Julian recognized the speaker instantly. "I heard a rumor you'd refused to die, but not a whisper that you were already back and up to no good!"

"Thorne, only you would underestimate me. What is one small bullet compared to a man's need for the degenerate company and unspeakable entertainments available in London proper?" Julian stood to clasp hands with the young Lord Crestford, then spied the ever cynical Mr. James Linville at his elbow. "James, cheerful as ever, I see."

"With Derek Thorne to drag me merrily from door to door, how can I complain?" he replied solemnly. "Good evening, Lord Andrews."

"Mr. Linville, Lord Crestford." Elton nodded at two empty chairs. "Join us and add to the fun."

"With gratitude," the handsome young Lord Crestford said as he gracefully took a seat, openly pleased. Linville was slower to settle. "I hesitate to interrupt your private conversation, but I told James it was too fortuitous a chance to catch Julian Clay out in public and miss it."

"You weren't interrupting and I'm not that elusive, for God's sake." Julian's brow furrowed at the thought of playing phantom. He'd missed several months of the social calendar while recovering in the country, but since then he'd hardly been hiding from his old friends and acquaintances.

Then again, I've hardly been lighting up my old haunts either.

Derek laughed. "Come down to the fencing club this week and give Sergeant Worth a fit! You look well enough for a round or two."

"I am well enough." Julian lifted his glass. "And I thank you for noting it."

Andrews leaned forward with a conspiratorial gleam in his eyes. "Perhaps you've not seen much of him lately because Lord Westleigh has been distracted by industrialists."

"Industrialists?" Linville remarked in surprise.

"In the way of investments or a quest for a professional trade of your own beyond a reliance on your fading good looks and musty title?" Thorne jibed casually.

"Very amusing." Julian took a sip from his glass. "And I am *not* distracted."

"Have either of you heard of a Mr. Warren Reynolds?" Andrews was relentless.

"Chesterfield mentioned him, I think. Something about new blood at the tables. Why?" Derek asked before helping himself to some of the port. "Is he a friend of yours, Clay?"

James's brows rose sardonically. "The industrialist in question, no doubt."

"Well," Derek continued, "Reynolds isn't much of a distraction, but I understand he has a niece who is quite lovely. My cousin told me she looks like a Spanish beauty with her black hair."

"Oh, my! Does he have such a niece?" Andrews asked innocently.

Linville missed nothing. "The source of the distraction."

Julian stretched in his chair, as if he'd been having trouble staying awake for such a dull subject.

"Hardly. But Andrews is desperate for new gossip. Quick, Thorne, tell him something wicked you've heard and give an old friend a hand."

Derek bit his lip in concentration. "I understand the eternally upstanding Lord Colwick has fallen into the arms of a brothel madame. Surely that's worth noting!"

Andrews laughed. "Impossible! Even I wouldn't fall for that silly rumor!"

Linville raised his hand. "Isn't your younger sister threatening to seek a professional trade instead of coming out next year? I'd think that was quite the scandal if—"

"And at that, we retreat." Derek unfolded from his chair, his cheeks flushed in good-natured embarrassment. "Come on, Linville, you grim bear. Let's withdraw to the safety of Crow's and see if we can't cheer even you. Good evening, gentlemen."

Linville bowed to the men before following his friend. "Gentlemen, a good evening."

"Interesting fellows," Andrews said when they were once again alone. "Perhaps Lord Crestford will give you a little competition for the lovely Miss Eve Reynolds, eh? He's young and handsome enough, I'd say, and has a fair enough income to go along with that little estate he's inherited. Linville's off the chase. Word has it he's one of The Jaded."

The Jaded. Julian had only heard whispers of it. It was a secretive and elite gentleman's society that had sworn off "the chase." Rumor had it that they were all misogynists and cynics but notoriously successful at protecting their own and breaking the hearts of any woman foolish enough to attempt to reform them. Julian wasn't sure he believed such a club even truly existed. *And even if it does, by God, it sounds like a dreary bunch!*

Andrews continued. "Then again, Thorne won't be the only one looking out for her. I'm sure her uncle will be pleased at all the attention Miss Eve Reynolds is attracting during her debut."

Julian's eyes narrowed. Just the thought of Thorne or any other man touching her made him feel murderous. *Damn! And I'm still floundering trying to find out where she'll be next.* "All right, Elton. You've set the stage. Out with it."

"Whetford's having a gathering tomorrow night—a lively little ball to try to catch himself a new young wife. Seems his luck at the tables has run out recently and he's decided a marriage will be far more entertaining than the poorhouse."

Julian tried to hide his revulsion. He recalled now seeing an invitation, but he hadn't paid much attention. From Elton's description, it was easy to surmise why. *Is that why the name Whetford sounds familiar?* "A ball?"

Lord Andrews shrugged. "Nothing you'd ever bother with, but—"

"But?"

"I imagine the guest list will include the gentleman you asked about—and his niece as well. Did you wish to borrow my invitation?" Andrews's expression was too indifferent to be sincere. No matter what Julian said, the damage couldn't be undone.

Then again . . . what damage? He can't do more than I do myself, especially after what transpired in Hutton's garden. My God, I almost had the girl within a hundred strides of the house. The thought carried no hint of remorse, just an acceptance that whatever line he should have towed had long been crossed.

"I have my own." Julian leaned back in his chair, satisfied that he had a much better feel for Miss Reynolds's situation and his next move. "But you'll not find me at some foolish dance bouncing around like a jackanapes."

"Oh, no, old friend!" Lord Andrews inclined his head, only marginally chastised with a knowing grin on his face. "But I shall certainly look for you at the card tables."

If there was one topic the ladies were eager to shed light on, it was the Earl of Westleigh. Eve's encounter with the man was all too fresh in her mind, but she was using all her skills to make sure she gave nothing else away to fuel the lively firestorm of speculation around her. Most of the ladies had witnessed only a fraction of his "interest" in her at Mrs. Wickett's, but Lady Morrington had witnessed her introduction to the earl at the Huttons' ball last night. Having no doubt imparted her observations of their lively interchange to her friends, she now had the entire group completely aflutter with excitement. The cards lay abandoned in the middle of the table as they instead refilled their sherry glasses and settled into their chairs.

And what would they say if they knew how close I came to letting him make love to me? A man I had just met, a man I know nothing about except that when he looks at me I forget everything—even how to be afraid.

"Who would have foreseen it?" Mrs. Cuthbert said. "Though perhaps it really is true what they say about men being changed by a brush with death!"

Mrs. Seward, a member of the group that Eve had just met that afternoon, was quick to agree. "Oh, yes! A dear friend told me she knew of a man who was a terrible drunk until he was run over by a mail coach."

The women exchanged amused, quizzical looks, but they were too kind to laugh. Lady Morrington shook her head kindly. "Be that as it may, the earl's story is far more illustrious and . . . relevant to Miss Reynolds's situation."

Eve wanted to nudge the ladies to reveal the

useful facts about the earl's brush with death without appearing to actually care about the dratted man. "I cannot imagine that a mail coach would do much to change a man who appears as set in his ways as Lord Westleigh."

"Oh, no." Mrs. Wickett shook her head. "But he was shot! And I imagine that did the trick!"

"Shot?" Eve said, astonished. "By whom?"

"Not by a jealous husband!" Mrs. Cuthbert replied, and they all chortled knowingly. "A surprise to all of us, I can assure you!"

So, he's a womanizer. Why is that revelation not a surprise? Eve forced herself not to give in to the urge to roll her eyes.

Once again it was Lady Morrington who tried to temper their comments. "Now, now! The earl is very handsome, and it is natural for a robust man of passion to . . . sow a few wild oats. If there was an indiscretion or two in his past, surely he has paid the price for it! His estrangement from his old friend the Duke of Sussex is legendary, and yet Lord Westleigh demonstrated that the loyalty he'd pledged to Sotherton in his youth was stronger than anything else." She made a point of addressing Eve. "He saved the duke's fiancée from a crazed servant and stepped in front of the bullet intended for her. He is a hero!"

A hero? Eve could only nod as a dozen new questions occurred to her. *Why would he risk his life for another man's fiancée? Especially if it was a man he truly disliked? Unless—unless the lady in question was of interest to Lord Westleigh. Had he been in love with the lady?*

"That was a wedding we wished we could have attended, wasn't it, Daisy? It was obviously a love match, for I heard that the duke couldn't take his eyes from her." Mrs. Cuthbert fanned her cheeks. "I haven't yet met her, but Mrs. Wickett saw her at a garden party and swears she is a sweet girl with impeccable manners."

"So shy and pretty, the Duchess of Sussex! I heard that the Deadly Duke swore never again to speak ill of Lord Westleigh in public just to please her." Mrs. Wickett sighed. "So, it's love without a doubt!"

Lady Morrington nodded. "In any case, Lord Westleigh demonstrated his good character and bravery in the face of certain death."

"I heard the earl was shot in the face!" Mrs. Seward chimed in.

The women gasped in astonishment. "No, no, Daisy!" Mrs. Wickett told her firmly. "Everyone knows he was shot in the stomach!"

"Oh!" Mrs. Seward looked contrite and took a sip of sherry. "Perhaps I'm thinking of Mr. Gilbert. He was a neighbor of my mother's and he was shot in the face—though he is none the worse for it from her report. She said his cat did it."

"Oh, my!" All eyes turned to Lady Morrington for rescue and a return to reasonable discussion.

"There will be no more talk of shooting or cats." Lady Morrington's edict was met with general relief. "Now, as changed as Lord Westleigh may be, he is still just a man. As your friend, Miss Reynolds, I must advise you to proceed with caution and compassion."

"I cannot remember the earl ever showing interest in an eligible woman," Mrs. Wickett said. "What a relief to think he has discovered our young friend here!"

Lady Morrington nodded. "You are a young lady of impeccable character and naturally will be shy with him. But I am sure that you will be a good influence and perhaps offer him the balance and solace that every rogue longs for."

"Courtship is fraught with obstacles!" Mrs. Cuthbert noted sagely before refilling her sherry glass.

"The earl is hardly courting—" Eve began.

"No need to protest, my dear! We know a great deal when it comes to this delicate point in time—don't we, Margaret?" Mrs. Cuthbert said.

Mrs. Wickett sighed. "Too soon to talk, too soon for declarations . . . ah, the delicious wait for the courage he needs to try to hold your hand for the first time!"

"Lord Westleigh does not strike me as a man

prone to courtship, ladies," Eve said, her words falling on deaf ears. *And he most definitely doesn't lack the courage to hold my hand!*

"Many a man not prone to courtship can find himself happily wed!" Lady Morrington observed. The ladies burst into laughter, leaving Eve awash in guilt at their misguided kindness and dear advice. They each seemed to truly wish the best for her, and Eve had never experienced such care from strangers. It made the wretched business of cards and wagers feel even more wrong.

Noting the time, Eve reluctantly made her farewells and left the table to gather her reticule and wrap. Lady Morrington pulled her aside to speak privately while the others continued to gossip over their sherry glasses. "I know we seem like hopeless busybodies, but it is meant well."

"I know it, dear lady. I'm sure if . . . my mother were alive, she would have given me similar advice." Eve almost winced at her own words. She hadn't meant to mention such a maudlin subject. "Truly, Lady Morrington, I have no interest in the Earl of Westleigh."

"Of course not!" Lady Morrington's smile belied her speech. "And why would you? He is a terrible rogue, too handsome and too charming for his own good, while you are a lady of serious philosophies with a practical nature, yes? It is too impossible to even consider!"

"Y-yes, just as I said. Good afternoon, your ladyship." It was all she could think to say as she bit her tongue to keep herself from adding anything more to some ridiculous argument against the "impossible."

Once safely inside the carriage, Eve checked the buttons on her gloves and then closed her eyes to try and calm herself before she reached the house. She wanted to marshal her emotions before facing her uncle. Even with the lost time talking about the "impossible" Earl of Westleigh, it had been a marginally successful afternoon. She'd demonstrated remarkable control, winning just enough to show improvement as she'd played the role of student to Lady Morrington, who'd continued to teach her the finer points of whist. It was a delicate strategy. She must innocently improve and earn their trust so that when the game's stakes increased and her "luck" improved, none of them would suspect that they'd been duped. She couldn't up the ante suddenly, even though her uncle might wish it otherwise. This was a test of patience and resolve—to keep her eyes on the ebb and flow of each hand and *not* on Mrs. Cuthbert's fine ruby earrings or Lady Morrington's superb opal-and-diamond choker.

Worst of all, she found herself growing overly fond of the dear ladies and their silly conversations—and she feared that in her efforts to get away from her uncle, she might have more to lose than to gain.

The ride went all too quickly, and before she really desired it, the carriage pulled to a stop in front of their rented town house. Eve gathered her skirts and made a graceful exit. Inside, she handed over her bonnet and gloves to Barnett just before her uncle emerged from the library doorway to beckon her inside.

He closed the door behind her and began without prelude. "Well?"

"It's just as you'd hoped. Lady Morrington's cousin will join us next week, and she is known to play with several ladies that have far more money than sense. I am days away from securing an invitation, and so long as things continue to go well, it's happening just as you planned."

"And why shouldn't they continue to go well?" Her uncle held out his hand, as excited as a schoolboy reaching for treats. "Why in the world don't you look more cheerful?"

She retrieved a small fold of notes from her reticule and passed them to him. "I'm just a little tired."

"Another headache?"

"No." It was like him to be kind when he thought he was getting his way, and for a moment, she wondered what her life would have been like if Warren Reynolds hadn't been a gambling man.

Would we have a history of conversations that didn't revolve around cards and odds and the weight of his wallet? Would I have worth to him for more than my skills across the tables?

"Well, wash up at least. I'm not spending a fortune so that you can lie abed with imaginary maladies. It's time you earned your way!" He laughed at the jest and returned to his chair. "I still can't believe you just left me at Hutton's. Took the carriage without so much as a by-your-leave and let some silly headache keep you from the business at hand! Mr. Chesterfield told me that there was a duchess dripping with diamonds who was looking for an opportunity to play! And where were you?"

It was a rhetorical question, so she kept silent.

He went on, "Do I need to remind you of what we have at stake here?"

"No, Uncle Warren, and I promise I will be available to engage the very next duchess dripping with diamonds in a lively game of cards, bless her."

He smiled, reluctantly charmed at the promise. "Well, tomorrow night is Whetford's, and if you so much as hint that you are not in top form I'm not sure what I'll do! Lock you in your rooms and send up nothing but bread and water."

It was a hollow threat, but she decided to take the opportunity to retreat. "Yes, Uncle. I'll just go upstairs and rest to make sure we're at our best—if you don't need me?"

"Go! Do whatever it is that delicate ladies do to recover their constitutions, and just remember—a clear head always wins the day!" He kissed her on her cheek, then immediately sat down to his desk to add her afternoon's winnings to his account book, instantly distracted with dreams of the money that would be his.

She left quietly, grateful for the reprieve and swallowing the bitter taste of resentment she felt for her only living relative. She'd earned him a dozen small fortunes over the years, but it had never been enough to remove them from the games. She'd given up the naïve hope that if she just won enough, he would quit and settle down. She certainly wasn't proud of the way she'd abetted her uncle in his schemes, but she was angrier with herself for blindly believing the best of him and ignoring all his flaws for so long.

She thought of the motherly look in Lady Morrington's eyes, and her fingers clenched the banister until her knuckles were white. *Forgive me, your ladyship, but you are a means to an end. One last Season, and I'll repent a thousand times. I just need you to hand over a few of those jewels and stop looking at me like I'm the daughter you've never had!*

She reached the stark sanctuary of her rooms and threw herself onto the bed. "One more Season," she whispered, "and I swear I will never touch another foul deck of cards as long as I live!"

She groaned and buried her face in her pillow. The Earl of Westleigh's wicked words still haunted her, and Eve knew that never had rebellion tasted so sweet—or potentially cost so much. *If he is at Whetford's ball . . . oh, God, I think I'll have a headache after all.*

Chapter Five

Julian deliberately chose to arrive late to the Marquess of Whetford's ball to make sure that all the other guests would already be in place. He was fashionably late, but not so late that she might slip past him. After all, if she preferred exchanging cardboard bits with aging paragons of virtue, it wouldn't make for a long evening.

Unfortunately, it also meant that Andrews and a few other acquaintances might be present to spot him and make a few comments—but what was the chase without risk? And admittedly, he couldn't remember being this aroused by the pursuit of a woman before. But then, Eve Reynolds wasn't like any other woman he'd come across.

It was a large party, and he did his best to navigate the crush without incident. After almost twenty minutes of searching, he spotted her at last. The tilt of her head and a graceful movement of a fan caught his eye, and he allowed himself a moment to admire her from afar and relish the game ahead.

A different blue gown, he noted, with a slightly more daring bodice. It was still more modest than the gowns most women her age selected to show off their figures and bounteous assets. The jewelry was the same, and that made him wonder. Wouldn't the niece of a wealthy industrialist be sporting a ridiculous tiara? But Eve Reynolds hardly needed ornamentation to set her apart from every other woman in the room. Amidst clattering, animated birds, she was an island of calm beauty, her energy restrained, with sapphire eyes alert to everything around her.

Everything.

Just then, she looked directly at him, and once again Julian marveled at this creature who drew him like a moth to a flame. She shifted her stance, ensuring that he would see that her uncle stood at her right elbow. *As if Warren Reynolds is going to frighten me off.*

He crossed the room, weaving in between the various groups of guests, until he reached the pair. "Mr. Reynolds? I apologize for being forward, but Whetford has spoken so highly of you that I felt an obligation to introduce myself. I am Julian Clay, the Earl of Westleigh."

"Lord Westleigh," Mr. Reynolds said as he took Julian's hand, smiling warmly. "I am honored. I believe I may have seen you at the Wicketts' salon last week."

"You may have." Julian waited politely for the next step in the ritual.

"May I present my niece? Miss Eve Reynolds."

"Lord Westleigh."

Julian bowed over her hand, playing the perfect gentleman and ignoring the urge to linger over the slender fingers that rested briefly on his.

"A pleasure, Miss Reynolds." He straightened, politely watching her out of the corner of his eye while turning back to Mr. Reynolds. "She is a treasure, sir."

Warren's eyes gleamed as he stepped closer to Eve. "She is that. A joy to me, I readily admit it. A true joy!" He seemed to assess the costly embroidering on Julian's cuffs before asking, "Are your estates near London?"

Julian stiffened at the directness of the question. "Far enough away to keep my friends in town from intruding without an invitation."

Reynolds was oblivious of his error. "Do you keep a large stable there, Lord Westleigh?"

My God, I think the man is about to ask me what my income is. Julian surmised that he didn't like the man's bluntness, but one glance at Eve confirmed that she liked it even less. "For large stables, if you've an interest, I recommend asking Mr. Frederick Wilkinson. He is famously proud of his stock and loves to show them off."

"I shall look forward to it, Lord Westleigh. Is he a married man, this Mr. Wilkinson?"

"I don't recall." At the sight of Eve's flushed cheeks, Julian was inspired to spare her any further embarrassment. He exhaled in order to overcome the urge to punch the man in the face, then surprised the hell out of himself. "Would you care to dance, Miss Reynolds?"

She looked as shocked as he felt. "I'm . . . That is so . . ."

"What an honor! Of course she would!" Mr. Reynolds practically pushed her forward, and Julian instinctively slipped his hand under her elbow to steady her.

"Miss Reynolds," he murmured as he led her away, her uncle calling after them, "Enjoy yourself, my dear!"

She was completely flustered by the time they reached the crowded dance floor, and her cheeks had turned a lovely pink. It likely added to her ire, this inability to manage these blushes, but Julian thought it a charming weakness.

They took their positions, the orchestra began, and Julian pulled her into his arms and into the first turn before she could change her mind or execute another retreat. She was not a skilled dancer, but it didn't really matter. With the floor so crowded with revelers, it was easy to hold her a few inches closer than decorum would have dictated. "I thought you were jesting when you said you didn't like to dance," he murmured into her ear, smiling when she trembled in reaction. "But you don't even seem to have a dance card."

"I said I hated it, Lord Westleigh, and I wasn't planning on dancing tonight." She kept her face averted from his, a cool Venus uninterested in his existence. Except that she was warm in his arms, and unconsciously moving in harmony with him, the slightest pressure of his hands leading her through the steps.

"No, I don't imagine you were." She was completely under his physical control as he guided her around, and he deliberately began to take every opportunity to touch her wherever he could under the guise of a waltz. She gasped in surprise when the hand at the small of her back pressed her closer against his hips so that she could feel every firm inch of his arousal against her stomach.

"You!" She wriggled away, but not before he saw the flash of heat in her eyes. "Behave, Lord Westleigh!" she hissed, then was forced to smile as Mrs. Cuthbert caught her eye to wave a greeting. "Behave or I swear you'll limp off the dance floor."

He relaxed his hold slightly. "As you wish."

She looked up at him, and Julian cheerfully

braced himself for the lecture he'd undoubtedly earned. "Is this how you usually approach women?" she asked.

"Whatever do you mean?"

"You know what I mean. As if one look from you is enough to set a lady ablaze—as if the more uncivilized you are, the more irresistible you become!"

"I'm not irresistible?" His pretended innocence hit the mark. "You aren't . . . ablaze?"

"I'm not some foolish girl fluttering at the thought of your attentions, Lord Westleigh."

"Not in London to catch a husband?" he asked in a shocked tone, his eyes twinkling with mirth. "How singular of you!"

"I'm not in London to catch the likes of you! And I doubt that that makes me unique."

He winced theatrically. "I'm afraid I'm having a bit of trouble believing you, Miss Reynolds."

"Really? And why is that?"

"Obviously you didn't run home and tell your uncle about that kiss the other night."

She stiffened in his arms, her face losing color. Julian almost swore beneath his breath at the flash of concern in her eyes, but it was gone before he could react. "There was nothing to tell him." Her chin lifted defiantly. "Bored yet?"

"Hardly."

"Well"—her breath caught in her throat, betraying her emotions—"you will be, Lord Westleigh!" She lowered her voice. "I have no intention of allowing you any more liberties."

"I admire your desire to follow the rules."

"You do not! But despite your own announcement that you don't give one whit about rules, the other night was . . . a mistake."

"I regret you didn't enjoy it."

Her fingers tightened against him. "Whether I enjoyed it or not is not the issue! I suggest you look elsewhere for your entertainments and leave me to mine!"

His smile never faltered, and to any casual observer, they must have made a lovely couple on the dance floor, with her dark coloring offset by his golden tones. As the music ended, he released her gracefully after bowing over her hand, only his breath caressing the bare skin at her wrist. "Off to more parlor games, Miss Reynolds?"

Her eyes darkened with frustration, but her expression was calm. "Good-bye, Lord Westleigh."

He straightened slowly, wicked pleasure infusing his body. *God, she's actually lovelier when she's riled like this. Barely restrained and controlled, but she's one breath away from kissing me again.* "Until next time then."

She *almost* stamped her foot but instead narrowed her gaze with a look that might have given another man pause. Then she sailed off without an escort into the crowd back toward the salons and her uncle's protection.

Julian, however, wasn't going to let a mere look of disdain do anything more than spur him on. *He who hesitates is lost, isn't that how the saying goes?* Well, the lecture she'd given him to send him packing had definitely backfired. Julian shook his head, bemused at her efforts to dismiss him. He noted the scandalized whispers in her wake as she cut him publicly and crossed the crowded room unescorted. Whatever her plans and entertainments entailed, he was more determined than ever to know what it was she needed to accomplish and what role her uncle played. *Reynolds comes across like an open book. Perhaps it's time to read a few pages and see what I learn.*

He would uncover Miss Eve Reynolds's secrets, and before he was done, Julian would see to it that the only thing she commanded him to do was to take her to bed. Once she was spread out beneath him, her passions would ignite like—

"Lord Westleigh! What a marvelous and happy chance to find you here!"

Julian was wrenched from the sensuous path of his thoughts by Barnaby's effusive greeting. Red-cheeked and slightly unsteady on his feet, Lord Shelbrook was openly tippled. Beatrice was a vision of aristocratic beauty carved in icy disapproval. As they publicly greeted each other, there was nothing in her countenance to betray the fact that she'd done more for her current houseguest than offer to refill his coffee at the breakfast table that morning. Lady Shelbrook was formidable in more ways than Julian cared to consider. He could only hope the couple hadn't arrived in time to see him waltzing with Eve.

God, there's a nightmare I hadn't anticipated.

"A lovely evening, is it not, my friend?" Barnaby observed in a booming tone, indicating just how far into his cups he was. "Whetford certainly knows how to put on a good show! Is it my imagination, or does the man's waistcoat match the decorations in the hall? Does one even do that?"

"Indeed," Julian replied in an offhand way, as if he'd been to ten thousand balls that Season and didn't really care.

"It is *entirely* a show," Beatrice added, her own voice low enough that only Julian could hear her. "I heard he took a beating at the tables on the Continent and is hanging on by the barest thread."

His bored expression unchanged, Julian's eyes met hers, but his heart began to pulse in sick anger. The insinuation in her tone was unmistakable—she wasn't just talking about Whetford. She smiled, a calculated light making her ice-blue eyes even colder as she continued, "He has less than a month to make a match to retrieve his feet from the fire."

"As dire as that?" Julian glanced back across the glittering room with a new perception of how close he stood to the precipice. *There but for the grace of G—*

"Such a tragedy when men lose their fortunes and must rely on the hospitality and friendship of others."

Beatrice's cutting comment brought him back with a jolt. "Yes, a tragedy."

Beatrice shrugged. "Don't stay out too late, Lord Westleigh. We do worry about your health and . . . a man needs his sleep." Her pout was so practiced and perfect that he almost smiled.

Almost. *I'm starting to hate you a little bit, Lady Shelbrook.*

"Your wife is so kind, Barnaby." Julian clapped the man on the shoulder, ensuring he was a little more alert. "If you're not careful, I shall steal her away from you."

Barnaby laughed, oblivious to the dark currents that flowed between his wife and his friend. Beatrice looked supremely pleased and flattered, and Julian decided he'd said just enough to keep her satisfied.

For now.

But God help me when she realizes that I'd rather sleep in Lady Morrington's potting shed than let her lay one cold finger on me again.

Chapter Six

The stroll the next day had not been her idea, but Eve had to admit that Hyde Park on a lovely summer afternoon was a dreamlike experience. It felt as if all of London's fashionable inhabitants had come out for a breath of fresh air and the chance to show themselves off on the park's famous paths. Carriages slowly paraded by, and several were parked in the shade to allow their illustrious passengers to either greet friends or snub enemies.

It was like a vast and complex play, and Eve knew that without Lady Morrington to push her along, she'd have never risked it for fear of making a social blunder or critical misstep. The rules of elite English society were proving more challenging than most, and her "Tuesday Ladies" had gently chided her for her terrible miscalculation at Whetford's. Apparently stranding poor Lord Westleigh on the dance floor had been bad enough, but walking through the crowd unescorted to cut him, then leaving the ball alone was beyond comprehension.

As far as Eve was concerned, no matter how much the man's touch weakened her knees, losing the attentions of the Earl of Westleigh was the best of all outcomes, and she wasn't going to explain to anyone that etiquette didn't apply to men like Julian. She had more important things on her mind than his distracting kisses and uncanny talent for shattering her composure. Eve told herself that no matter what suspicions he voiced, she wasn't going to let her temper get the better of her. She would just smile sweetly and ignore him.

Lady Morrington had invited along two other young ladies who were also coming out this Season, apparently hoping that they would befriend Eve and demonstrate the behavior of proper English debutantes. Miss Gloria Finch and Miss Delilah Pratt were an education that Eve had never had, and she was doing her best to try to take them seriously as they walked behind Lady Morrington.

"I would be in tears, if it were me," Miss Finch confessed with a dramatic sigh that came across as a bit of a squeak because of a lingering summer cold. "It's one thing to snub your second cousin during a picnic because he's a prig, but an earl!"

Miss Pratt was quick to nod in agreement. "I'm afraid you've lost your chance with the Earl of Westleigh. My mother said that gentlemen are very sensitive to these things."

Eve smiled. "I'm sure Lord Westleigh will recover."

"Perhaps it's your travels," Miss Pratt noted.

"Pardon?" Eve was sure she'd missed something.

"That makes you so different," Miss Pratt explained. "I think you are very brave."

"Brave?"

Miss Finch interrupted them with the firm authority of a seventeen-year-old. "It isn't bravery if you find yourself without a suitor by the end of the Season. But I do love your taste in clothes! I wish my mother would let me wear anything besides pastels!"

"Oh, dear! Yes," Miss Pratt exclaimed. "My mother said that it just wouldn't do to wear anything darker than peach this year." In yellow chiffon, Delilah looked as if she'd been drowning in meringue, and Eve bit her lower lip to keep her opinions on fashion to herself.

"Are all your dresses that shade of blue?" Gloria asked.

Lady Morrington finally seemed to detect that Eve was outnumbered. "It is a most flattering color on you, Miss Reynolds. It makes your eyes look like sapphires, and I think it charming to stay to a theme for your entire wardrobe."

The two girls exchanged glances but seemed to take Lady Morrington's comment as an end to it.

"Thank you, Lady Morrington," Eve said. "I never meant to have just the one color, but—"

"Oh, my!" Miss Finch's squeak was a combination of excitement and horror. "It's him!"

"If he cuts us all, I think I'll faint." Miss Pratt reached up to make sure the matching yellow flowers in her hair were in place for an impending swoon.

"I'll faint if he doesn't!" Miss Finch whispered happily, her eyes widening as the man in question drew nearer.

Eve knew before looking in the direction in which they were staring that the young women were referring to Julian. Even Lady Morrington gave a telltale flutter of feminine preparation as he approached in his fashionable morning coat. "Lord Westleigh! What a delightful shock to see you!"

He bowed, then gave her a playful wink. "A shock before sunset? Is that what you meant, my dear Lady Morrington?"

The older woman laughed. "I know you better than most, your lordship!"

"You do, indeed." As he straightened, he bestowed her young charges with a heart-stopping grin, but he didn't look at Eve. "Though I admit I don't know all of your beautiful companions."

"May I present Miss Gloria Finch and Miss Delilah Pratt? They are just come out this Season and enjoying a great society. And of course, Miss Eve Reynolds you have met. Ladies, Mr. Julian Clay, the Earl of Westleigh."

"Delighted." He gave them a short bow, and Eve briefly held her breath to see if either girl would make good on her promise to lose consciousness. After a few seconds, it was clear that neither one wanted to miss a single moment of the encounter with the earl, though she suspected they might faint later for good measure. Not that Julian would dare—

"Would you walk with me, Miss Reynolds?"

"I— I suppose . . . only if Lady Morrington wouldn't rather . . . ," Eve struggled, amazed that she hadn't anticipated this simple question from him.

"Go ahead of us! I can keep Miss Pratt and Miss Finch company well enough!" Lady Morrington offered cheerfully, though the young misses looked slightly less pleased at the prospect. "Enjoy the air, my dears."

"Thank you, Lady Morrington." Julian held out his arm to Eve, his golden eyes full of sinful temptation. "Miss Reynolds?"

She took his arm, unwilling to look hesitant

or foolish in front of the others, and they began to stroll ahead until they had a small measure of privacy. Even so, she kept her voice low. "The ladies were concerned that I'd dealt you a mortal blow by leaving you on the dance floor last evening. If only they knew how close you'd truly come to injury . . . How did you find me here?"

"The weather is fine, and frankly, I had a feeling that Lady Morrington's curiosity about our encounter last night at the ball might demand an outing."

"How astute of you, Lord Westleigh." The compliment was far from enthusiastic.

"Let us start again, Miss Reynolds."

"I'm not sure that's possible." She eyed him warily. "Have you changed your mind about me, then?"

He nodded solemnly. "Somewhat. You are definitely not a pickpocket and I think if you wish to outlive your husband, it is a brilliant plan for a practical young lady. May I suggest Lord Harding? At eighty-three, I'd say he's a solid choice."

She opened her mouth to give him a verbal lashing, but then she caught the gleam of mischief in his eyes. Her anger evaporated against her will as her gaze met his. "This is your idea of starting over?"

He shrugged. "I am making a sincere effort, Miss Reynolds."

His humor was contagious. "Then I'll try not to take off at a run down one of the footpaths, Lord Westleigh."

"My reputation is restored!"

"Excuse me?"

"Well, after you were so publicly cruel, I imagine this walk of ours has gone a long way to repair my damaged social image," he said.

"I don't think anyone cares whether I dance with you or not, Lord Westleigh."

"Nonsense! Everyone cares about every little thing. What else is there to do while one is in town?"

"Attend lectures? Visit museums and art exhibits? Enjoy concerts?"

"You are a very odd girl, Miss Reynolds." His tone made it an unmistakable compliment, and Eve had to look away to remind herself that the affable man at her side was the very same one who had vowed to seduce her without mercy.

She looked back at him, tilting her head to see if he looked any less wicked when viewed from another angle. "So everyone keeps telling me."

The path curved under a line of lush elm trees, and they walked in silence through the dappled sunlight for a few minutes. He made no move to misbehave, but Eve was aware of his every exhale, of the heat of his arm through the soft cloth of his coat underneath her fingers—even of the subtle friction of his leg against her skirts. Even when Julian Clay was being a consummate gentleman, her thoughts strayed to how close she'd already come to giving in to him and his declaration that he would have her in his bed.

"Tell me why you hate dancing."

The command was gently issued, and Eve smiled. "I have no gift for figures and steps. I always worry too much about my partner's toes and end up injuring my own." She shrugged. "It's probably one of the few social skills where a failure to master the basics involves public humiliation."

"So it's the risk of looking foolish in front of others you truly hate."

Her eyes widened a bit at the revelation. "I never considered it that way."

Julian placed one gloved hand gently over hers as it rested on his arm. "Who taught you to play cards?"

"My father." As she spoke the words, memories flooded back. "I used to cherish our games because I knew that for however long they lasted, I had him all to myself." She sighed. "He never just let me win. I had to truly struggle and focus to defeat him, and I loved him for it."

"You miss him."

"Naturally!" She forced herself not to sigh again. "He died five years ago, and I don't think a day passes that I don't wish I could hear his laughter again." She marveled at the ease of their conversation. "Many women play cards, Lord Westleigh. I'm not a novelty."

"Many women dabble at cards. But you . . . you have a true talent. I've gamed for years, but when I saw you play, I felt like an amateur at my first table."

She tried to keep a defensive tone from her voice. "I am not a professional."

"Oh, but you could be . . ."

Dratted man!

She forced herself to smile, all too aware of the eager audience that trailed behind them and all the curious bystanders along Hyde Park's grand thoroughfare. "No, Lord Westleigh. And on that, you can place any wager you wish."

Thanks to Beatrice's comments the night before, the final piece of the puzzle about Warren Reynolds, the wealthy industrialist, had fallen into Julian's hands. He'd been so intent on achieving his seduction of Eve that he'd almost let the key to the mystery slip through his fingers. After tracking down Eve at the park earlier that afternoon, he'd met Lord Andrews again at White's, where he'd casually confirmed everything he'd heard. This time Julian had had no trouble placing the Marquess of Whetford in his memory.

Apparently, Whetford's debts were as extensive

as Beatrice had intimated, and his creditors were losing patience. No wonder the name had seemed familiar! They'd run in the same circles for years but had managed only a distant and passing acquaintance. The man certainly had Julian's sympathies, but from the looks of the ball, it seemed like the poor devil was opting for a young, unwitting heiress to repair the damage.

Coward! One good evening at the tables and any man can turn the tides of fortune. Or at least that's still my *plan!*

A few well-aimed questions and Julian felt very proud of the portrait he'd managed to create of the lovely Miss Eve Reynolds and her ambitious uncle. Whetford's introduction of the pair to London's elite had undoubtedly been due to a pile of notes that Mr. Reynolds had been holding against him. If Reynolds had threatened to call in the notes, it would have been easier for Whetford to vouchsafe for the villain and his niece than manufacture payments he didn't have. But apparently Whetford was so well connected that few had blinked at the new faces in their midst when they'd arrived with personal introductions. And Reynolds was touting himself as an extremely wealthy industrialist. New money was always welcome, so long as it had no plans for reaching too far up the ladder. Old money often resented rough interlopers, and they could close ranks at the first hint of poaching.

Mr. Warren Reynolds and his beautiful niece hadn't had to make anything of their lack of "family" connections. It was perfect. They'd slipped onto several guest lists, and by not overtly overreaching their social circles—no one had really asked too many questions—they'd managed to climb steadily upward. Besides, most people, when looking for a con artist, scrutinized the man and forgot to look at the innocent young thing trailing behind him.

They were charlatans. Every instinct confirmed it. Reynolds wasn't known as a good gambler, but his niece . . . she was the one with the hidden talent. Warren was too ham-fisted and crass to have gotten this far on his own. But Julian imagined that with the lovely Eve Reynolds in his arsenal, the uncle had made the most of it. Her card play was like poetry, and Julian of all people admired the siren's song of a truly good player. He had no proof against her, but for what he wanted, Julian decided he might not need it.

Because tonight he was at Chesterfield's table at the Boar's Head, a seedier gaming establishment that attracted a few of the more daring gentlemen amidst the Ton to mingle with the regular and rougher crowds. Tonight, Mr. Warren Reynolds himself had joined the game and was congenially regaling them all with tales of his travels and extensive adventures. Tonight, the ale was flowing like water, and Julian discovered that he was in just the right place, at exactly the right moment.

"Ah, I feel lucky this evening, my friends! Consider yourselves fairly warned!" Reynolds chuckled as he gathered his cards.

"I'm considering another round," said Mr. Chesterfield. "And who needs fair warning? You never win, Reynolds!" Chesterfield boldly tossed a hefty ante on the table to test their courage. "Whilst I, on the other hand, never lose!"

"Never?" Julian asked quietly. "Remind me to ask you your secrets later, or to make sure I don't play you too often."

Chesterfield laughed loudly, and Julian watched beneath hooded eyes as the regular inhabitants of the bar took note of their merry corner. Discretion and habit had made him choose the seat against the wall with the greatest vantage of the room. Julian laid his cards down to withdraw from the duel and refilled their glasses from the decanter on the table.

"You'll never win if you do not play, Lord Westleigh," Reynolds expounded with the sage wisdom of a man supposedly deep in his cups. He threw in coins to match Chesterfield's bet and raised the amount with a reckless flick of his wrist. "Am I not right?"

"You are indeed!" Chesterfield nodded, then helped himself to his brandy, oblivious to the drips and drops that splattered over his cravat and cards. The sloppy movement would have diverted Julian's attention entirely had it not been for the tiniest dull flash of light from Reynolds's cuff links as he exchanged a card from his hand for one up his sleeve.

Julian's expression never changed, and he sat back to watch Chesterfield's fall. His plans to ply the man with even more liquor so that he could ask some pointed questions of his own evaporated like smoke. Reynolds had made the one underhanded move that had told Julian everything he needed to know.

"I have lost after all!" Chesterfield proclaimed.

"Indeed." Julian raised his own glass and caught Reynolds looking at him over his own cup, as if he'd suddenly been wary of the company he was keeping. Their gazes held, and Julian wondered if the older man wasn't worrying about the other cards up his sleeve. Reynolds's look was full of the cunning of an animal when cornered, but before Julian could say anything, the moment passed and Reynolds turned in his chair to hail a barmaid.

"More ale here!" Reynolds's jovial demeanor returned, and Julian decided he would let the matter lie—for now. A wicked plan coalesced and formed in his mind's eye, and Julian marveled at the simplicity of it. It *was* wicked.

I have you, Eve.

Every gambler enters the game by choice, he told himself. She'd known the risks and accepted them. He would make a feint and see if he could get the lovely Miss Reynolds to take the bait.

Chapter Seven

Dearest Eve,

Your last letter at once gave me the assurance that you are well and full of spirit, but also some cause for concern. I cannot help but feel that you aren't telling me everything. We are such close friends, you and I—and yet now, it's as if you don't trust me with the truth of your situation.

You mentioned in passing something about a "good string of luck" and I confess I was alarmed. I know your uncle would never hear of you gambling, so please set aside this interest. Stay clear of the gaming tables and you cannot go astray.

Have a marvelous time in Venice and enjoy yourself!

Eve, if I have misread things, forgive me. It's been so long since I've seen you. I miss you and pray that you are safe on your travels. Please write soon!

Your friend,
Jane Kingsley

Eve refolded the old letter, its corners worn and frayed from too many viewings, and tucked it back into the drawer. It was the last one she'd ever gotten from Jane. They'd become best friends after Eve and her father had been guests at one of Jane's family estates in Malta. She'd been fifteen, and it had been a summer that still stood out in Eve's mind as perfect. Her father had been in fine form, she'd spent every waking moment in the gardens or exploring the village with Jane at her side, and there'd been no foreshadowing of things to come.

She'd received this note from Miss Kingsley just a week before she'd gone to Venice. Eve had never told Jane that Uncle Warren had not only been happy to "hear of her gambling" but he'd also been the one who had encouraged, cajoled, and gently pressured her every step of the way while he'd pocketed her winnings toward their growing expenses. Dear, innocent Jane! Eve had valued her friendship and opinions too much to risk a full confession, so Jane's suspicions had been well founded. Eve had written her a reply, a long letter describing Venice in all its glory at Carnival and omitting every painful detail of her own heartbreak. She'd done everything she'd been able to do to reassure her friend that all had been well.

But she'd never received another letter from Jane.

Eve had stubbornly continued to write to her, refusing to believe that Jane would have cut her off without a word of farewell or explanation. And then it had evolved into a ritual of putting pen to paper and imagining Jane's expressions when she read the letters. It made Eve feel connected to happier days, and it was worth the cost of a few stamps to cheer herself.

" 'Stay clear of the gaming tables and you cannot go astray.' " Eve recited the words with a smile. "Oh, Jane! What would you say if you knew just how far off the path I've come?"

She began her letter to Jane as she always did, with a fervent wish for Miss Kingsley's health and happiness, and then she wrote as honestly as she could of her current dilemma and the doubts that plagued her. But she couldn't bring herself to mention Julian Clay directly. Seeing him in Hyde Park the day before had thrown her off balance. She was trying to dismiss him as an ordinary rogue, but his approach and demeanor had been so . . . different than they had been in the garden, so open and sincere. If he was bent on seduction, the dratted man had done more to unsettle her with his kind questions and sharp wit than she wanted to admit. She couldn't stop thinking about him, trying to guess at his tactics and wondering just how far he would go to have her.

A knock at the door brought her head up, and Eve instinctively covered the sheet with blank parchment before calling out, "Yes?"

"Just me! Just me!" Uncle Warren came in without any formal preambles. "Writing love letters?" he teased.

"Hardly." Eve set her pen down. "Just writing a few thank-you notes to keep us in good standing with all your new friends."

"Ah, the domain of ladies! All that frippery and note writing makes the world go round, and I am grateful for it." He took a seat on the edge of her bed. "I do hate to trespass above stairs, but we've been so harried lately, it seems I never see you to talk." He glanced around the threadbare room, as if noticing it for the very first time. "The . . . ah, morning light is very nice in this room."

Oh, dear. He was after something, she had no doubt. But she knew better than to try to anticipate the path he would take. Uncle Warren never just wanted to talk without a scheme on his mind. "Yes, it is."

"Well, time is money, as they say. We're doing well here, Eve. I know you were worried, but if you continue to apply yourself, my plan will come off brilliantly!"

He looked so inordinately pleased with himself and her that for a moment she wondered if this might be her chance to reach him and avoid hurting him somehow. "Uncle Warren. It is a good plan, but what if we—"

"I'll tell you what is a harder business!" he interrupted with a wave of his hand. "Sorting through all the bachelors in London to make sure I'm selecting only the best candidates for you. What a chore!"

"Only because I suspect you're coming at the problem backwardly. I think the suitors are supposed to do the selecting, and *then* you sort them out so that I can refuse them." She smiled. "That doesn't sound difficult at all, does it?"

"I like the young Mr. Thom Farley, don't you? He'd make an amusing husband, wouldn't he?" he asked, openly ignoring her jest.

"Uncle Warren, I don't remember him, so I'd say that's a bad omen for a match." Eve's stomach began to ache. "Can't we discuss this another time?"

"Well, of course." He rose and kissed her on the forehead before heading toward the door, but he turned back at the last moment. "Oh, I meant to tell you! The Earl of Westleigh is off my short list of prospects, dearest."

"What?" Her voice was hollow with shock. "What was that about Westleigh?"

"You'll see to it that there are no more of these public walks or waltzes with the man, eh? But I understand that a very handsome Lord Crestford has asked about you recently. He is titled and far from poor! So there's an eligible young man for you to consider! What do you say?"

"I don't know what to say." She took a slow, calming breath. "May I ask why you're suddenly set off the earl?"

"Nothing for you to concern yourself about. But you'll obey me, Eve. Not one word to the bounder in public, understood?"

The bounder. She nodded, dazed but unwilling to admit that this sudden change was surprisingly upsetting and painful. "As you wish."

For days, she'd sworn that if Julian abandoned the chase, she'd breathe a sigh of relief. But now . . . she felt anything but relieved. "Please, Uncle Warren, for my sake, no more matchmaking."

"Don't you want to be married?"

"Yes. I want very much . . . a place of my own and a family. I want to settle down someplace quiet and live a simple country life away from—"

"Bullocks! There is quiet enough in the grave, and besides, my dearest niece, you have no potential as a country wife, I am sad to tell you." He took her hand to gently pat it in sympathy. "What vicar, gameskeeper, or farmer will desire a wife whose only skills are playing cards and discerning when someone is bluffing?"

"What makes you think such a wife is desired by anyone?" She tried to hide how much his words stung. He was right, of course. But it was hard not to lash out in frustration, since he was the very man who had seen to it that all her talents centered around her ability to keep his pockets full.

"Rich men care only for wit and beauty! And those qualities you have in abundance! Besides, you are extremely eligible as the niece of a wealthy industrialist."

She shook her head, looking at him with a sad smile. "I am *not* the niece of a wealthy industrialist, Uncle Warren. And when this proposed husband discovers the truth of his bride's imaginary fortune and conniving uncle, how happy do you suppose he'll be?"

"Well . . ." He pouted, unable to fend off the implacable truth of her logic. "Let's stay with our original plan, then. I came up to tell you that we've been invited to a card party at Major Hayes's tonight."

"Oh."

"It's going beautifully, Eve! You are playing brilliantly, as I knew you would, and we'll make off with our trunks full of money at this rate. I thought a few months in Stockholm would suit us next. I understand that when it gets cold, there's little else to do but wager, and we have a standing invitation from a baron I met once in Paris. What do you say?"

She nodded, unable to say anything past the lump in her throat. There was no end to it. No escape from his endless schemes and plans, and nothing to look forward to beyond a lifetime of tables and odds, wagers and risk.

I have to get away. No matter what I've managed to save. I'll leave before the end of the Season and just pray that he'll let me go.

The card party at Major Hayes's was much larger and livelier than Eve had expected. She surmised that her uncle's confidence must have grown with every invitation they'd received. Since Lady Morrington's patronage of her, he'd probably decided that they were ready for more discriminating circles.

Eve certainly hoped they were.

This was far from Wickett's. With almost a hundred in attendance, the party was crowded with revelers elegantly attired and cheerfully engaged in conversation or looking for sport. Music drifted from the corner as a trio of musicians contributed to the pleasant scene and guaranteed that guests were properly entertained while they played at the tables or stood about conversing. They were surrounded by glittering wealth, and even after a lifetime of seeing such rooms, Eve had to admit that the setting made an unforgettable impression.

Brightly lit, the room sparkled in welcome, showcasing the quirky and expensive taste of their host's furnishings and artwork. Carved elephant tusks crowned the mantel, and Eve had to smile at the sight of a sculpture of an Indian god holding a box of chocolates on a priceless pedestal from Italian antiquity. It was a kaleidoscope of cultures that announced the major to be a world traveler, if nothing else!

The room was longer than it was wide, dominated by a wall of great windows at one end and awash in army red and gold wherever one looked. It was clear that Major Hayes was not a man who favored subtlety in anything he did.

"Glad you could come!" Eve's hand was swallowed entirely by his bearlike grasp. The unmistakable Major Hayes, in his bright red regimentals, his chest puffed out to display all his decorations and medals, was a sight to behold. His waxed handlebar mustache wobbled as he smiled, and at every exclamation, his black enamel-rimmed monocle threatened to leap from his face. Major Hayes boomed, "We've games for the ladies, too! Though I deliberately kept a room for dancing and whatnot, since it's hard to please everyone."

"Your parties are famous, Major! We are honored to be here," Uncle Warren said. "As for games for the gentlemen?"

"In the adjoining library, Mr. Reynolds. The ladies scowl if you smoke in their presence, so I do what I can to accommodate their more delicate senses. I've invited the men to play there if they prefer a cigar or a less cautious approach to their conversation—but I warn you, the women do wander in from time to time."

"How can you keep them away?" Uncle Warren teased, giving Eve an ungenteel wink, which she did her best to ignore. He was in a buoyant mood, but she wished he would be a little more guarded when they were in good company.

"Are all the tables segregated then?" she asked.

"Oh, no! There are tables on that side of the room for all to play, and the smaller red salon is set up for casino. So you can play as you wish!" He bowed, "Pray forgive me, I just spotted a friend who I must torment for old time's sake!"

He left them without another word, and Eve gripped her uncle's arm. "Stay."

She looked for a familiar face but saw none. None of her Tuesday ladies were in attendance, but her uncle was not in the mood to stay at her side.

"There's Chesterfield, dearest! Enjoy yourself and don't look at me like such a prim! I'm a grown man and entitled to a bit of fun." He kissed her cheek and retreated before she could say anything.

He was sure that she would successfully find a place of her own at the tables, but Eve shook her head. *What would Miss Gloria Finch advise now?* Restrictions of etiquette kept her from inviting herself into a game or approaching anyone she didn't know without her uncle's introduction. He knew this, of course, but Uncle Warren had a childlike knack for conveniently forgetting the rules when they kept him from his amusements.

She circled, surveying the various groups of gamblers in one of the two adjoining rooms set aside for cards, trying to look for an open chair or opportunity. Her uncle would complain if she didn't manage a few hands, but Eve wasn't worried. Polite manners would ensure that their host or one of the guests noticed her solitary state and offered her a remedy eventually. So for the moment, she enjoyed an insular quiet and moved to look at a wall covered with artwork. Hunting scenes, epic battles, and oriental prints proclaimed the major's manly tastes, but Eve was drawn to one small, plain frame.

It was a miniature painting of a young woman. But unlike a traditional portrait with the subject staring out with solemn eyes, the girl in the picture was perched at her desk with a mischievous expression in her eyes. Caught in the act of sealing a letter, she'd tipped her head to one side in an unabashedly coquettish challenge. Her smile made Eve wonder about the contents of the note in her hand and who it was for.

"The major's sister, I believe." A soft feminine voice spoke at her elbow, a gentle intrusion on Eve's reverie. "She is a woman grown now, and keeping house for their youngest brother living in Egypt."

Eve turned to meet the lady. Grateful for the company, she curtsied. "She's beautiful, and apparently an adventurer as well. May I introduce myself? I am Eve Reynolds."

"Merriam Sotherton," the lady replied shyly. "I admit I came over because it looked as if you'd been cut adrift, and I used to dread any gathering where I found myself studying china collections and trying to blend in with the drapery."

Eve laughed. "You're jesting! You don't strike me as the sort of woman who could ever blend into a window treatment, but I thank you all the same for the courtesy."

"Ah! If only you knew . . ." Merriam stepped aside to bring Eve over to a small group standing in conversation. "Miss Eve Reynolds, may I introduce you to my husband and friend? This is Drake Sotherton, the Duke of Sussex, and his niece, Miss Callie Singleton."

Eve curtsied again, lowering her eyes as she absorbed the new connection. *Duke of Sussex. Which makes you, dear lady, the Duchess of Lady Morrington's salacious stories about Lord Westleigh's brush with death. Which makes me wonder at my strange luck . . .* "My pleasure. Do you enjoy playing cards, Your Grace?"

"Not at all."

Eve almost laughed at the dour and succinct reply from such a tall and brooding man, especially when his lovely wife gave him a look that immediately altered his manner. "That is to say, I prefer to watch others and keep a safe distance."

Miss Singleton's eyes widened in a mocking show of amazement. "And what distance would *that* be?"

"Harridan," the duke pronounced quietly, but a gleam of amusement in his eyes gave away the game. No matter how forbidding the man appeared, he had a strong affection for the women at his side.

"Drake Sotherton! Behave! What is Miss Reynolds to think of you? The both of you!" The young duchess struggled to keep her tone stern as her husband instantly looked subdued and the lovely Miss Singleton put her fingers over her lips.

"I'm sorry, Merriam. I know we should be better behaved, but must Drake always try to frighten people on first acquaintance?" His young niece shared a feminine version of his dark good looks but little of his serious countenance.

He leaned over conspiratorially to Eve. "It's become a habit."

"You're very good at it," Eve noted. He didn't look "deadly" to Eve, but she wasn't about to ask how a man earned such a dreadful moniker. "I imagine you'd be a hard man to intimidate across a card table."

His brows lifted in amusement. "Perhaps, Miss Reynolds, I'm missing an opportunity to apply myself and overturn a few fortunes."

It was the duchess's turn to laugh. "Major Hayes would have a heart attack from the shock of seeing you at his tables! Come, dearest, let's see if we can—"

An excited burst of shouts and laughter from the library cut her off, and conversations all around them trailed away as everyone craned to see what the commotion was about.

"No trouble, I hope," Merriam said.

Eve shook her head, her instincts keen when it came to these things. "No, someone is on the brink of winning a vast sum, or has just done so."

The three of them drew closer to see for themselves until one of the men in the doorway, his voice full of awe, informed a friend behind him, "It's the Earl of Westleigh!"

Drake's expression was unreadable, but he stopped immediately and reached out to catch his wife's arm. "We're going."

Miss Singleton looked displeased. "Must we?"

"Forgive us, Miss Reynolds, for abandoning you so abruptly," the Duchess of Sussex smoothly intervened. "But we have one or two more stops to make this evening, and I don't want to keep Callie out too late."

"I'm hardly—" Callie began, but she ended her protest at the duchess's pleading look. "I didn't realize it was so late, Miss Reynolds. It was a pleasure to meet you."

"Yes. I hope we have another chance soon." Eve bobbed a quick curtsy at the sudden loss of her small circle of new acquaintances but was assured that the Duke of Sussex had his reasons for going.

"Another time, Miss Reynolds," Merriam added gently before taking her husband's proffered arm and letting him lead her briskly toward the door.

Eve wasted no time in pondering the nature of the feud between the two men but instead turned back to the library doorways and began to weave her way through the gathering. Despite her uncle's admonitions, she was not about to miss seeing what was happening inside that room.

The whispers as she drew closer helped fill her in on the event at hand.

"Too rich for my blood!"

"He was down a staggering amount, but my God, I think he's about to take poor Mr. Sweetley for a year's worth of income!"

"Sweetley may regret this in the morning!"

"It's not over yet!"

The crowd shifted and Eve slipped inside the room. The library was outfitted in the major's signature red and gold, but it was muted by the leather volumes and carved wood of the inevitable shelves that gave the room its name. There were six tables set up, but only one was currently occupied. All the other players had abandoned their seats to watch and bid on the game of écarté that had caught everyone's attention.

The cards were being reshuffled for another deal, and Eve watched Lord Westleigh with the eyes of an expert. There was nothing aggressive in his posture or movements, nothing to betray the fact that he had any personal interest in the outcome. He was reclined in his chair with his legs outstretched and crossed at the ankles, in casual disregard for the polite rules regarding a gentleman's posture in public. One look at the ramrod-straight outline of Mr. Sweetley told her everything about his character.

The earl is deliberately making the man crazed—distracting him by letting his drink drip onto the cloth and keeping his elbows out like that. Lord Westleigh is not a slovenly man, but he's playing it well now.

As was the custom, those in company were encouraged to bet on the play and could advise the players as things unfolded. So both men were now drowning in earnest calls of advice and commands, strategies and tactics for luck as Julian dealt the cards again.

Mr. Sweetley, though rattled, was not a soft mark. Eve couldn't see his cards, but as the play began and the trump was declared, it was clear he knew how to make his calls and discards with merciless skill.

But it was Lord Westleigh she focused on, clearing the rest of the room and its noisy occupants from her attention until it was as if just the three of them had been sitting in Major Hayes's library.

Julian Clay was a golden lion, lazy and rested, but hungry enough to go on a hunt. The game took shape, and Eve absorbed the rhythm of his moves and the hidden aggression that was nipping at the heels of Sweetley's icy strategies.

The amount on the table was frightening. *Too much money to lose, I don't care who you are, Lord Westleigh.* Shouts of advice escalated around them, and suddenly Eve saw how he could lose. How he would lose . . . How it was inevitable . . . and something in her was seized with genuine fear for the earl.

Without hesitation, she spoke up firmly but didn't try to shout over the others. "Lord Westleigh."

His eyes snapped up from the cards in his hand, his fingers frozen in place above a single card. Somehow he'd heard her above the din, and Eve felt a rush of emotion at this strange connection between them.

"Don't give him the choice of a finesse. Look hard at the trump before you touch the queen. Play it out and then take command." She bit her lower lip. "Trust me."

The gold in his eyes seemed to churn and smolder, and when he finally smiled at her, she swore at the bolt of lightning that wound its way around her spine. *Impossible man!*

Eve turned on her heels and pushed her way from the room. She couldn't bear to watch him anymore, couldn't bear to see him lose, and she didn't want to see the smug arrogance on his face when he won. She wasn't even supposed to talk to the man in public, much less address him in front of a crowd!

She looked across the room and realized that her uncle Warren must still be in the smaller salon with Chesterfield, so she'd at least saved herself one potential lecture in the carriage on the ride home.

A cheer went up behind her, and Eve resolutely sank down into an open window seat, where she pretended to admire the carriages on the drive below and count the horses. The minutes ticked away, and she knew without looking up when he came up behind her.

"I owe you my thanks, Miss Reynolds."

She stood and turned to face him, wondering

why she was surprised, every time she saw him, how strikingly handsome he was. "You owe me nothing. If I'd been quicker, I'm sure I'd have placed a small wager of my own, but—"

"Everyone else was urging me to throw caution to the winds," he noted. "But you kept a clear head."

"Everyone else was looking at the money on the table and not the cards."

He shook his head. "You never cease to amaze me, Miss Eve Reynolds."

Eve's breath caught in her throat at the compliment, and she struggled to remember her purpose and place in the world. "Lord Westleigh," she murmured, keeping her voice low, "there is something you should know."

"If it has to do with declaring the king in a hand, I'm sure I can manage."

"My uncle . . . has forbidden me to speak to you." She bravely lifted her chin and awaited his disapproval.

"Nonsense." The earl was clearly unaffected by the news.

"I am serious, Lord Westleigh. He insists that I end any further public exchanges with you! I know you're not in the habit of paying attention to these things, but I'm not in a position to cross him."

"I see," he replied, attempting a more serious expression. "Is he going to call me out?"

She rolled her eyes. "No! Nothing has happened between us as far as he knows beyond a waltz and a walk—and that's where it ends." She took a deep breath. "My uncle's word is . . . final."

He gave her a skeptical look but kept his own counsel. Instead, he rewarded her with one last, searing look that rendered her speechless. Then he bowed a very formal farewell and strolled back to the library.

Eve sank down onto the cushions and sighed. She had no illusions of victory as he withdrew without looking back. A man who ignored the rules wasn't going to alter course because her uncle commanded it.

How do you dissuade the devil from asking you to dance?

"Especially if a part of you doesn't want him to stop asking . . . ," she whispered, unaware that she'd spoken aloud and forgotten not to watch him go.

Chapter Eight

Her hands shook as she read the note for the sixth time, as if repetition would have changed the elegant scrawl.

Miss Reynolds,

Meet me at 420 Bell Street tomorrow at noon. We need to talk about your uncle. It is an urgent matter.

Julian C.

It was probably a bluff to get her to meet him alone. But if it wasn't a ruse, and she didn't meet him, Eve wasn't sure what the consequences would be if she ignored this "urgent matter." Was this just the earl's reaction to her uncle's edict to Eve to stay away from him? Or had something else happened since the card party at Major Hayes's? What had Uncle Warren done now?

The threat was unspoken, but it radiated from the crisp white page.

Come or else.

Curiosity overcame her doubts. She had no choice. She would have to slip from the house after breakfast and make her way to meet him, if only to discover what it was he knew about Uncle Warren.

Was her uncle's change of heart regarding "the bounder" part of this?

It made no difference. Julian had all the answers.

I have no illusions of this man's honorable intentions.

Why doesn't that frighten me?

No matter what revelations he had in store, they would be alone, and it was too wicked an opportunity for a man like Julian Clay to forgo. He was going to do his best to seduce her, she knew. But something inside her began to thrum and dance in anticipation of the game.

She wanted to see him again.

She did favor strong leads, but what Lord Westleigh was about to learn was that sometimes giving someone an illusion of being in the lead meant that she would be the one to stay in control.

Julian waited for her at the Bell Street address. It was actually owned by Shelbrook, a small townhome he'd acquired and kept secret from his wife. Apparently, a few years ago Barnaby had had a mistress, but he'd dropped her when his new young wife had treated him to an ice storm of relentless hysterics. He'd never given up the fashionable address, though, either to keep his peers from discovering that he'd failed to stand up to his wife on such a critical matter or because he one day hoped to have the courage to cheat on her again. He'd given Julian the key in a bit of male bonding over brandy recently, and Julian had decided after his first inspection of the place that it was a godsend. He'd promised Barnaby he wouldn't use it too often so that there would be little danger of Lady Shelbrook's discovering its existence.

Right on time, she arrived on the doorstep. When he opened the door, she handed him her hat and gloves without a word, as if he'd been a mere servant. Julian escorted her into the parlor with a wry grin. "May I get you some tea, Miss Reynolds?"

"It's a bit early in the day for tea, Lord Westleigh." She faced him squarely, clearly bracing for battle.

"Wine? Brandy? Sherry? Port?"

Her eyes narrowed, and she crossed her arms defensively. "In the middle of the day? Exactly the sort of hospitality one might expect from a man who sends a rude summons to a woman to meet him alone. My uncle—"

"Forbade you to talk to me in public. But as you've already pointed out, this is a private meeting, Eve."

"Why don't you get right to the point of your summons, Lord Westleigh?"

She was so beautiful and fearless standing there. He was drawn to her and the delectable and precarious nature of her situation. She was no more the niece of a wealthy industrialist than he was eligible for the clergy. But her attempted ruse was necessary if she had certain aims. It wasn't as if the Ton would bother to invite someone to play unless they believed they had the money and cachet to make good on their wagers. Bloodlines, credit, and reputation were the delicate instruments that kept the riffraff out. If she intended to sit in on the best circles, theatrical touches were vital.

But he wasn't entirely convinced that it was that simple. Nothing about her seemed simple. "What are you up to?"

"That's the second time you've asked me that question. I thought it was my uncle you wished to discuss, Lord Westleigh. You proclaimed to know all in your note, and here I am. Or am I to understand that among your many notorious traits, you're a liar as well?" she asked sweetly. "Or is this just another revision of a previous conversation? If it is, I assure you that I won't linger long to waste your time."

He raised his eyebrows, amused at the insult. "Oh, my! Did I say that I 'knew all'? I never thought I would relish notoriety, Miss Reynolds. But when you look at me like that, I swear I can think of a dozen ways to enjoy it without a moment of regret."

"I'm not sure how to look at you, Lord Westleigh. But why do I have the feeling it would be more dangerous not to keep an eye on you?"

"My father used to say, 'Always trust your instincts.'"

"And mine used to say that you could never trust anyone."

"We are at an impasse then." Julian turned to pour himself a small glass of port. "I'm sure if I asked you to trust me—"

"I never could." She finished the thought. "Are we done then?"

"Yet you asked me to trust you at the major's."

She crossed her arms, openly flustered at the reminder. "You won, didn't you? And this is my reward for helping you?"

"Absolutely. Just assure me that your own plans don't entail anything too criminal."

"Why should I tell you anything?"

"Because I might just keep asking and asking until others start to wonder as well."

She took a deep breath before answering him calmly. "No, Lord Westleigh, nothing *too* criminal." He raised a skeptical eyebrow, and so she added hastily, "The last I knew, gambling and perjury weren't entirely acceptable, Lord Westleigh, but it isn't always considered criminal."

The woman made a good point, since he didn't know anyone who didn't gamble or lie on occasion. "That's all?"

She spread her hands. "It is the vast extent of it, yes. So what do you intend to do now?"

"Nothing."

"Nothing?" It was her turn to play the skeptic. "You feel no urge whatsoever to warn your friends that there is a commoner in their midst with an eye on their fortunes?"

"If that's the worst of it, I'm sure they can take care of themselves. And if they lose fairly, so be it." He rolled the stem of the glass in his fingers. "You pulled me back from the brink at Major Hayes's. I want to return the favor."

"Am I on the brink, Lord Westleigh?"

"Do you play fairly at your parlor games, Miss Reynolds?"

"Yes." Her chin lifted proudly. "Always."

"But your uncle . . . fairness doesn't come to mind when he's at the tables, does it?" He polished off the port in one swallow, setting his glass down to savor its effects. Then he watched her composure falter, her eyes blinking in surprise as a new wariness entered her beautiful blue eyes.

"Are you saying . . . that he . . . ?"

"Cheats? Absolutely. I witnessed it myself at the Boar's Head, and while the others were too drunk to take note, I'm sure it would only take a word or two for things to become decidedly more dangerous in London for Mr. Warren Reynolds."

She gasped at the prospect, and Julian marveled at the novel notion that she genuinely might not have realized what her uncle was up to. *Is that even possible, or are you acting the innocent again, Lamb?*

"What do you want?" she asked.

He held his breath, trying to choose from a wicked list of possible responses to that question. God help him, she was reading his mind, but instead of blushing and running from the room, her lips parted as her breath quickened, and he knew that if nothing else came of this delicious exchange, he would sample the taste of those lips again. Anticipation at the sweet, soft feel of her beneath him only brought the simmer in his veins to a sensuous boil, the weight of his lust flooding lower, like warm sand, until his cock was rock hard.

"I'm not a villain, Miss Reynolds. I admire anyone who strives to make their fortunes as best they can. And while your uncle may foolishly choose an unsavory shortcut or two, I promise you that I won't be the one to out him." He took a single step closer. "On my word of honor."

To her credit, she didn't laugh at his pledge, and

he watched the silent debate in her eyes yield to him. "What do you want?" she asked again.

"I want you to trust me. I want to play, Miss Reynolds."

Long seconds bled away as she seemed to make a decision. "Do you have a deck of cards, Lord Westleigh?"

"Yes." An ornate wooden box sitting on the corner table yielded a deck when he opened it. He'd brought them with him in the hopes that Miss Eve Reynolds would answer his summons.

"Why don't we start with something simple?" she said.

"As you wish." He held out the deck to her, forcing her to come closer. She moved warily, as if she expected him to suddenly spring forward or hurt her somehow. He had no such intentions. *But neither am I a gentleman without aspirations of seeing you completely on your back, dear girl. Make no mistake, Miss Reynolds, I'm going to enjoy getting you there. I simply see no need to rush.*

She took the cards from his hands and began to shuffle them. He watched closely as the act calmed her. The tension flowed from her frame, dispersed through the deft movement of her fingers. The sound of the whispering friction of the deck made him smile. *Never did I think that sound would make me so aroused . . .*

"A quick game of high card, Lord Westleigh?"

He nodded, then followed her over to the elegant overstuffed settee. She pulled a side table over to serve as a makeshift playing surface, and Julian sat down next to her.

"Why don't you deal?" she asked, setting the cards down. "To keep me honest?"

He picked up the deck and began to randomly divide the cards into two equal hands. He kept his eyes on hers, wondering how many men would wager their fortunes to take his place.

"You didn't reshuffle them, Lord Westleigh."

"I didn't need to, Miss Reynolds." He studied her for a moment. "Before we begin, shouldn't we decide on what the stakes are?"

She nervously moistened her lips, her tongue touching each pink curve in a slow sweep that sent shock waves across his body. Julian wondered how long he'd be able to maintain even a vague hold on polite decorum if he was going to be treated to the sight of the tip of that sweet, wet tongue. He wanted to enjoy this seduction, lingering over each advance, unlike the heated rush that had swept over him in the garden at Hutton's. They were alone, in no danger of interruption, and Julian felt like a man on the brink of paradise.

"Why don't we name a forfeit after each victory?" she proposed calmly.

Paradise found. "Agreed."

With their respective stacks facedown on each

side of the small table, Julian gave her a brief nod. "Ladies first."

She slid the first card off the top of her pile and laid it down.

The six of diamonds.

He drew his and knew he'd won just by the sudden intake of her breath. He glanced down at the ten of spades with a surge of euphoria. He looked back to her, unable to hide his pleasure. "Ah, fate!"

"And what prize will you claim?" she asked.

"A kiss."

A soft gasp escaped her lips, her eyes darkening as she looked up at him. "You—wouldn't rather ask a question? Demand the forfeit of a truthful answer?"

He shook his head, smiling at the maidenly attempt at negotiation. "Perhaps another time."

"This may be your only chance to play, Lord Westleigh."

"Then I would be a fool not to insist on that kiss, Miss Reynolds." He deliberately stood his ground and waited to see what she would do. He didn't need to remind her about the prime rule regarding the honor of a wager, and he knew she was weighing it all out in that clever head of hers. *And remembering what happened at Hutton's.*

"Very well," she conceded. "A kiss, then."

There was no further debate. Julian was relieved to discover that Miss Eve Reynolds might be many things, but she was definitely a woman of her word. She leaned forward, balancing herself by placing a hand against his heart. Her splayed fingers seared his flesh through the silk of his shirt, and he wondered briefly if she could feel his pulse racing at her touch. He forced himself to hold perfectly still to allow her the power to truly initiate this kiss.

Her lips grazed his, a warm, wet friction that was gone almost before he could register it.

"There," Eve said, beginning to shift back, but Julian wasn't about to be cheated out of his prize. His arms encircled her and prevented her escape as he captured her mouth with his. Within the space of a few heartbeats, she softened against him and pressed closer, capturing his lower lip with her mouth only to taste him with her tongue—a flicker of hot flesh across the most sensitive curve of his lips that ended his resolve to be still. He shifted to repay her in kind, arcs of sensation pushing every nerve ending into a white-hot dance that demanded he taste every part of her mouth until she moaned and writhed on the seat, her weight sagging against him. His teeth grazed the softest corners of her mouth, and Julian suckled her tongue, in a rhythm that matched his heartbeat. She yielded to him, the duel of their mutual need spiraling out of control. She moaned, and Julian drank that in as well, the womanly sound of it setting off an answering growl he couldn't contain deep within his chest. His arms reached up to encompass her, to press her closer against him, increasing the fiery tempo between them.

Finally she withdrew, disengaging with a bit of difficulty, her lips swollen and her eyes darkened by passion. It struck Julian that his enthusiastic gypsy queen was magic—so sweet and ready, but not overly practiced in the arts of love. She shifted back to rebalance herself on the sofa next to him and, with trembling hands, drew another card to set it down on the table.

The two of hearts.

Julian smiled. "I love this game. I can't imagine why it isn't played more often in public."

He tossed down his next card, not surprised in the slightest to win with a humble four of the same suit.

"Well?" she asked. A shiver of anticipation worked through her, and Julian's hands captured hers, then released them to gently trail his fingertips up her arms, across her décolletage, and over the sweet curves of her breasts as her breathing hitched and teased his touch. She pursed her lips, inadvertently drawing his attention back to her mouth.

"I want to touch you."

"I suppose . . ." Eve blushed as she caught her

breath. "I suppose it would be useless to ask you to consider a more gentlemanly request?"

"Completely useless." Julian knew he would press her only as far as she desired, but he also knew that if her kisses were any indication—he'd already achieved the field. "Just let me touch you," he whispered.

She nodded. "As . . . you wish."

It was like touching warm velvet. Down her cheeks to the slim column of her throat and downward over the planes and firm curves of her chest, across her ribs and then up again to cup her breasts, he traced her body through the layers of her clothing, marveling at how wicked it was to stroke a woman like this, to possess and tease with only the use of his hands. He deliberately left every button and fastening intact, watching the desire in her eyes as he disregarded these chances to stray beneath to touch the creamy soft skin that was surely burning for the contact she craved.

"So many layers . . ."

"For modesty—" she gasped, and started to pull away, but his gaze caught hers and she froze, unable to deny the tension building inside of her. "Julian, you—" Her words abruptly stopped as his fingers worked their magic despite the layers of clothing and boned undergarments he was complaining about. The day style of the gown denied him easy access, but Julian Clay's efforts were slowed, not deterred. Each hindering button gave his hands a chance to linger and press, to tease and caress her body through the offending cloth.

"How can it be modesty when it only inspires a man to think of how to get the damn things off?" At last, he gave in to the yearning he read in her eyes. Julian kissed the edges of her collarbone, nuzzling the indents and hollows of her throat even as his fingers brushed across the rising curves of her breasts, deliberately using the friction of her gown against her. His touch excited her, and her breathing hitched the firm mounds against his palms in an unspoken supplication for him to uncover all that her beautiful body offered.

"Not every man thinks as you do, Lord Westleigh."

He lifted his head in mock astonishment. "Really?" It was just too bewitching—to hear her voice rough with arousal while she attempted to be so prim and proper. He moved swiftly, his tactic changing without warning to effectively find a shocking way to end the debate on ladies' fashions and press his advantage. His hands caught the fabric of her skirt and swept the layers up over her knees while his fingers swept over the curves of her calves, then upwards to the supple flesh of her thighs.

"Oh!" Her head fell back with another moan, her eyes closing as she succumbed to his hands. "I believe this . . . is where modesty insists . . . that you stop."

"Does it?" Julian pressed her back into the cushions, kneeling above her to use his hands in a relentless campaign to draw her past all ladylike reason—and without disturbing a single gusset on her corset. Instead, his fingers navigated the forbidden and warm terrain of petticoats and lace to find her skin, slipping through the opening in her pantalets to find their goal. Her eyes fluttered open to meet his as he touched skin that felt like smooth, wet silk and beckoned him to linger and invade and take all that he could.

She gasped, her knees tensing to draw together, but he began to move his fingers against her flesh and she relaxed beneath him, letting out one long, trembling sigh.

"Lord . . . Westleigh, I . . ."

"I want to touch you, Miss Reynolds." It was a wicked mockery of modesty that he allowed her skirts to ride no higher than her knees but had her spread out to his hands like a feast—and he relished the delicious discovery of her just by feel. His fingers were slick with her arousal. His thumb moved across her tight, hot little clitoris, and she started against him, arching her back and gripping the pillows as he stroked her there. He imagined the dark coral of it, a swollen pearl sweet and small, and wondered how many men had tasted it. Julian deliberately increased the tempo, teasing and working the tiny bud until she moaned and began to tremble beneath his touch. Julian spread his free hand around her hip to guide her movements and bit his lower lip in concentration.

God, she's beautiful—so wild now, but even so, she is about to bid me stop, or I've forgotten everything I ever knew about women.

Her hand caught his wrist, and she strained back against the pillows to escape his hands and the powerful pleasure he'd evoked.

"A-another round, Lord Westleigh?"

"Most definitely."

She sat up, pushing her skirts back down with a show of prim modesty that belied the raucous tenor of her breathing. "You cannot win . . . every hand, you realize."

"I don't expect to, Miss Reynolds."

She turned over the jack of clubs and held her breath.

Julian revealed the jack of hearts from his pile and grinned. "A tie."

"Another card then? To determine the winner?"

He nodded and watched as she confidently drew another card—the seven of spades. A degree of confidence fled her eyes when she looked back up at him, to be replaced by a flare of wanting and confusion.

He flicked his card over, the snap of paper to wood pleasant and cheerful. It was the ace of hearts. "It looks like my luck is holding."

"Name my forfeit," she whispered, her eyes meeting his without a flutter.

A gentleman would ask for something trivial and innocent. A gentleman wouldn't push this game any further. But Julian acknowledged to himself that there was little use in proclaiming himself a gentleman now. He'd already come much too far for that. There was no sound in the room but their breathing—hers, erratic and labored, his, the steady draw of a man invigorated by the hunt. *God, she's like an opiate.*

"I want you to touch me."

He leaned back against the settee to marvel at the war of desire and innocence in her dark blue eyes. It was the most alluring mixture he'd ever seen. He watched her consider exactly what he expected his demand to entail. Unless she asked, Julian decided that he would leave it entirely up to her.

Her eyes raked the path she wanted to take, and Julian's breath caught in his throat, his blood already warming in response. He stretched his arms along the back of the small sofa to casually offer himself up to her attentions. She inched closer, and he waited patiently for her approach. Long, slim fingers gently reached out to skim up his chest, and it was his turn to experience the torment of being touched through the silk and cotton that covered his skin.

Her eyes locked with his, and he forgot everything as he saw delight and power come into play. *You are in charge, Lamb. Until the turn of the next card . . .*

She rocked up to lift one knee onto the settee, then leveraged herself up to balance for better access to him. She smiled and began innocently tracing his face, then she drew her fingers into his hair, her nails sending shivers of pleasure down his spine as she ran them across his scalp, unsettling his golden curls. Then down his throat and lower, fingers splayed as she mimicked the teasing explorations he'd made, invoking fire from his nerve endings without disturbing a single button.

He groaned as he edged toward frustration, and then no longer felt like complaining when her hands dropped to his thighs and pressed against the muscles of his inner thighs and slowly circled upwards in a lazy massage that made his cock rock hard. The outline of his erection was unmistakable, its length prodding unapologetically against the fabric of his trousers, demanding attention.

She lowered her gaze and stared at him as her hands caressed the shape of him, stroking the shaft and gently squeezing his balls until he thought he would embarrass himself inside his clothing. "Eve . . ."

"Once more . . . one more time, Lord Westleigh. And this time . . . I think we should raise the stakes." Her eyes were still lowered to his engorged anatomy, but she was already retreating, her hands shaking.

"Yes."

"One more . . . and the winner . . . can have . . . *anything* . . . they . . . want . . ." Eve finished and looked to him for his decision. "Unless you think it better to stop now."

He didn't wait but leaned forward to toss a card onto the table. *Thank you, God.* It was the queen of diamonds. He began to reach for her, but she held out her hand to turn over a single card, her fingers trembling.

The ace of spades lay on the table between them.

"What will the lady have then?"

He was so confident. He knew she was swollen and ripe, wet for him, so ready to yield. She hesitated for a moment, a beautiful and wanton creature perched on the sofa, and he held his breath. His cock was screaming for release, and Julian knew she couldn't deny her desires. She was clearly so ready to tumble into his arms that he thought he might explode if she didn't say the words he longed to hear.

Finally she took a deep breath, and her eyes met his with a sapphire blue fire all their own. "I never want to see you again."

Chapter Nine

"A little early for social calls, isn't it?"

Eve froze, her right hand still on her bedroom doorknob. The house was still, and she had thought herself safe enough to just slip back into her room without notice. She turned back and tried to brazen her way out of trouble. "Is it?"

When he didn't react, but stayed still and silent, she abandoned the tactic.

"Uncle Warren, I—"

"Tell me where you were."

"I just went out for a short turn in the air. The weather's been so beautiful and you're the one who always complains that I should get more color."

"I don't believe you, Eve." He pursed his lips, and Eve recognized the signs of an impending tantrum.

"I stopped at the chemist and got a mix for Barnett." She pulled a small plainly wrapped package from her pocket. "The poor man's hands trouble him, Uncle Warren."

His mouth fell open, and he stared at the brown square she held out. "It's— I'm sure he'll appreciate your thoughtfulness." He took it from her quickly, tucking it into his coat pocket before he gave her one last searching look. "I'll see that he gets it. But I swear, you nearly gave me a heart attack with this foolish disappearance! I could only imagine the worst, and . . . as you well know, your judgment hasn't always been sound."

She nodded, praying he wouldn't say any more, especially about V—

"Remember Venice? Remember how you wept for weeks afterward?"

"Of course I remember."

His expression softened. "I'm cruel to mention it. It haunts me, how I should have taken better care of you and never encouraged that bounder Moore to pursue you. I can't tell you how many sleepless nights I've endured."

She almost laughed. "You poor man!"

"Poor is right! It was almost six months before you could play with any sense! I thought we were going to end up in some foreign debtor's prison!"

Eve felt all her humor bleed away at his words. "Uncle Warren. You're not . . . cheating at cards, are you? After all that we've been through and when it's going so well—tell me you're not up to your old tricks. Not after you swore to me you would never do it again."

His guilty silence spoke volumes.

Eve moaned. "You promised!"

"And I've kept my promise!" His gaze faltered. "Well, perhaps I have given the Fates a nudge now and then. But only on the rarest of occasions and when it's absolutely necessary! And who is the cad who accused me? I certainly hope you came to my defense, for there's no proof to be had! Not one shred!"

"It doesn't matter." She turned back toward the doorway, retreating to her room. "I saw to it, Uncle Warren. I'm going to bathe and get ready for this evening's party. Please, just . . ." Her words trailed away, for she was unsure what plea would reach him.

"Yes, a wonderful idea!" He recovered his affability with his usual amazing speed. "A bath will set you right, and a nice rest before this evening will make sure you're in good form for écarté. Lady Winston will be there, and though we've never had the pleasure before, I understand she is always eager to play."

"Then we'll make sure she is entertained. If you'll excuse me," Eve said as she shut the door behind her, unable to endure any more talk of the business that consumed him. She pressed her forehead against the wood once it had latched, listening to the hollow sounds of her uncle's return to his comforts below on the ground floor.

The day's amazing events struck home, and Eve began to undress, the ritual slowed by the distracting storm of her thoughts. She'd met Julian alone and deliberately indulged in a wicked fantasy over a game of cards. He'd set the game's goals, but her own desire had quickly come into play. She'd wanted to beat him at his own game, but Eve realized she'd underestimated her own hunger for his touch. She'd risked everything for the sweet taste of rebellion and for a few minutes had ignored the rules and restrictions of the world around her. But when that final card had offered her an honorable retreat, she hadn't wanted it. Victory over this rogue earl hadn't been nearly as satisfying as she'd thought it might be.

Perhaps her uncle was right and she couldn't trust her own judgment ever again when it came to such men.

She sat on the edge of the bathtub, running the water with both taps open, even though the hot water pipes would do little more than yield a faint tease from the warmth below stairs. Still, anything to keep the water from a stinging cold was welcome. She turned off the water and dropped her wrap across a clothes stand to keep it off the floor.

Standing, she entered the water gingerly, sitting slowly to slide down, letting the cool temperature soothe her skin and assuage the heat that still pulsed through her body. The tender flesh between her legs tingled at the contact, and she held her breath for a moment until her nerve endings gave in to the change, allowing the cold to numb her body.

Her skin marbled in the cool air. The lamp she'd lit and set on the shelf above her made the room seem less stark and empty. It was early to bathe, but she wasn't sure she could sit through an evening out in polite society with any telltale evidence of Julian Clay's attentions remaining on her body.

She retrieved a flannel and a bar of her favorite soap to begin the task, aware as her hand worked over her skin that it would take more than a single cold bath to erase his touch from her memory. She glanced down at herself, pondering the fact that despite whatever maelstrom of emotions the man's hand had elicited, there were no marks or physical signs of their encounter. *Shouldn't there be? Shouldn't that kind of passion leave something behind?*

But there was nothing. Her skin was as pale as ever. She held up the cloth to her cheek and sighed. She took a deep breath and decided that life was too full of ironies—a person could waste a lifetime wondering how hatred and violence left marks, whereas tenderness and passion evaporated off one's skin like water.

Despite all the complications Lord Westleigh presented, a part of her wished that there had been some way to harbor the heat and fire of his hands. She wanted to keep the sensations he elicited from her like a forfeited jewel and hoard them away.

Uncle Warren can rail all he likes, but this is one thing he can never take away from me. I know what it is to be wanted again. And I'm beginning to wonder how long it is that I'm supposed to atone for one stupid mistake, punishing myself and letting him browbeat me every time it serves his purposes.

She'd let things with Julian go too far.

She leaned back, watching the light cast on the ceiling from the lamp's cheap wick, and listened to the sound of the water dripping from her fingertips as she lazily moved them across the tub. Nothing she'd planned with Lord Westleigh had been as she'd expected. *Every player has a weakness—but all I know now is that he is my weakness. I wanted to lose. God help me, I wanted it even when that blasted ace fell across the table. And then I ran like the coward I am.*

In his presence, none of the rules had any power over her. He spoke of desire and touched her as if this had all been a simple matter; when he looked at her, she almost believed it—that it was normal to find yourself on your back clutching pillows and struggling not to cry out with a man's delicious hands up your skirt. It was blasphemy of a most intoxicating nature, and Eve knew she had never before experienced anything like Julian. Nor would she ever again.

Her hands slipped down, as if of their own accord, beneath the surface of the water, moving over her breasts and lingering to test their weightless state. He'd teased them only hours earlier, his fingers taunting her growing needs until she'd been sure she was mere seconds away from begging him to taste them, to suckle them and kiss them and have his wicked way with every inch of her. Her nipples hardened at the thought of such a blissful surrender—the forbidden freedom to voice such a thing. Her palms hovered over the sensitive points, and Eve closed her eyes before squeezing each one as she imagined that it was his hands touching her.

A slow arc of heat unfolded at the pressure of her fingertips and she rocked her hips to arch her back, moving with the pleasure that began to course through her. She freed one hand and let it creep down her ribs and over the soft swell of her stomach until she reached the aching flesh that lay beneath a triangle of dark curls. She felt completely wicked, but she refused to answer the part of her that protested as her own hands imitated the dance his had performed on that couch at Bell

Street. *Later . . . I will think later . . . right now, I wish to feel.*

The water was cool, and she slid farther down—a sensual Ophelia lost in thoughts of her Hamlet. Her hair fanned out beneath her, brushing her skin and adding to the dream that overtook her. The water lapped at her ears, and all she could hear was her own heartbeat and the air rasping through her lungs faster and faster as the fantasy took hold.

Julian was with her. A handsome golden lion perched above her, watching her, directing her, admiring her. He wanted her pleasure. He wanted her to keep nothing from him, and this time there was nothing to stop him. Naked with nothing between them—not even fear. They will play another game, but this time, every card comes as she wills it. He helps her to stand from the water, his touch innocent at first as he offers her a towel and then helps to dry her, dragging the warm cotton across her body and drawing it under her arms and breasts and even between her thighs to ensure that she is ready for him. Turning her to face away from him, he kneels down behind her. Before she can ask his intentions, his hands smooth over her body, tracing the shape of her legs up to her bottom and then up the curve of her spine. Then his tongue takes the place of his hands, moving up her legs in hot kisses that send new shivers through her body. He teases the back of her knees with a soulful sweep of his mouth and gently bites upwards to learn the curve of her thighs.

He grazes the places where her bottom creases above her legs, his hot breath christening the sensitive fold of her flesh, his hands cup her curves and ensure that she cannot fall.

Too wicked, he parts her thighs and sets her foot on the smooth tub's rim so that he can press his face into her, his tongue darting forward and licking her slit until her knees start to buckle. She leans forward to give him the access he needs. And then his mouth is there—where his fingers were earlier that day—on the tiny nub that sends uncontrollable jolts of desire up and down her spine to pool between her legs. It is so sweet and still such a torment—this delicious pleasure that heralds an emptiness only he can fill . . .

The raw pressure of the release building inside her overtook the fantasy and Eve gasped, her eyes fluttering open as a bone-melting climax tore past her control, catching her by surprise. She bit into the washcloth to stifle a moan and then sat up abruptly, water sloshing onto the floor as she struggled to regain her balance.

She'd never done such a thing before—never felt such things. Her hands shook as she pushed her cold, wet hair from her face, a little shocked at the nature of her exercise. She'd never even considered that such things were possible. But it was as if Julian had kicked open some hidden door inside of her—and she knew without question that it was a door she would never be able to close completely. *I am the wanton I always feared after Venice. And I said I never wanted to see him again. Liar! Yet another sin to add to my tally, but oh, if I could take it back I would, Julian. I would take so much back. I would throw those cards on the floor and name a prize to shock even a rogue like you.*

Oh, but you must hate me!

She accepted that Julian had every right to be furious. She'd pushed him too far, and he was probably going to very happily decide to comply with her wishes and avoid her for the rest of their time in London.

Or would he?

Out of habit, she considered all the potential outcomes and finally decided that she had no choice but to stick to her original plan.

And if he wants revenge?

It wouldn't be the trifling revenge of spoiling her card games. She could only pray that he would be a man of his word and keep her uncle's shameful habits to himself. Eve closed her eyes again and put her head into her hands, suddenly feeling cold and utterly exposed.

Or, he'll make me beg for him to finish what I started tonight.

And God help me, I hope he does.

Chapter Ten

He'd stayed away for a week. Not because she'd bid him to, naturally. Rather, Julian told himself, it was to let the Lamb stew a bit. He didn't have the slightest inclination to alert her victims to her schemes or betray her uncle's indiscretions at the Boar's Head, but Eve didn't know that. The only danger threatening her was the eroding net of civilized behavior that kept him from stealing a horse and riding over to her uncle's town house, taking her over his knees, and spanking her into submission.

He hated a tease.

But it was hard not to admire the brilliant maneuver that had left him in a glorious state of frustration. Never before had a woman so deftly led him into such a blind corner and caught him so completely off guard. That she'd been as aroused as he, Julian still had no doubts. That she'd been able to walk away as if they'd been discussing orchids and the state of London's roads baffled him.

He winced as he shifted back against the cushions of the carriage to make sure he wasn't visible from the sidewalk. The weather was damp, and it set off the ache in his chest, though he did his best to ignore it. An easy enough task for a man on a mission, he noted. *When I think of Miss Eve Reynolds, I'm sure I could ignore a broken leg.* Within minutes she would emerge from Lady Morrington's house, and Julian relished the afternoon ahead of him. Miss Reynolds was going to settle her overdue account with him in full, plus interest.

As if the lustful fire of his thoughts had summoned her, he heard her steps approaching quickly, and the flurry of activity as she juggled her umbrella and the carriage door provided exactly the distraction he'd hoped for. She didn't realize he was sitting across from her until the door was firmly shut behind her.

"What are you doing here?"

"Waiting for you."

He rapped on the carriage wall and the driver pulled out into the lane, effectively eliminating her chance to jump out.

"What do you think you are doing? This is my hired carriage!"

"I outbid you, and I think I'm taking you back to Bell Street."

"I . . . oh! But that's . . . kidnapping, Lord Westleigh!" She was speechless. Julian surveyed her, with her bedraggled bonnet feathers, rain-spotted skirts, and muddied boots, and decided she looked absolutely ravishing. *Hard to stay angry with you, Lamb, when you are just as beautiful as a man recalls.*

"I thought it would be the best location."

"The best location?"

"To finish the game of high card we started last week."

Some of the shock was beginning to wear off, and he could literally see her getting her bearings. "I won that game, Julian."

He shook his head. "You cheated."

"I did nothing of the sort!"

"Of course you did. You deliberately lost those first hands until I was whipped into a frenzy, and then you cruelly left me in a state of—shall we say, I was less than satisfied?"

She folded her arms defensively. "I apologize for your 'state.' However, that has nothing to do with your current foray into crime. You said you wanted to let the fates decide, and I'd say they did. You lost and were never to see me again!"

"You cheated and any prize is forfeit," he stated calmly, and waited for her to change tactics.

"I never cheat, but I . . . I can't just disappear—my uncle is expecting me!"

"Your afternoon game with the ladies ran long. Lady Morrington asked you to stay to supper. How could you refuse?"

"I would have sent a note then to—"

"You did. Or rather, Lady Morrington will. Such a sweet woman and so considerate to make sure your uncle doesn't worry."

"Lady Morrington? But then, she—"

"Knows that I am set on you, I'm afraid. I didn't even have to ask twice for her assistance, she is so fond of you and eager to see you happy. Her late husband was quite the rogue in his day, and I think she has a soft spot for me. Naturally, she has a different interpretation of things than you or I, but I saw no need to correct her assumptions."

"Her assumptions?"

"Something about having a chaperone and taking you out in public for a respectable afternoon and swearing to behave impeccably—I may have been vague on the details."

"You lied to her." Eve shut her eyes for a moment. "Even if she thinks this is an innocent outing, she'll talk, Lord Westleigh, and if my uncle hears of it—"

"Nothing. Besides, she wouldn't dare. If she talks, she'll have to admit her own role in the conspiracy. If it comes to that, you'll threaten tears and tell her how horrible it was to be a virgin thrown to the wolves."

She opened her mouth to argue and then shut it quickly, unwilling to protest his reference to virgins and wolves. He took the liberty of continuing. "Your plans, *whatever* they may be, are not jeopardized. This"—he took her hand, peeling off her glove to run the pads of his fingers over the sensitive well of her palm—"business is just between us, Eve."

The carriage stopped, and she looked at him, her eyes luminous and full of amazement. "Business?"

"Come, let's argue inside. You'll have far more room to throw things and the privacy to say whatever you wish. You may rant as you desire, and I will swear an oath to have you home safely before your uncle begins to wonder how many courses Lady Morrington can have served to keep you so late." He opened the carriage door. "Agreed?"

"I'm not agreeing to anything." She crossed her arms, refusing to leave the carriage.

"I can carry you in, Eve, but then that gives me all the physical advantages of having those pretty feet of yours off the ground, and . . . that's going to be *quite* the public scene."

She glared at him, obviously considering her options. "Since, as you pointed out, there will be things to throw inside—I'd say it's your skull at risk, Lord Westleigh." She made a show of checking her reticule and straightening her skirts. He knew without question that she was taking every second she could to gain her equilibrium. "Very well."

She climbed down without taking his arm, and he escorted her up the stairs and unlocked the door to let them in. He removed his coat and hat, tossing them carelessly on the sofa as they entered the parlor. "Your uncle seems a unique character."

"I won't discuss him with you."

"I see." He watched her closely as she slowly drew out her hat pin and set aside her bonnet with her gloves. "Well, we'll leave him out of it for now."

"For always, or I am leaving this instant." Her chin lifted a fraction in defiance before her eyes fluttered and dropped to focus on his chest. "Please."

It was the first time he'd heard her use the word, and it distracted him completely. It was a word he very much desired to hear her say again and again.

"What do you want, Lord Westleigh?"

"I told you what I wanted. In the garden. And if my memory is accurate, I think I also made it clear the last time we met despite that disastrous first game of high card." He held his place. "Not that you haven't consequently added a few new motivations to my original designs, but the result is the same, Miss Reynolds."

She nervously licked her upper lip, as if she could already taste him there. "You . . . are a determined man, Lord Westleigh."

"Most definitely."

Eve shifted her weight to the balls of her feet, a part of her contemplating escape even while the rest of her considered how very much she wanted him. "I'm having trouble understanding that of all the women in your many . . . social encounters, you've managed to select me to . . ." She just wasn't sure how to finish.

"Seduce? Tumble? Ravish?" He offered a few salacious suggestions without a hint of embarrassment.

She crossed her arms. "Why me?"

He seemed to take the question very seriously, pausing to consider before answering. "Because I cannot remember why. Anyone else, I think I could list a few relevant facts or even blame boredom or happenstance. But you . . . ever since I first saw you, I seem to be able to think of nothing else. It makes no sense, Miss Reynolds. But I won't ignore this, and I won't relent. Especially since we've already initiated this game." He took a step closer, a panther testing the open air. "I never leave a game unfinished. Never."

It was rebellion, pure and simple, everything he was suggesting.

Her uncle had forbidden her to even speak to him.

She wanted this—wanted him to force her hand. Even if he hadn't invaded every daydream, every restless corner of her soul already, something about his presence felt right to her. Days of nervous anticipation were finally alleviated.

The most dangerous game of all . . . he ignites every forbidden longing I have ever had and several I wasn't aware of. Why not take what pleasure I can? In a few weeks it will all be over, and if I have my way I'll be enjoying a new quiet life in the country—and this will be a world away. He will be a world away. Never again will I cross his path. Never again will I have such a chance to experience the decadence of his golden eyes locked onto mine.

The decision was made in a single heartbeat. Never had she felt so vulnerable or so wild—as if none of the rules of polite society had any power to protect or restrain her. As if they'd ever done either. Her father had taught her long ago that the rules didn't apply to "such as them."

"No children from . . . *this,*" she whispered. It was the last obstacle she could think of. If he had been going to blackmail her, he already had more than enough to make a convincing case. But her instincts told her that no matter what else this rogue might be, he was not a liar. If Julian Clay had proven himself to be anything, it was stunningly straightforward.

He nodded. "I swear it. We'll use condoms." He took one step forward, as if preparing to spring on her. "Anything else?"

"Only one thing."

His expression didn't change, but Eve sensed the dangerous flash of frustration he held in check—barely. "Yes?"

"Do you really think I cheated you at cards the other night?"

He laughed in surprise at the question.

"Don't laugh, Lord Westleigh. You impugn my honor when you say such things."

He openly struggled with his mirth. "Exactly what I would expect a professional cheat to say!"

"I am not a cheat." She took a deep breath as a daring and dreamlike idea took hold of her. "And I shall prove it to you."

He sobered slightly. "And what will you prove? That you are unnaturally lucky?"

She made a quick, wordless prayer that her own desires wouldn't overwhelm her and spoil the game. Now was not the time for a show of vulnerability or fear. "Oh, I can assure you that my gifts are entirely natural. But why not judge them for yourself?"

She tugged the first pearl button free at her

throat and was rewarded by the sharp intake of his breath. She'd managed to surprise him, and that was good. It would buy her the precious seconds she needed to steel her own nerves against the wave of heat shimmering through her. The brazen idea to end his accusations had taken on a power of its own. Ever since that first card game, her flesh had ached with a need to completely surrender to this man.

The buttons slid from their moorings without protest, her fingers moving with a grace that belied the storm within. "I can think of no better way to demonstrate that I have no cards . . . up my sleeves."

Chapter Eleven

"Shall I lock the front door in case you decide to flee again?"

She shrugged. "If it will make you feel better, but surely you can trust me, Lord Westleigh?"

He shook his head, his eyes darkening. "I refuse to answer that question. And if you have to ask . . ."

"I have no intention of tormenting you." She continued to release more buttons, her voice steady even if her knees were trembling as she stepped out of her shoes. "In fact, no matter who wins this card game, Lord Westleigh, I expect there will be . . . satisfaction for both of us." Eve slid her blouse off her shoulders and dropped it to the floor. "Do you have the cards at hand?"

"Let me understand this completely before we

get too far along . . ." He took a slow breath and held his place, watching her every move as she began to unfasten her skirt. "You are going to disrobe to play cards in order to demonstrate that you are not, in fact, *cheating*?"

"I could keep them on," she offered as she stepped out of her skirts, standing before him in her chemise, corset, crinoline, and petticoats. "But I'm not sure you'll truly withdraw your accusation otherwise, and I am determined, Lord Westleigh."

"Determined?" He echoed the word as if bemused, while she put a leg up on a footstool to roll off her stocking, then delicately shifted to remove the other in the same fashion. "It is one word among many I'd have chosen to describe you, Miss Reynolds."

He swallowed hard, and she knew he was having trouble keeping track of the conversation. "Do you have a better idea?"

"Not one."

She smiled, a wave of shyness washing over her at the intensity of his gaze, but the power of her own desires pushed her forward. "Would you help me with this?" She turned around, and within seconds his hands were expertly releasing the crinoline's ties. "You can unlace the corset to—"

He circumvented her request in one breathtaking maneuver by placing his hands at her waist, his fingers splayed to press inwards in one smooth, strong push that popped the busk on the front of the corset, spilling her out of the garment far faster than she'd ever imagined possible.

"I—one would think you had some experience with women's undergarments, Lord Westleigh."

His look was pure sin. "A gentlemen never discusses such things."

Her first instinct to try to hold the corset together to cover herself gave way when she realized that it was futile, and would have been relinquished in any case. She faced him and let the heavy boned garment fall to the carpet.

He was closer now, not having retreated after assisting her, but he made no move to trespass any further. Instead, his eyes roamed appreciatively, like a man surveying his plate before a feast.

Eve untied her crinolines and let gravity pull them downward to join the rest of her clothes, stepping out of them when he held out his hand to help her stay steady on her feet. The gesture was as smooth as a courtier's and made her smile in light of the fact that she now had on a thin cotton chemise and single petticoat with lace trim. The fabric would hide nothing, yet she was standing in a sitting room as boldly as if they'd been about to have tea.

Perhaps you have the right of it, Lord Westleigh. There is no sense to the why—and I no longer seem to care.

He waited, and Eve knew that she could "dangle" him no longer. Her fingers shook but the buttons gave way, and she slowly slid the chemise straps from one shoulder, savoring the raw fire in his gaze. This wasn't going to be like the awkward encounter that had haunted her for two years. This was going to be an experience like no other, and she welcomed it.

"Faster, woman." It was a rough growl, and his expression warmed her all over.

"As you wish, Lord Westleigh." She pushed the cotton past her breasts and shimmied from skirt and pantalets in one swift and graceful move that left her as naked as the day she'd arrived in the world. She knew the sight of her body pleased him, and his reactions bolstered her confidence and kept her from giving in to every instinct that was screaming for her to cover herself and flee. "Where are the cards?"

"I can't remember."

"Ah, here they are." She held out the deck she'd retrieved from the same wooden box on the table. "Piquet? Casino? Whist?"

He took the cards out of her hand and dropped them carelessly onto the carpet at their feet. "We don't need those."

"Lord Westleigh, you're the one who said you wished to play," she said, wishing she knew how to properly look at a man through her lashes.

"Impossible." He stepped over the cards, slowly reaching for her. "Utterly impossible."

"Are you . . . forfeiting this game?"

"No, Lamb. You are." Julian took her into his arms and gently seized her for a kiss that ended flirtations and foolish debates. His lips were firm over hers, claiming her mouth without apology, and Eve found herself clinging to him to keep her balance, unsettled by the raging hunger that surged inside her. There was nothing gentle in his kisses, but something in her celebrated each rough touch, and she gave in to that primal drive with a moan. The delicious friction of his waistcoat against the sensitive peaks of her breasts and the brushed wool of his pants against her soft belly made her wriggle with naughty delight. To be embraced without a stitch of clothing—it was positively sinful. He was in control, and before she realized it, he was lifting her up off the floor to carry her up the stairs, his mouth still tasting her, nuzzling her neck, until they reached the small upper hallway, where he was forced to raise his head to kick open the bedroom door. In three strides they were in the tiny bedroom, and he unceremoniously tossed her onto the bed, making her gasp at the unexpected landing. She presented him with a lovely and fetching picture as she lay there breathlessly naked and splayed just for him. She tried to cover herself, but he shook his head and began to pull at his cravat and shirt front. "Don't you dare, Eve Reynolds."

Her eyes widened. "I believe I've already proven that I'm . . ." She swallowed hard as he quickly bared his chest and threw his coat and shirt on the floor. She'd known he was fit from the sweep of her hands through his clothes, but the sight of his naked chest was another matter. The dusting of golden fur across his chest and the faint trail of it downwards across the rippled landscape of his abdomen almost made her forget the debate at hand. " . . . I'm the kind of woman who will dare whatever I want."

"Are you?" He began to unfasten his pants, aware that his "daring" Miss Reynolds was quickly losing her composure—a flush was creeping up her cheeks and adding to her beauty. To her credit, she was not averting her gaze, and it inflamed him to think of her eyes on his body, just as his were on hers.

"The ladies seem to think you were shot in the stomach."

"Evidently not." He guided his fingers to the two-inch scar on the left side of his chest, two inches below his collarbone. "Not exactly where my heart would have been, but close enough to prove I may not have one."

"Liar." It was a soft whisper that sent an arc of heat into his hips.

"Cheat." Before she could protest, he dropped his pants and freed himself from the last confining bits of his clothing, his erection springing away to jut proudly from his body. With efficient hands, he retrieved a tin of condoms from the bedside drawer and applied one over his sheath. A jar of lubricant was next to it, but he didn't think he'd need it.

He grabbed her ankle and slid her toward him and the edge of the bed, kneeling between her legs. Pink glistening folds parted as he pressed her thighs wider, luxuriating in the sight of her, already wet and ready for his touch. Scent of musk and salt, his fingers traced each sensitive crease until he dipped a finger inside of her, at the same time using his tongue to lathe the hard bud of her clit. Her muscles clenched around his finger, working against his hands, and she bucked as he kissed and tasted her. Faster and faster he moved, the frantic pace of his tongue underscored by miniature thrusts of his hand. She groaned, and he added another finger, stretching out the amazingly tight confines of her and pressing harder into her just as he lightened the touch of his mouth to keep her in check. She moaned again and he could feel her racing now, desperate for her release.

But he had other plans. *Ace of spades, Miss Reynolds? You'll play by my rules, you little minx.*

He withdrew his hands and gave her clit one

last, lingering kiss before standing up to put one of her feet against his shoulder. Her look was delicious confusion, but it changed quickly to anticipation when he pressed the head of his cock against her, moving it against her deliberately—just as his mouth had—faster and faster, the wet friction of the searing warm heat of him gliding back and forth over her until she was writhing on the bed, her arms outstretched and whimpering as she began to climax.

He pushed forward, his eyes closing at the glorious rush of sensations as her body gripped his, taking only the swollen head of him—she was so tight. Julian held still until her climax eased his path, and he was lost to everything but the need to bury himself inside of her. He thrust forward, a deep, slow stroke that absorbed the waves of her pleasure and sent his own body beyond his control. She was so snug—almost virginal—that he meant to take more care, but the intention was swept away from his thoughts when she lifted her hips to take more of him, wordlessly begging him to ride his fill. He held her hips in a ruthless grip and pumped himself inside of her, the air pulling through his teeth as if her flesh scalded his—but it was pure ecstasy that made him groan, lost in the primal drive to claim her, possess her, mark her with his body until he couldn't feel where he left off and she began. There was nothing genteel in the workings of his hips, only the blinding quest for release that came in a ragged, white-hot explosion that seemed to come from his soul.

He gritted his teeth to keep from shouting at the strength of it, shuddering as jets of crème continued to spill from him. Finally, he felt a few tenuous threads of reason return, and he was jolted by the sight of her beneath him—so thoroughly ravished, so beautiful, and so . . . *upset*?

Tears shone like diamonds on her cheeks and Julian let go of her instantly, withdrawing to assess the damage he'd done. "Are you hurt? I should have realized I was—"

"No!" She sat up, reaching for him and laughing. It was ridiculous to find herself crying, but she hadn't been prepared for any of it—not the power of his touch, the frightening loss of her self-control, and certainly not for the sensation that she'd broken apart into a dozen pieces and left her own body behind when he'd sent her over the edge, filling her with his beautiful cock and making her forget why she'd ever fled from him. She put her hand against his chest, determined to right this misunderstanding quickly and ensure that his pride wasn't wounded. "Not at all! It was just . . . overwhelming. I didn't expect to feel—so much." She knelt on the edge of the bed, and he pulled her into his arms, raining kisses onto her hair in relief.

"Damn it, Eve. You scare a man with those things."

"Tears?" she asked, unable to hide her merriment. "I shall keep that in mind, Lord Westleigh."

"And you must call me Julian."

"Must I?"

"I insist on it with every woman once I've navigated a good game of naked piquet," he teased. "Besides, you had another preference?"

A dozen naughty nicknames fleetingly suggested themselves to her before she realized he might have the better idea. "I'd prefer you didn't use the word 'must,' but I'll concede the name does suit you."

He laughed, pulling her back down into the bed with him, rolling her onto her back to press her close. "You are a willful thing, Eve Reynolds. A willful and naughty thing, indeed."

"Somehow when you say it, Julian, it sounds like a perfectly wonderful thing to be." She reached up to pull his face down to hers, nibbling on the soft and sensitive flesh of his lower lip before kissing him as she longed to. Need and fire were reignited in a slow, sweet burn.

He was hard again, and she relinquished her hold only so that he could retrieve a new condom and sheathe himself once more. And then he was back in her arms and the embrace was restored. She kissed his neck, nipping and teasing him, her tongue flickering over his Adam's apple and downward to the well at the base of his throat.

He reared back and slid into her so slowly that Eve was sure it was a new torment—this conquest by inches until she was completely enmeshed, until she could feel his heart pulsing inside of her.

This time she was ready for the power of the connection between them, and she just gave in to it. She lifted her heels to press them against his back, spurring him on, driving him forward. This time momentum came slowly, but looking into his golden eyes with each stroke, she found herself unable to look away as she climaxed in indolent, bone-melting waves. Eve cried out and finally closed her eyes to taste his name on her lips. "Julian!"

His own cry followed quickly, and Eve buried her face against his shoulder and savored this new power, however fleeting it would turn out to be.

He helped her dress a few hours later and sent her home with a nagging feeling of reluctance. It was impossible to linger any longer than they had—a dangerous pastime for a woman in her position—and Julian was struggling to pay attention to the rules.

Off you go, Lamb, until next time.

If she was using him for some scheme, he couldn't care less. It made no sense, but he believed her when she assured him she meant no harm. Julian went back upstairs to collect his coat and make sure he wasn't leaving anything behind. There were no servants to worry about—only a weekly housekeeper who checked in to tidy up and see to the dusting. Even so, he didn't like the idea of arrogant carelessness. It was one thing to be reckless at the gaming tables, but this . . .

This was an arena where the best gladiator could still unwittingly meet his match. But defeat wasn't in the cards. He decided it was easy enough to stay in control, and he would just enjoy this affair while it lasted.

In Julian's experience, these things always faded after the first coupling . . . or two. Though naturally, at the moment, he couldn't see an end to the desire, not for a woman like Eve Reynolds.

Chapter Twelve

"Well?" her uncle demanded.

"Lady Morrington said her cousin might be there," Eve replied, praying, as she lied, that her countenance was as steady as her hands. It had been two days since she'd left Julian's bed, and Eve was sure that it was only the memory of his hands against her body that had kept her sane while Uncle Warren's obsessions over her progress at cards had escalated. "She may be at the lawn party today, although Mrs. Cuthbert hinted she thought otherwise."

"Don't get too confident!" he reminded her, his usual affable temper suffering from a head cold that made him growl in frustration. It was keeping him from accompanying her this afternoon, and he was lashing out irrationally as a result.

"Let them start things, and don't forget to watch the leads!"

"Yes, Uncle." It was all advice she'd heard a thousand times.

"Nothing easier, dear niece." He smiled. "You're doing well. Don't mind an old bear."

Eve nodded, distracting her mind by studying her uncle's face, thereby leaving no room for errant thoughts of just how fantastic the Earl of Westleigh looked without his pants. It was too dangerous an image to entertain, and she had to subtly dig her nails into her hands to stay focused.

They had arranged to meet again this afternoon, and Eve could hardly wait to see him. Every moment with Julian was precious to her, and she protected it as she protected one of the brooches hidden in the wall of her bathroom—every stolen kiss was all hers and had nothing to do with her uncle.

Eve glanced at the clock on the mantel. "I should go."

"You'll be home by supper?"

She shook her head. "Sometime afterward, I think. The weather looks like it will drive the party inside, and I plan on taking every advantage to avail myself of the games that will come about."

He nodded. "See that you do! Time is flying and you need to apply yourself."

"I will, Uncle Warren." She crossed over and

kissed him on the cheek before leaving. "Feel better, and ask Barnett to heat up some of that beef broth for you."

"Enjoy yourself, Eve."

I will, Uncle. I believe I absolutely will.

As she'd predicted, a summer rainstorm overtook the Dixons' annual lawn party, and guests were forced to take shelter inside. Plans for badminton and bowling now naturally transformed into faro, cribbage, and écarté, and Eve kept her eyes on the flow toward the games to see if there were any friendly faces she could join.

"Écarté, miss?"

Eve turned at the welcome invitation and came face-to-face with one of the most stunningly beautiful women she had ever seen. Blond, with eyes the blue of a winter sky, she was a perfect English doll in expensive frills that declared her wealth and status. Eve found her voice quickly. "I would love to play."

"I understand you have some interest and skill in cards . . . Miss Reynolds, was it?"

"Yes, interest certainly! As for skill," Eve said as she made a self-deprecating gesture, "I do hope I am improving."

"Lady Andrews mentioned you, so I thought to be forward and meet you today. I am Lady Shelbrook."

Eve curtsied. "I'm honored."

"Come, let's have a round or two, shall we?"

They located a small table and the cards they needed, then settled in near a window to enjoy what distractions they could. Outside, the rain danced on the windows, and Eve wondered how long she could wait before rushing to Bell Street.

"—deal?" Lady Shelbrook said.

"Oh, dear! I'm sorry, what?" Eve was horrified to realize she had drifted from the business at hand—and before they'd even shuffled the cards. "It's the rain. I'm afraid it makes me think of my father."

"I asked if you wished me to deal," Lady Shelbrook advised, either ignoring Eve's bid for sympathy or not being a woman with an ear for subtle remarks.

Eve wasn't sure how to read the woman, but she had no choice but to continue as if nothing was amiss. "That would be lovely."

The cards were sorted and dealt, and Eve discovered that Lady Shelbrook was a worthy opponent but one who played with reckless abandon. As the games progressed, and Eve struggled to keep the initial takes equal, she began to wonder why Lady Shelbrook really wished to play at all. She seemed so unhappy in the exchanges.

"Does the rain affect you as well?" Eve probed gently.

The lady shook her head. "I think only weak people allow something as trivial as the weather to affect them. Not, of course, that *you* are weak."

The correction did little to amend the sting of her words, but Eve knew better than to snap back. Clearly the woman had more on her mind than the turn of cards. "Thank you. Did you wish to bet?"

Lady Shelbrook pushed her bet out without looking at it. "You are sweet to put up with me. I confess"—she leaned in and lowered her voice—"the truth is that I am nervous in cramped quarters and can be wretched company when confined."

Eve smiled as a surge of relief washed through her. She hadn't given offense or engaged "the enemy," yet she'd uncovered her partner's cause for unhappiness. "Would a change of location suit? I'm sure Mrs. Dixon wouldn't mind if we moved to another, less crowded room."

"You are too kind. Let us stay here. It's a comfortable enough place to lose my husband's money." Her smile didn't quite warm the icy blue of her eyes, but Eve decided that it didn't matter. *I have the lady in hand now, and we shall see how attached she is to those emerald earrings.*

Within an hour, she'd achieved a handsome amount to convey to her uncle, as well as a pair of delightful emerald earrings for her own secret cause. With Lady Shelbrook's odd propensity to bet without regard to the amount, Eve had been able to escalate the game without a single moment of uncertainty—and, even more important, without alerting anyone else in the room. The last thing she wanted at this stage was an audience to note just how much she was taking in.

"It has been a wonderful afternoon, Lady Shelbrook," Eve remarked as she discreetly tucked away the earnings. "If my uncle were not unwell, I would linger, but regretfully—"

"Yes, another time, then?"

Eve pivoted to leave the table and almost collided with Mrs. Cuthbert. "Oh, my!"

"Oh, Miss Reynolds!" Mrs. Cuthbert began breathlessly. "I was afraid I might miss you before getting a chance to ask if you saw the Earl of Westleigh again. He was—"

"No, Mrs. Cuthbert, though my uncle may have. I'll ask him, but I really must go, I'm afraid. I'm so sorry to rush off, but please, I cannot wait to see you on Tuesday and hope I will be welcome even if I cannot manage any good gossip of my own." Eve gently cut her off, not wishing to link herself to Julian in front of strangers and hoping her discretion would be enough for both of them.

"Tuesday, then." Mrs. Cuthbert kissed her cheek, and Eve made a quick and quiet retreat with her winnings, blissfully unaware of the cold eyes that followed her until she was out the door.

* * *

"Let's get you out of these wet things, shall we?"

"You're t-too kind." She was doing her best not to ruin the carpets, but she'd arrived a bit worse for wear and soaked to the bone after her cheap umbrella had disintegrated in the wind outside the Dixons'. Her teeth were chattering, and she shook her head in defeat. "Y-you realize th-this was a l-lovely d-dress intended to imp-press you, Julian."

He stopped his efforts to peel the wet articles from her and stepped back to survey her from head to toe. He made a single circle around her, and she couldn't help but smile as his hand brushed over the limp fall of her bustle and trailed down her back and around her waist. "Silk?"

"P-poplin," she amended, "with a taffeta underskirt."

He nodded, as if her choice in fabrics had made all the difference in the world to his appraisal. "Hmm. Well, I'd say you look lovely, if only a bit—"

"Damp?" she suggested.

"Not at all. I was going to say wilted." Wicked thoughts of what his previous courteous offer to help her out of her wet clothes might entail made his eyes look like molten gold, but even wilted, she had enough of a spark left to give him an answering wicked look of her own.

"Let's get you upstairs, Lamb," he said in reply.

He threw a warm wrap around her shoulders before leading her gently up the narrow staircase. She kept waiting for his hands to stray as they climbed, but instead it was the gentle heat of his hands politely at her back and on her shoulder that fueled her nervous anticipation.

If he'd stripped me in the hallway downstairs and bent me over the banister, I don't think I would have been surprised. But this! I've never had a man treat me as if I might break like glass.

Inside the cozy bedroom, he led her over to a small overstuffed chair. "Here, Lamb, sit here."

"And ruin the cloth? I should stand and . . . get out of these."

He nodded but pushed her gently back into the waiting chair's comfort. "Agreed. Let's see to you before you catch your death of cold." His skilled hands made quick work of her clothing, and even without the sensual preambles of their first encounter, she found the experience difficult to absorb. She had to rise for some of the more complex layers, but he was as efficient as any ladies maid she'd ever seen and was undoubtedly more handsome. Once she was down to her skin, he pulled the coverlet from the bed and swamped her in its folds.

She laughed at the strange comfort and odd state of being once again entirely naked while he retained his clothes, if even just for the moment. "Thank you, Julian."

He knelt and began to set up a fire in the grate. "Let's see if we cannot get you warm again."

Within seconds, a bright blaze crackled in the little grate, and he sat on his heels and studied her. "Something is lacking."

"Besides my clothes?"

His gaze narrowed and traveled over her, wrapped as she was from the top of her head and downwards, until she realized he was staring at her bare feet against the floor. "I believe I have just the thing."

A kiss? She blushed at the wanton bent of her thoughts, apparently unable to think of anything else but Julian Clay and the feel of his body against hers, inside hers. *Does he know what he's done to me? How his touch has changed me already?*

He stood and crossed the small room to open the top drawer on a small bureau against the wall. He turned back with a look that made the bones of her hips feel liquid and hot. "I took an inventory when I was here alone. I think these will suit."

He knelt before her again and set about pulling a pair of clean, thick, woolen socks onto her feet. Eve wrinkled her nose but reveled in the soft fleece against her toes. "Julian, they are hardly the fashion!"

"A woman wearing bedding doesn't get to fuss about fashion, Eve."

"Does she not?"

Julian's hands strayed up her calves, the raw primal desire in his face there for her to see, and she felt a jolt to realize the wild power he was reining in even as he tended to her mundane comforts and put socks on her icy feet. "Julian, please—"

He unfolded from the floor in an easy move, silencing her with a kiss. His mouth covered hers, commanding the fire that spread through her limbs and drawing her into a world where it was perfectly normal for an earl to attend to one's every desire.

Her hands moved over his shoulders and she reached upward to touch his face, feeling like a vine entwining itself around an oak, but he withdrew when she began to stand.

"Wait, Lamb."

"Wait?" It was mortifying to feel put off, and it must have shown in her face. Jullian's hand was warm against her cheek and he was smiling, a devilish grin that denied any hurt in the tactic. "Julian, what am I waiting for?"

"For this." He pulled a large flannel from the back of the chair and set it over his arm. He began pulling out her hairpins and combs and dropped them into a pile on a shelf above the grate. "I want to see about drying your hair."

"You're . . . deliberately drawing this out, aren't you?"

He shrugged, continuing to work his fingers

through her damp braids to free them. "I think a bit of vengeance can be a good thing sometimes."

"I thought—"

"That you had settled your accounts on your last visit?" He captured her hair in the fold of the flannel and worked the length to rub her tresses and massage her bare shoulders. "Hardly. Now, tip your head back."

She dutifully leaned back. Her hair was almost long enough to touch the floor. She'd once thought it her best feature, though undoubtedly the wrong color to be fashionable in London. *His gold locks are so much prettier and all the rage,* she thought, and smiled. *I am jealous of my lover's hair.*

"What amuses you?"

"That you are undoubtedly prettier than I am, Lord Westleigh."

"Am I?" He shook his head. "Not from where I am standing."

With her head tipped back, he bent over and kissed her again. The strange sensation of being upside down added to the impact of his touch as her lower lip was suckled. She could taste only the most sensitive curves of his mouth with hers. Her tongue dipped out and she was sure that no kiss was as sweet, though her inability to reach him fueled her growing desire.

Spreading the coverlet open, he caught her arms and pushed them out from her nude body, his fingers trailing across her shoulders and then down over her breasts. "Ah! The view from here definitely defies description, Eve. You are all things beautiful."

"Even in wool socks?" she countered, a throaty laugh escaping from her at the delicious play of his hands over her chest. He lifted her breasts and she arched her back, her nipples hardening under his attentions. She ignored an inner voice that chided her for not feeling shy or ashamed. But when he looked at her, she just wanted to laugh and beg him to take her back to bed.

"As a punishment, I should make you wear them every time we meet, Miss Reynolds."

"And how is that a punishment?"

It was his turn to laugh. "Not much of one, but it will keep those icy toes of yours off me while I'm soundly rogering you."

"Oh!" She sat up in a dignified huff, then squealed when he scooped her up inside the coverlet so that the wool-clad feet in question were completely and helplessly off the floor. "Julian!"

"I think I've had enough vengeance for one afternoon!" He threw her over his shoulder like so much baggage and headed for the bed. "Time is wasting, Lamb!"

Into the bed they tumbled, and Eve reveled in the wonderful weight of him as he pinned her easily to the soft mattress. "You were the one drawing things out, Julian," she chided him gently. "Now let us see to your clothes."

You're not the only one with a taste for vengeance, your lordship.

She lifted herself onto her knees to attend to the task, aware that with her thighs parted and her breasts suspended a few inches from his nose, she might not have long to play out her game. She began to undress him but mischievously lingered when she could—just enough to make his breath quicken as she kissed all that she bared and took her time sampling the salt off his skin. She daringly dipped her head to flick her tongue over his chest and playfully bit one of his nipples, loving the way his body's reaction mirrored her own.

"You would make a wretched valet, Eve."

"How so?"

"Because I think I would only ever want you to help me out of my clothes and never into them. A social downfall"—he kissed her throat—"to attend dinner without one's pants."

"Oh, hush!" She shyly unbuttoned his pants, then forgot the witty rejoinder she'd meant to make about his next social downfall. His erection sprung free in all its male glory, and her fingers traced the silken skin, gripping him and marveling that her body could accommodate such a thing without injury. She stroked him with varying degrees of tension, admiring its power and the lively way his flesh reacted to her touch. Her study was an innocent exploration, but Julian clenched his jaw as each fan of her breath threatened to send him over the edge. He hissed through his teeth as her long fingers pulled on the length of him, each point of pressure making his heart stop.

"Did I hurt you?"

"God, no . . . it's heaven, Eve." He let out another long, slow whistle as she mischievously stroked him again, her fingers deliberately dragging along the sensitive ridge beneath the underside of his erection. "There is no . . . chance of damage unless you decided to use your teeth, Lamb."

Eve gasped at the shocking thought, then considered what his words implied. If his mouth could send her out of her head, what would her tongue do to this delightful bit of his anatomy?

But he read the gleam in her eyes and circumvented any further mischief. "Another day, wicked little Lamb."

Within seconds, he'd shifted away to cover his sheath in another condom from the bedside tin and returned to her arms. "Enough dawdling for one day, Eve." He reached down to assure himself that she was ready before he positioned himself between her thighs. He'd meant to go so much slower this time, to make up for the rush he'd made of it that first night, but she was so eager, so responsive that it was hard to remember anything of slow torment or ridiculous punishments—or any reason not to take her as hard as he could.

He drove into her, one fluid movement to bury himself inside of her, and then gave in to the inner voice that urged him to speed, to plunge into her again and again until there was nothing in the world but this woman.

He dipped one hand between them to make sure the sensitive clit wasn't ignored in the exchange, the rhythm of his hips moving his fingers against her. It was all he could manage, lost to the sweet pull of her body on his, her slick channel gripping him like a wet fist. Julian closed his eyes and rode into her, reveling in the stretch and surrender of her delectably tight core against him. *Made for me, she was made for my cock . . .*

Deeper and longer, each stroke pushed them further and further out past the boundaries of civilized façades. She clung to him and rocked her hips up to meet each thrust, and his focus narrowed until there was nothing but the point where their bodies became one. The sound of his hips plowing into the saturated velvet between her legs was a melody that surrounded his senses and cut off the last of his reserve.

Without thought, he used his arms and the momentum of their joining to lift her up, keeping her legs around his waist and settling her on his upper thighs as he knelt in the center of the bed. Eve blinked at the shift, still impaled by his cock and held in place by his hands. She looked uncertain at first to find herself upright, but Julian waited for a moment while she realized all the advantages of the new position. With the smallest press of her thighs, she could lever herself up and down and ride him as if he'd been some kind of living erotic swing.

He cupped her bottom and their breath intermingled as they moved together, in an ancient rhythm and dance that left nothing of games between them. She gripped his shoulders and arched her spine, eyes closed and lost to sensation, mindless with the quest for release.

Julian moved his hand around to find her clit, once again letting the rise and fall of her body put pressure on his fingers—only what she desired. Julian added to her control by holding his hand as still as he could. "My Eve. Let it happen."

He lowered his head to capture a taut pink nipple, sucking on its firmness as it grew taut against his tongue. Then he tugged at it with his teeth until she began to shudder.

"Julian!" She came around him, and he rode each wave as each spasm of her body flowed over his cock. He held himself back, unwilling to spoil her climax, and just held her against his chest as she trembled and sighed.

"Julian . . . that was . . ."

"Not over." *I'm not that generous, Eve. My turn.* He lowered her onto the bed, pulling out only so that he could push her over onto her stomach and then lift her hips against his raging erection, guaranteeing that she was aware of the "situation at hand." He positioned himself against her, aligning himself even as she instinctively moved to accommodate him.

She was on her hands and knees before him, and at the sight of her swollen, pink, wet lips waiting for his cock, he knew he wouldn't be able to hold back any longer. He thrust forward, plunging into her until he was buried completely within her, a pulse in his lower abdomen measuring out the impact as his shaft twitched and jerked at the glorious sensation of her body's pull to his. He began to move in hard, relentless strokes until he could feel the head of his cock brushing up against the very entrance of her womb. It set off a cascade of power and fire down his spine, and his climax began to gather momentum. He looked down to drink in the sight of his body and hers, the vision she presented—her beautiful bottom like a pale peach spread for him, her supple spine yielding to him in a timeless position of surrender of female to male . . . it was just enough to send him finally over the precipice.

He growled at the scalding release, unable to stop the roar of triumph as he gripped her hips and gave in to the white-hot implosions of pleasure that robbed him of control and reason. It was all he could do not to smother the poor thing, and he tried to keep from crushing her as best he could as he collapsed onto the bed.

"My God, Eve . . ."

"My thoughts exactly, Julian . . ."

"How do you feel?"

"Warm." She began to giggle, and Julian held her close, drowsing and listening to the sound of the rain on the windowpanes and running along the gutters.

She sighed and burrowed her face into his chest. "Why don't you have a wife, Julian?"

"Why don't you have a husband, Eve?" he replied without hesitation.

She punched him lightly on the shoulder. "Touché!"

He drew her closer and began to place gentle kisses at her temple and along the sensitive curve of her cheek in a sweet assault on her senses. "Why *don't* you have a husband?"

She sighed. "Because I prefer to wait until the choice is mine and not my uncle's or anyone else's. I don't need to be married to prove my worth, Julian."

"Remarkable."

"Is it really so extraordinary? I would think that a lot of women wish to be free to decide their own fates."

"I never considered it." He answered honestly, before realizing it might not make him sound like the most enlightened of men.

"And you?" she pressed. "Why have you not married?"

"I loathe the idea of a warden tapping her foot and giving me dirty looks until I behave."

She giggled. "As if you ever would!"

"Precisely!" He rolled over, tucking her beneath him. "Come to me after your ladies' game on Tuesday. I'll make sure that Lady Morrington will send word to your uncle and we will have the evening to ourselves."

She said nothing, and he slowly realized his mistake. "Please," he added softly.

"Tuesday then." She kissed his shoulder, her tongue laving the pulse that ran up his neck and making his skin marble with goose bumps.

"God, I think you know me too well." The minx was reading his mind.

"You are not such a difficult mystery to solve, Julian."

His cock jerked a bit at her words, reflexively nudging between her thighs. Her wet flesh, so swollen and sensitive, met his, and he knew that if he took her again so soon it would be an intoxicating blend of pleasure and pain.

But she melted against him, her ankles drawing up the back of his legs, until she'd hooked them behind his thighs to guide his thrust forward. He looked directly down into her eyes as he complied in one smooth, merciless stroke that made them both gasp in surprise.

I am not a mystery, Lamb, but you still are.

Chapter Thirteen

Eve entered the house, humming to herself as she handed over the battered remnants of her umbrella. The rain had stopped, but her clothes were still relatively soaked from her earlier dousing. Julian had hung them up in the bedroom, but there hadn't been enough time to dry them. Even so, the chill of damp skirts did nothing to spoil her wonderful mood. "Barnett, I hope you had a good evening? Is Uncle Warren feeling better?"

"No, miss. He was quite insistent th—"

"Barnett, you're dismissed for the evening!" her uncle barked from the library door. "Eve, get in here immediately!"

"What is it? I thought you'd be resting."

"How could you cross me? How could you lie to me, of all people? Do I not see to your welfare? I spoil you, I'd say! And what do I ask in return? One thing! One singular thing! Loyalty! Obedience!"

That's actually two things. "Uncle Warren, I'm not sure what you're—"

"Where have you been? You left the Dixons' hours ago! And now you walk in without a care in the world, and here I sit like some doddering fool . . . This is how it started before—you begin to keep things from me and disappear without a word. Some man is flattering you and telling you lies, and you forget all about those who have sacrificed so much for your well-being! It's Venice all over again!"

"It's hardly Venice."

"You left early to go where? To see someone, yes? Damn it, we're so close, and you're going to ruin everything! There'll be a scandal and I'll be left with nothing!"

He knows I left early, but that's all. Whoever his source is, they've given him only enough to make him suspicious. If he knew it was Julian, it would have been the first words he uttered. Just breathe through it and wait until he winds down a little.

It was the only strategy she could summon.

His face grew more and more splotched from his exertion as he began to pace. "You're lying to me again. You're up to something, I can see it in your eyes."

She shook her head and gently tried to lead him

back to his chair. "With those red eyes? I'm worried you can't see at all. You're ill and tired, and you're having hysterics over nothing, Uncle."

"Very well!" He flopped into the chair, his arms crossed. "Tell me about this 'nothing'!"

"I won."

She retrieved the pound notes from her skirt pocket and held them out to him calmly. "I won almost five hundred pounds. It happened so fast, I thought it best to end my afternoon early and not make a show of it."

He took the money with a pout, clearly less sure of his accusations. "But that was hours ago."

"Frankly, I wanted to enjoy a little quiet. Every time I step over this threshold, you've accepted another invitation or you're barking about your short list of potential husbands for me. I'm tired of parties! And I wasn't in the mood to argue about marriage tonight."

"Well—"

"On top of all this, you weren't feeling well and you are supposed to be resting, and I thought, foolishly, that I'd earned a few hours on my own to just ride in the carriage and listen to the rain." She put her hands on her hips, as if daring him to oppose her. "I went nowhere."

The lie held, and Eve watched him take it all in and accept that he *might* be mistaken. It was the best she could do before heading up to her rooms, smiling at dear old Barnett as she passed him in the hallway. *Whatever he's paying you, I warrant you're thinking it's not enough.*

The rain had started again, and in the gloom, she wondered about the lies that had finally flowed from her lips. It meant more than she could say to have something untouched by the rest of her world. What she and Julian shared was theirs alone, and the power of having a secret was too sweet to relinquish. Eve's fingers found the small cloth bundle she'd hidden in a pocket underneath her skirt's ruching. She clutched the hard-won emeralds and finally fell asleep listening to the rain, dreaming of Julian in a garden.

"You lose again, Lord Westleigh. I fear it is not your night."

God help me, the man has a point. But even with the night's setback, he was even in his accounts for the first time in a long time. It was an odd sensation to know that he was on the brink of either getting ahead or sliding back into debt. And instead of fear, he couldn't help feeling that his luck was about to turn for the better. He'd just spent the most glorious afternoon in memory and was sure nothing could unsettle his good mood. It was difficult to complain about something so trivial as a few bad cards after a rainy day in Eve's arms.

It's only money. And what is that to the allure of Eve? Changeable and impossible, I'm beginning to look forward to our every meeting as this girl surprises me each time.

"I'll take your advice and turn in early then, Mr. Crane. A man should know when to cut his losses."

"Remarkable!" Mr. Crane began to clear his side of the table.

"Remarkable in what way?" Julian asked.

"I never thought to see the Earl of Westleigh leave a card table at a sensible hour and with such a cool head." Mr. Crane spoke candidly, but then he seemed to recall Julian's past and erratic reputation, and he began to regret his words. "N-not that you aren't known for your . . . strong sensibilities, Lord Westleigh."

Julian smiled. "Am I? I wasn't aware of it, but a man can be famous for worse things, so I'm grateful for it, Mr. Crane."

"Yes, yes." Mr. Crane pocketed his winnings and gave a quick bow before leaving. Julian watched him go, amused as he heard the man mumbling the word "Remarkable!" to himself over and over.

A change in reputation never hurt, at least not if it leaned toward a more reserved or disciplined bent. Julian doubted his reputation could get much worse when it came to his favorite vices, but if Crane and others saw him differently now, there was no harm in it.

Could be an advantage at the tables, if I play it rightly. Or an advantage with Eve's uncle, another part of him whispered, and Julian smiled.

On the carriage ride home to Shelbrook's, he considered the implications and all his options. His pursuit of Eve had certainly led to some unexpected consequences—one being that his strategy of accepting only the more respectable invitations that crossed his breakfast tray had smoothed his path. He'd never paid much attention to the disregard of others, but now that it was lacking, he found that being liked and admired wasn't at all unpleasant. "Heroic endeavors" aside, the effort it required to open unlocked doors was minimal, as opposed to the social struggle when certain venues were barred completely.

He couldn't honestly say that he was better behaved these days, but no one seemed to be noticing if he wasn't. He wasn't sure if he should be more insulted or not, after a lifetime of reveling in his notoriety, but once again, he resolved that at the very least it might add to his abilities to recover his fortunes.

As the carriage stopped before Shelbrook's door, Julian took a deep breath to brace himself before alighting and heading indoors. Facing his lovely hostess was awkward on a good night, but as he crossed the threshold he had to admit that recently she'd been better. If anything, Beatrice had been strangely polite, omitting the seductive looks, proposals, and even the veiled threats. Not that he was stupid enough to relax his guard. *Still, perhaps she's moved on and found a better candidate.*

He glanced through the library doors as he passed and realized that Beatrice was there. To be polite, he veered in his path to greet her. "Are you keeping vigil tonight for me, Lady Shelbrook?"

"Don't flatter yourself." She waved him in, an invitation to an open chair across from her. "A glass of wine, Julian?"

"One glass might help me sleep. Thank you." He helped himself to a glass from the tray and refilled hers. "Has Lord Shelbrook retired for the night?"

"The rain makes his bones ache. He took a draught for the pain and I don't expect to hear anything sensible from him before noon tomorrow."

"He has my sympathies. They usually make my bones ache a bit as well, but that's my own fault for breaking a few of them over the years in reckless stunts and idiotic endeavors." He stretched out and took a sip of the expensive vintage, letting it roll over his tongue. "You could spare him a few more kind thoughts, I should think."

"I have none to waste on Barnaby. But if you're going to sit there and lecture me on the role of a good wife, I'll have my wine back, thank you very much."

He smiled. *Point taken, Beatrice. I'm not exactly in a position to preach, am I?* "Well, save one or two gentle thoughts for me, then."

"Have you earned them?" She gave him a coquettish look over the rim of her glass. "Are we not at odds, Lord Westleigh?"

"Were we?" He took another sip of the wine. "I'm not holding any grudges."

She laughed humorlessly. "How generous of you!"

"Come now, Beatrice. Shall I apologize and make us friends again?"

She shook her head, settling into her chair and relaxing a bit, some of the icy starch leaving her eyes as she did so. "No apologies. I hate apologies."

"I thought women in general loved the damn things. Lord Hood says his wife writes all his down or makes him put them into letters so that she can relive them later whenever she likes. Dangerous hobby to allow a wife, but there you have it."

Her humor seemed to be returning, and Julian was glad to see her smile at his jest. "She's a fool! To accept a box of letters when he could write a few cashier's checks instead?"

"There's the mercenary I've come to know."

She shrugged, then blushed, as if he'd just offered her the supreme compliment. "Enough of that, Julian. I think I know the source of this change in you—this offer of peace and friendship."

"Do you?"

"I heard a rumor you were besotted with some little debutante nobody. Is it true?"

"What rumor ever is?"

"Not that I care, Julian. I have no claims."

"No, you have none." He restated it, to ensure she felt the weight of his words, then tried to divert her. "Was that the best of the rumors? I heard that I was going to sell all my worldly possessions and go off on an excursion to Africa."

"You are known to enjoy the chase."

"But not the kill?"

"Oh, you relish the kill." She shook her head. "But you take more than you can eat, my love."

He pulled in his legs, preparing to stand. "Thank you for the wine, Lady Shelbrook."

Her hand stretched out to gently restrain him. "I would forgive you anything, Julian."

"I never asked you to, Beatrice." He stood to take her hand, bending over it to kiss the bony rise of her knuckles before letting it go. "Good night, my dear."

Julian turned and left the room without looking back, thereby missing the cold smile of satisfaction on Lady Shelbrook's face.

Chapter Fourteen

"You're late." It was only ten in the morning, and Julian marveled that she could look so fresh after so many late nights at the tables with her uncle. It was getting harder and harder to slip away from their busy lives, but he'd have met her at dawn if he'd had to.

"I thought I was early," she replied, dropping her reticule. She began to untie her bonnet ever so slowly. The hours and days had crawled since she'd last seen him. "You're impatient, perhaps?"

"Most definitely." He leaned against the door-frame to the sitting room, his casual stance belying the alert heat in his golden eyes. "It's a wicked trick to keep a man waiting, Eve."

"I would never deliberately toy with you like that, Julian." Though he would never know how close she'd come to sending him a note to say she wouldn't be there. *I still don't know how Uncle Warren knows I left Dixon's early—or if it's safe to be here. But I just don't care anymore.*

Seeing him so strong and handsome, an oasis of attention and warmth, she didn't believe that anything would have merited sacrificing this appointment. In the days since her uncle's tirade, she'd attacked her plans with a new zeal, aware that the lies she'd told might hold for only so long. She'd finally begun to win in earnest, with an appropriate sprinkling of "beginner's modesty" so that her new popularity wouldn't be dampened. Providing a good show meant she was a more entertaining guest and partner at the tables, and new blood with old money had taken note and started to ask for their turn to challenge her.

As the risks had increased, she'd fought to stay calm. Her uncle's scrutiny hadn't faded; while he'd apologized for his temper and the need for his, as he called it, "harsh lecture" after her disobedience following the Dixons' lawn party, he'd been no less vigilant.

It would have been so much safer not to see Lord Westleigh, but she hadn't been able to stop herself. Time was the relentless enemy. No matter what happened, Eve wanted to actually do something and not just hide in her rooms for the rest of the Season.

"Then again, you seem to know far too much about wicked tricks, Julian." She turned from him and headed up the stairs, pausing briefly on the fourth riser. "Would you like to come upstairs and teach me a few of them?"

"I'm not sure I should give away any of my secrets," he said as he began to climb the steps. "But I could never say no to you, Miss Reynolds."

"Never?" She paused outside the bedroom door. "Hmmm, a remarkable admission, Lord Westleigh."

"Why don't I clarify, then?" He put a hand against the doorframe and leaned over her. "Within this house and for this afternoon only, I shall be your willing servant."

"I'm going to test that." Eve smiled as she considered all the implications of Julian's potential enslavement. "You'll do anything I ask?"

"Anything except leave you alone," he clarified ruefully. "No more banishments."

"Fair enough." She drew him into the room and stood him at its center. *What would it be like to command such a man?* She circled him slowly, a mistress enjoying the study of her new possession. "My willing servant."

"As you wish." His voice was rough, betraying how much he was already aroused by this game.

She sat on the small overstuffed chair in the corner, as regal as any queen. "My shoes . . . are tight."

Julian smiled and knelt smoothly in front of her. "Then I will see to them, mistress." He pulled off her shoes slowly, sliding them from her feet and setting them beneath her chair out of the way, ever the dutiful valet. "May I rub your feet, mistress?"

She smiled at the very thought of it. It was a decadent thing to command an earl to touch such a mean and humble part of her body. *He can't be serious!* "Very well. See to my pleasure, servant."

She expected him to make quick work of it and suggest another task, but her servant had other designs. He retrieved her right foot and began with slow, strong strokes that worked into the tight muscles of her foot, until her toes curled with the startling sensations he elicited. His thumbs pressed into the delicate arch of her foot, and with each circular caress, her eyelids fluttered. His warm hands cradled her heel, and she marveled that she'd no idea that her feet were wickedly connected to every nerve ending in her body.

He gave her left foot equal attention, and Eve pushed back into the chair and bit her lower lip as a flood of bliss began to rob her of her ability to command.

Then he set her feet against the top of his thighs, so that he could slide his hands up over her calves, the massage making her moan in pleasure as he worked the muscles of her legs. It was a delirious sensation to relax against his hands, knowing that she was in control. The knowledge made her hungry for more, but also hungry to turn the tables. His palms slid up to caress her knees and began to brush across the tops of her stockings. Eve sat up and abruptly slapped his hands.

He was instantly still, his look questioning but warm with approval.

"You take liberties, servant."

The reprimand increased the heat and the tension between them. Eve was dizzy with desire when he finally replied. "My apologies, mistress. I just wanted to see your—"

"You'll see only what I wish you to see." She took a long, slow breath to try to rein herself in. *This is a game better played slowly.* "I want the room to be dark this time."

"Dark?"

"Dark," she insisted. "It is far too bright in this room. Draw the curtains and extinguish the lights, please." She walked to the bed to await his obedience. "I did say please, Julian."

"Are you telling me that you are shy?" He did as he was told, albeit with some reluctance. A gloom enveloped the cozy bedroom as he shut out the afternoon light and turned off the lamps. "Eve, this wasn't exactly the scenario I was hoping for with my indentured service."

"No? But the dark gives me courage."

"Courage? Courage for what?" he asked impatiently, and Eve had to bite the inside of her lip to keep from laughing.

"For this." She took a single deep breath and then seized control, feeling more wicked and wild than she ever had with him. The dark was more than just a veil to cover his eyes. It was the freedom to act. Eve pulled his face down to hers, her kisses voracious and without a hint of feminine reserve. For the first time, she was the aggressor, and from his response, he was not offended in the slightest.

She pushed his jacket from his shoulders and removed his clothes, eager to follow her hands with her mouth. His words from their last encounter had haunted her, and Eve wanted to taste him, to experience the salty, sweet musk of his arousal—the essence of his power, there on her tongue for her to savor and absorb. His erection was massive, the weight of it in her palms making her heart race at its raw beauty. Her hands explored the shape of him, emboldened by his reactions when her fingernails gently scraped over every inch only to be soothed by a cooling exhale of her breath. She traced the pulse of his blood along the sensitive root with her mouth and teased the silky ripe head of him with maiden-sweet kisses she knew would drive him mad. His flesh was searing to the touch, but she felt like a moth drawn to the flame. His hands fisted into her hair as a groan slipped past his lips, and Eve instinctively suckled the ripe swollen head of his cock, listening raptly for each hiss of pleasure and moan he rewarded her with.

"Eve—not to . . . rebel but . . . if you don't stop that . . ." He took a slow, steadying breath. "This will be a very one-sided afternoon."

"Is my servant complaining?" she purred, her mouth still against him so that the question reverberated at the base of his shaft.

"No! Your servant is . . . most content."

She pulled more of him into her mouth, then released him in a slow pull before using his body to climb to her feet, deliberately ensuring that no part of him didn't endure the brush of her clothes and the friction of her curves against him.

Julian tried to pull her into his arms. "Let's get you out of those clothes, Eve, and—"

She caught his wrists gently. "Lie down on the bed, Julian."

"So imperious . . ."

"So disobedient . . . ," Eve countered, kissing him again to undercut the reprimand as she propelled him backward until his calves were pressed against the bedframe.

"As you wish, miss." He lifted himself onto the bed, and in the shadows, his outline amidst the white bedding was compelling. It was a position she'd been in more than once, but to see him there made a coil inside her begin to tighten and grow heavy against her hip bones.

She unbuttoned her dress and removed her petticoats, not at as leisurely a pace as she'd planned, but it was hard not to hurry with him lying there waiting for her next command. She left on her chemise, stockings, and corset, instinctively aware of the extremely sexy effect of being only partially naked for him.

"Are you sure a single oil lamp wouldn't be . . . helpful?"

She laughed. "You've seen enough of me, Lord Westleigh, to allow that keen mind of yours to imagine anything you are missing."

His harrumph of disappointment was muffled as she began to climb into the bed, touching only his naked frame to navigate her way toward him. From his ankles, she slowly pressed upwards to claim him with every stroke of her long, slim hands. Up over his knees and thighs, she smiled as she realized that her disgruntled manservant had definitely stopped complaining.

Lingering over his cock again, Eve gasped in delight when it moved in her palm, as if eager for more of her. It was a bit daunting to be so utterly in charge, but she was discovering that there were more than a few advantages.

Wrangling with the condom was much harder than he'd made it seem, though the gloom no doubt added to the challenge. It was a minor struggle, and she did her best with it, until at last it seemed secure and she could settle down astride him, a beautiful if disgruntled stallion.

"Ah, mercy at last!"

He submitted to the indignities, but only because it quickly became apparent that this new position would free up his hands to touch her while he bucked upward and rocked into her. She only needed to hold on. He gripped her hips at their widest curve, guiding her down onto him but letting her control how much of him she took. Ever so slowly, she yielded one inch and then another, her body growing slick and stretching to take him, her muscles contracting as if to milk him and draw him up inside of her.

"Julian."

"Too much?"

"Not enough. It's not enough." She spread her thighs and in one movement encompassed every thick inch, making him groan at the sudden, complete connection between them.

And then he could do little but let her go, his hands reaching up to roam over lace and confining garments, gritting his teeth and wishing she'd bared more for his hungry hands. Still, he had no room for complaint.

Eve used her legs to try to stay above him, to minimize the impact on her back, and she learned quickly that the wild sensations of each pistoning stroke up into her core drove the pain away, its power fading as the coil within her began to unleash at last. She wanted it to go on forever, this wicked escape from the world, but her body betrayed her and gave in to the flash of lust that shook her to her very center. She cried out, sure that this climax had altered her irrevocably.

Still she rode on, unwilling to return to reality, unwilling to relinquish this singular sensation of power and surrender. Pain and pleasure dueled and danced, and she began to feel the coil of need tighten again, with another release just beyond her reach. "Julian!" Her head fell backwards, her arms outspread as it overtook her and she gave in to the wave of white fire that swept through her body. He held her upright, guiding each bucking stroke, each rise and fall, slowing and then faster and faster, his cry of release mingling with hers in the strange, gray world of shadows she'd created.

"Will there be . . . anything else?" Julian's wry question came through ragged gasps for air as they both recovered. Eve fell on top of him, marveling at the delicious sensation of riding his chest as it rose and fell with each breath, a gentler echo to her own heart's pounding.

"I cannot think of a thing," she chuckled at the honest admission, marveling at the impossible whirl of her thoughts. "Not a single thing."

"Good! I'll take it as a compliment."

She struck his shoulder playfully and began to extricate herself from his embrace.

He sat up. "Damn it, I can't see. Did I hurt you, Lamb?"

"No, no, Julian." She shifted off the bed and began to retrieve her clothes. "Only a twinge. Ladies are not used to . . . riding astride."

He laughed. "True! I shall attempt to be a kinder stallion on our next outing."

His tone changed, becoming more serious. "Though you do make it hard for me to remember my best intentions, Eve. I touch you and I forget caution."

"So do I," she whispered solemnly. *If only you knew, Julian, how much of caution and care you drive from my mind—I think I would shock you at last!*

God help me.

Her nerves felt frayed. One word and she was sure she would start to babble about her fears—that her uncle would discover that they were lovers and drag her from England or that he would be caught cheating and she would be implicated and disgraced before she could slip away. Her dream of freedom felt more tenuous than ever . . . and Julian's hold on her was growing with each encounter. She was in a trap of her own making.

His fingers caught her chin to guide her gaze toward his, and Eve realized that she'd worried him—that he'd read the fear in her eyes. "What's troubling you, Eve?"

"Nothing," she said as she pulled away from him and reached up to button his shirt. "You missed a button, Lord Westleigh."

His brow furrowed, thrown off by the mundane and unexpected shift in conversation. "What difference does that make?"

"You'll look like a man who dressed in a rush. Or worse, one who has no care for himself or the woman he just finished pleasuring to try to dress properly."

"I hardly think—"

"Not that I expect you to know how to button your own shirt. Poor man, a lifetime of attendants and valets! It's a wonder your pants aren't on backwards."

His eyes narrowed as her words hit the mark. "That was uncalled for."

"It's all so easy for you. You have no idea how the world really works. You're born to privilege, only to waste it on gaming tables."

Julian crossed his arms, unsure of how the afternoon had taken this turn. One moment she was heaven above him with her sweet thighs riding his hips and making his cock ache because he'd come so hard—and now he was definitely a man on the defensive. Was it Sotherton who had once joked at university that women were like wars—you could win a battle at sea and then realize you didn't have a port to land in? "Do you not gamble, Miss Reynolds?"

"You think I play for pleasure, your lordship? That it is some grand amusement that I let the turn of a card determine my fate—my survival?" Her voice broke, and he watched in amazement as his passionate and unflappable Eve transformed into another woman, one who was lost and sweet, defiant and frightened. His first instinct was to protect her somehow, but she stepped away from him. Her shoulders squared, and when she looked at him he saw only the strong and graceful vixen. "I play to win because I cannot lose. To lose is to starve, dear man. Not all of us are born so lucky that we have a future to throw away on a whim. I have no such future and nothing to lose, in fact. Can you see the difference?"

He saw it. Hell, he'd skirted closer to that line than he wished to admit. Born to privilege, he'd risked his fortunes for the sheer thrill of it. He'd won and lost and had never thought twice. But looking at her, he felt slightly humbled. She was the true gambler. With steady hands, she took up the cards that fate dealt her, and without fear, she played to win.

"Yes," he finally spoke. "I see it."

"Oh, dear." A new fire lit her eyes, and Julian marveled that a woman's temper could be increased by a man's admission that she might be right. *Difficult creatures!*

"I'm not an object to be pitied, Julian. I am not some stricken orphan with holes in her slippers." She stomped her foot as if to demonstrate the specific point, and suddenly he was trying not to smile.

"Make no mistake, Miss Reynolds. What I feel for you is not pity."

He pulled her into his arms, overriding the weak protest of her hands pressing against his chest. He kissed her, hard enough to ensure that she would surrender, drawing out her ire and infusing them both with a soft fire they could easily restoke. It was a passionate resignation of his servitude, and Julian let her go reluctantly. "If I cannot manage to catch a glimpse of you in public beforehand, then I shall see you next Tuesday."

"Julian, I—" He read regret in her eyes.

"Courage, Lamb." He kissed her again, a soft, lingering taste to apologize as well—for whatever the hell he'd done wrong. "Play well."

She nodded, her eyes full of unshed tears. "Thank you."

She left without another word, and Julian found himself alone in the bedroom, to take his time in dressing and absorb the familiar landscape of the room.

Brilliant little minx, got me all flustered and distracted.

And you aren't upset about shirt buttons, Eve Reynolds. So let's see if we can't find out why you suddenly have the look of a woman without a friend in the world.

Chapter Fifteen

"Is that all of it?"

Eve nodded as she watched him count and recount the stacks of cash and promissory notes from her recent games. It had been a very profitable few days. She'd taken Julian's words of encouragement to heart, stepping up her games whenever she'd been able, determined to accelerate her escape if she could. In a simple cloth pouch tied to her corset, she had the afternoon's secret take, contributed mainly by a very arrogant friend of Mrs. Wickett's—the Marchioness of Toxbury, who didn't seem to think a thing of playing for rings. Eve had suspected they'd be paste, but in the carriage she'd confirmed to the best of her ability that they were as valuable as they appeared. She'd wrapped each in a tiny patch of old rag to keep them from clinking against each other and giving her away.

Eve's risk had increased exponentially as the games' stakes had increased and her opponents had become wealthier. There were only a few weeks left in the Season, and if any of her unlucky card players commiserated with a friend and word spread that her skills were more than formidable—though there were always a few who enjoyed a greater challenge—she would find it harder to get anyone to really gamble with her. And if that word reached her uncle . . .

She didn't want to consider what would happen then. No, she would take whatever risk she needed to. She would see Julian in just three more days, and she would confess all. If only to let him know that when she disappeared after the Season, he wouldn't think the worst of her.

"Come now, Eve. You aren't still upset with me about our . . . misunderstanding after Dixon's, are you?"

"No, Uncle Warren."

"Well, I certainly hope it's not a lingering snit about the earl being put off. It's not as if a man like that was ever going to make an offer! I've heard the worst of him when ladies aren't present to censure the men's comments. Not to be crude, but it's best you know, he's tapped so many married women that word has it there's a bounty on his head if he so much as puts a foot inside certain counties."

Oh, dear. "I have heard something similar, but mostly just hints at a wicked past. Some brush with misfortune has transformed him a bit, according to Lady Morrington, and he may be a man on the straight and narrow. Your source may have been speaking in the past tense."

"That's not the sense I get of it, Eve."

An inconvenient flash of jealousy was swallowed with difficulty. "Men are known to exaggerate their conquests to impress others. I hardly think he's—"

He shook his head firmly. "I disregarded one report I received that you'd dallied with the man already. I told myself that I knew you wouldn't be so foolish. But looking at you now . . . I wonder."

"What reports? I'd say you have an imaginative gossip on your hands." She responded calmly despite the accuracy of his words, which made everything seem to slow down. "Who is this source?"

"Never you mind my source! The look on your face tells me everything I need to know." He crossed his arms and gave her his sternest look. "First things first, Eve. We've been invited to the Hightowers' for an intimate dinner in three days' time. I'm sure there will be a friendly hand or two afterwards, so see that you are at your best. Now, get upstairs and change to go shopping."

"I have clothes."

"This will be about more than a card game, Eve. Hightower is the best candidate for a husband that ever walked marbled halls! So, you'll need something to wear that's especially alluring but modest, just in case Mr. Hightower proves to live up to his potential. The man has more money than sense, but there are worse faults to be found!"

"The Earl of—"

He raised his hand, his face losing the last of its cheerful veneer. "I know the earl is not without his charms, but I would think that you, of all women, would be immune to such things. You've a soft spot for him, and that's Lady Morrington's fault for encouraging you, and mine, perhaps, for giving you too much freedom here. How can you expect the deliciously wealthy but notoriously staid and conservative Mr. Hightower to marry a woman who carries on a friendship with a known rake?"

"I can't imagine," she sighed. "Should I ask him?"

"This is no time for terrible jokes, Eve! This is business and that's all that matters. A clear head, Eve, rules the game."

She nodded. Cards, money, business were all that mattered to him—and now potentially ensnaring an unsuspecting Mr. Hightower.

"Upstairs with you! And don't worry, Evie. If we can't manage Hightower, then when all of this is over, we'll get you out of dreary London and find someplace much better, eh?"

"Perhaps something other than blue, miss? With your stark coloring, you will dazzle in these!"

She waved off the proffered gowns of daring red and burgundy. She was in no mood to wear scarlet. "The royal blue suits me, and it is already made."

It was a sentimental habit, the color choice. It had been her mother's signature color, and her father had said he always adored her in it. After she'd died, he'd made a point of insisting on buying only dark blue dresses for Eve, and it had become a connection between them. Eve had almost no memories of her mother, except for her wearing a sapphire blue satin dress with tiny ribbons at the hem.

So when her father had died and left her with a wardrobe full of blue, she'd decided to carry on the tradition, to honor him as well.

"I like the look of that one." She pointed to one of the dresses draped over the mannequin. It would flatter without overtly displaying too much of her shoulders and breasts. The silhouettes in fashion had changed a great deal in the last few years, and while she was thrilled to abandon foolish hoops, the crinolines and bustles were still a waste of material from her viewpoint.

The mistress clucked in disapproval. "So matronly for one so young!"

"We have a difference of opinion, Madame Dellacourt." She threw the price list down and began to gather her things. "Another dressmaker may have what I desire, so I will—"

"Oh, no! We are pleased to have your business, Miss Reynolds! I spoke rashly! Naturally, you will look lovely in that cut. Please, let me set you up in one of our back rooms to take your measurements, and we will have it pinned and tailored just for you."

The woman was a whirlwind of hospitality, ushering Eve toward a narrow hall of doors in the back of the store. At the last door, she brought Eve into a private changing room, replete with a silk settee and a folding set of mirrors in one corner. "The event is Monday evening, yes?"

"Yes, thank you."

"Yvette will attend you, and we will have all ready and delivered by midday tomorrow!" The woman curtsied and left quickly, as if to prevent Eve from making another feint at escape.

The girl came quickly. In a businesslike manner, she had Eve down to her skin for measurements in seconds. Then she laced her back into her undergarments and petticoats and put the blue dress over them. The adjustments needed would be minimal, and Yvette pinned the hem with a light and skilled hand.

Eve stared at the woman reflected in triplicate,

the dark blue setting off the sheen of her hair and making her skin seem even whiter. *Who is that woman? I only know one thing about her for certain,* she marveled. *I know she isn't going to let Mr. Hightower even think of twitching in her direction, damn it!*

Yvette gently removed the dress without exposing Eve to a single pin. "I'll be back to help you dress, miss. Excuse me."

"Oh, well, if you could just—" The door closed before she could finish, and Eve had no choice but to await her return.

She did what she could without aid, but she accepted that without someone to manage the buttons at the back, she would have to wait. The sound of the door reopening came sooner than she'd hoped, but at the sight of Julian Clay slipping inside the room, shock robbed her of thought.

She leapt up on the pedestal, avoiding his outstretched hand, clutching her dress to her throat. "You cannot be here!"

"And yet I am. I want to buy you something beautiful—perhaps a new ball gown. Don't you ever wear anything that isn't blue?"

"No! No! And what difference does it make what color I wear? You cannot buy me clothes, Julian!"

"Not even a sexy red silk chemise and petticoat? Something along the lines of a scarlet corset to match? Or black with sheer textures to make a man go wild? My pants are getting tighter just considering it. Come, Eve, your uncle will never see them, and think how wicked you'll feel wearing it while you play bezique with the old ladies."

"Julian, I already feel wicked while I play bezique with dear old ladies. Please don't complicate things." She tried to gesture toward the door without losing her grip on the cloth.

"I like this one." He'd retrieved a small stack of prints off the side table and held up a fashion plate of a sumptuous evening gown. "The bustle is a bit much, but they do move nicely when you stroll about . . ."

Her mouth fell open in surprise. "Lord Westleigh, are you choosing clothes for me?"

"Why not?" He stepped up onto the dais behind her, holding up another plate in front of her. "It's a day gown, but I love the décolletage." He caught her eye in the mirror, and she wickedly watched their reflections as his free hand began to encircle her waist. "It would flatter you."

"I don't . . ." She lost the trail of her thoughts as his warm hand moved up her rib cage to cup one of her breasts. Her body responded instantly to having him behind her, and Eve knew this was a battle she would enjoy losing—but couldn't risk fighting. "I don't need another day gown."

"Nonsense." He smiled, his eyes never leaving

her face in the mirror. He callously dropped the rest of the prints on the floor, freeing his hands to touch her as he wished. "A morning gown then? Something soft that embellishes that figure of yours; something easy to remove when I desire so that I can touch you as I wish."

"You . . . seem to touch me as you wish already, Lord Westleigh."

"Do I?" he asked in mock surprise. "May I?"

He read consent in her eyes. "Julian—"

She watched the woman in the mirror yield happily to each caress, the otherworldly quality of the encounter fueling her hunger. Julian trailed his fingertips up from her wrists over the bare skin of her arms and made her shiver with anticipation. His warm breath fanned the shell of her ear, and Eve tilted her head to silently entreat his lips to follow. He obliged her with a mischievous grin before lowering his mouth to taste the sensitive curves of her throat.

"Oh, dear!" She closed her eyes. *Yvette is going to be back at any moment!*

"I think I'm going to buy you a dozen gowns at this rate, Lamb," he said with a playful growl against her throat.

"I am not your mistress, Julian. I am not—" Eve tugged at the gown to cover herself in a fit of frustration and stepped down from the dais. It was splitting hairs to argue the matter, and she was in no mood to proclaim her right to sleep with a man without accepting gifts. "What are you doing here, Lord Westleigh? And how in the world did you find me?"

He followed her and stretched out on the settee like a sensual leopard lying in the sun, completely relaxed. "I wasn't completely satisfied with the way we ended our last conversation."

"That doesn't answer my question of how you happen to be here."

"I was across the street by chance when I saw you get out of your carriage. It was fate."

"Fate? This isn't a fairy tale, Julian. They'll find you in here, and Madame Dellacourt will talk even if they don't!"

"Nonsense! I'm one of her favorite customers, and besides . . . I paid off the seamstress. She knows better than to slander me."

Her eyes darkened with the implications of his claim that he was already a good customer of the shop's, but Eve knew better than to play the jealous lover with him. "I never imagined you as one of those men who find fulfillment dressing in women's clothes, Lord Westleigh."

"Such talk from a young lady! Careful, Eve, or I'll suspect you've seen more of the world than an innocent lamb should."

"Julian . . ." Eve took a steadying breath, attempting to regain her composure. It was terrifying to think of him there, and impossibly risky—but at the same moment, he was dreadfully handsome and charming as he reveled in this bit of bad behavior. The man was fetching. "Did our last conversation end so terribly that you would hide in a ladies' dressing room to finish it?"

He nodded. "I actually lost sleep last night thinking about it."

She smiled. "And that is . . ."

"An unacceptable inconvenience, in my opinion." Julian's scowl carried little weight, a vague mockery of a nobleman "most put out." "You are the first woman to *ever* disrupt my rest, and I'm not sure I can allow it, Miss Reynolds."

"I see."

"The solution is clearly . . . to say what I should have said at Bell Street when you intimated that I was being callous."

"I never said—"

"That I looked like a man in a hurry, because I didn't care about himself or the woman he had just tumbled?"

"Well," Eve said, biting her lower lip, "I'm certain I didn't mean to phrase it so directly."

"These amusements have become—important to me." The declaration hung in the air for a moment, and she marveled at the strange effort it took for him to continue. "I *have* been reckless with this affair and with you. And I suppose it is a terrible habit I have always had that made me treat it so—casually as I may have done. But I find I am not reckless in my regard. Miss Reynolds, I wish to take more care where you are concerned—"

"I am flattered, Julian. When I spoke in anger, I never meant to hurt you. It never occurred to me that you would take a word of it to heart. Or lose sleep . . ." A small smile escaped her, and she wondered if this was one of the strangest conversations of her life.

"Your uncle—"

"I don't want to talk about him, Julian. There is nothing to say."

"Say nothing then." He waved away her protests. "Like most men, I enjoy my own speeches, so I shall just make one now. You deliberately diverted me from it last time, and I let myself be diverted because I have no right to confront your uncle . . . and doing so would only expose us. It makes sense, if that was your logic. But I hate logic, and I think I let myself be diverted because I have a tendency to be a selfish prick."

"Julian, there is nothing you can do to . . . help me."

"Ah! I think that is the point that sticks in my craw." He sat up, his arms gripping the seat on either side of him as if to restrain himself from reaching for her. "Do you really believe that I can't help you because of some failing in my character that you perceive? Am I not the heroic type to intervene on your behalf? Do I seem . . . unlikely to take action, Eve?"

There was nothing about him that even hinted at inaction. "Julian, what action is there to take? Call him out as a liar and a cheat? Threaten to expose him as a charlatan? And how does this help me improve my situation?" Eve swallowed at a lump in her throat, an unnamed emotion she didn't want to comprehend. "Julian, you have always seemed to me a man who would make the very best choices."

"For myself, yes. That would have to be true, wouldn't it?" He shook his head, a sorrowful sphinx. "Especially if you've heard the stories. But I swear, when you look at me, I know you haven't."

"When I look at you? I'm not sure I'm following you."

"When you look at me, Miss Reynolds, I see a better man in your eyes. It's impossible, considering the nature of our relationship and my reckless approach to your company. Yet not once have you looked at me as if you judged me. It is . . . refreshing, Miss Reynolds."

"I'm in no position to judge anyone's behavior."

"Not even the way they button their shirts?"

She blushed. "That was a rough feint to change the subject, and you know it. You are a very capable creature, and I'm not going to stroke your vanity and enter into a ridiculous argument about how wonderful you are, Julian."

He rewarded her with a look that warmed her to her toes and made her suddenly wary, reminding her that she was not entirely dressed for the occasion. "Thank you, Eve."

"I've done nothing."

He came to his feet easily, his entire demeanor changing in a flash, the sad and thoughtful cast in his eyes thrown off and discarded like a coat. The playful and dangerous lion she was growing terribly fond of now once again stood before her. He straightened his waistcoat, slyly using the mirrors to ensure that his appearance was up to standards. "Why *do* you always wear dark blue?"

She shook her head. "And exactly *how* is it you were shot again?"

His wry grin was a sight to behold. "Touché!" He gave her a mock bow. "Well, I'd say that does it for today. We can trade secrets later. What a relief to have things settled between us so . . . amicably?"

Eve's eyes widened in confusion. *Is he dismissing me?* "Settled? Have I missed an exchange or two in this conversation, Lord Westleigh?"

He stepped forward, reaching up to pull her down for a kiss. "Not at all." His touch was possessive and firm, setting off a storm of sensations as he commanded her body's instinctive surrender. She consented with a sigh, reveling in the hunger that raked across her skin and flared with every nibble of his lips over hers. *I am a feast for you, Julian, and would feast on you in return until I forgot who I was and I lost the desire for all the things I cannot have.*

He released her slowly, making sure she had her balance on the dais before he stepped back. "Well, I'm afraid I promised an old friend I'd meet him at the club. I'll see myself out."

"Julian!" Her eyes fluttered in surprise. "Y-you can't just l—"

He bowed, his eyes raking over her. "Until Tuesday. It was a pleasure, Miss Reynolds. A true pleasure. Of course, if you wish to see me sooner . . . I'm sure you can find a way."

She raised her hand to bid him wait, but he was gone. *Damn it, I should warn him that my uncle suspects that we're seeing each other—before Uncle Warren steps in and ruins it all.*

She stepped down and sat on the settee he'd abandoned, trying to catch her breath and calm the storm of emotions sweeping through her. There was something so pure and impossible in the way he wanted her—the way it made her feel. Would he want her if he knew everything? All the pitiful details and sordid twists? She just didn't feel strong enough to lose him—not yet. Perhaps the truth would wait for a few more days. Uncle Warren had Mr. Hightower in mind, and until that business had failed, as she knew it would, he would do nothing about Julian. There was still time to pretend that he was truly hers.

She stood and pushed down her petticoats, smoothing her hair back into place before ringing for an attendant.

Yvette came almost instantly. "Yes, mademoiselle?"

"Tell Madame Dellacourt I wish to add a few things to my order."

Chapter Sixteen

Eve climbed out of the carriage. She was nervous, as she had not been in many weeks. It was not her usual day to arrive at Bell Street, but the fact that this was decidedly a Sunday and not a Tuesday had nothing to do with the invisible butterflies that fought to escape her chest.

I will tell him this afternoon about my uncle's schemes and . . . I will warn him off. As wonderful as this has been, I can't lie to myself any longer. Uncle Warren is bound to ruin it, and I may as well be the one to tell Julian to extricate himself before it gets ugly. It didn't matter that her uncle would gain nothing from his actions. Eve knew he was too caught up in his own lies to see reason, and would impulsively strike out if he thought Eve was acting on her own to create alliances. She'd sent a note of invitation to Julian at his club to be discreet, since Lady Morrington had advised her on some of his well-known haunts. Even so, there'd been no way to confirm if he would come or not, which only added to the jangle of her nerves. She did not have a key to the house, and so she had been forced to ask the driver to wait.

At her knock, the door opened, and Eve silently marveled at what a pretty butler Julian made before turning to wave off the carriage. "I'm . . . glad to see you, Lord Westleigh."

He ushered her inside, openly happy to see her as well. "I think Andrews caught a glimpse of your lovely handwriting, but I told him it was from an elderly aunt who was ailing and wished to see me right away."

"An elderly aunt?" She handed over her bonnet and reticule. "I suppose I am feeling a bit . . . peaked."

"What a shame! And how long have you been suffering?" he teased.

"Since I went dress shopping on Friday—and was accosted by a very cheeky scoundrel!" Eve did her best imitation of Margaret Wickett in a full snit and fanned her face with a free hand. "What is the world coming to, I ask you!"

"Well then, let us get you to bed, my dearest," he soothed, picking her up easily to cradle her against his chest and carry her up the stairs, taking them two risers at a stride. "I don't see how you can breathe in those clothes."

There will be time to talk afterward—yes, after.

She was coming to love the confines of the small upstairs bedroom that they had made their own. Eve buried her face in his neck and inhaled the familiar scent of him—sandalwood and smoke, and a masculine musk that quickened her pulse.

"I love it when you do that," he murmured.

"I can't help it. You smell divine, Julian." She kissed him up the strong column of his throat, nipping at the pulse she felt there. "Wicked man."

He set her back onto her feet and began to undress her without an instant's hesitation, reading the desire in her eyes as all the ready permission a man ever needed. The buttons of her demure dark blue gown gave way and his fingers froze at the first peek of what lay underneath.

"You didn't!" Julian almost swore in astonishment.

"You should be more careful if you didn't wish me to call your bluff, Lord Westleigh."

"Clearly." He pushed her gown from her shoulders and drank in the sight of Eve in a sexy red silk chemise and petticoat. As the dress fell away, she was a vision in scarlet, the half corset adding to the effect of a rose in bloom. Her pale skin glowed, and her lips and cheeks were flush with pleasure, and he did nothing to hide his approval of her daring surprise.

He pulled her hair down, eager to see the black silk curls cascading down her back over the sweet curves of her body encased in the red of peonies, her breasts pushed up by the half corset, her nipples already taut and eager for his touch. He tugged at the pins and dropped them carelessly on the floor in a race to keep up with the pace of his desire, drawing one long curl over her shoulder to circle one delectable orb of her bosom. "My God, Eve! You are a vision a man would cheerfully die to behold." He pulled her against him, unable to keep from kissing her, anchoring his hands in the heavy silk tangle of her hair. She was a pagan goddess wearing the colors of flames and blood and Julian was a warrior as he held her, ready to sacrifice anything she demanded for the pleasure of bedding her.

The petticoats and underlying crinoline were discarded, and he winced as the delicate chemise tore in his hands. "Damn it!"

He lifted his head to assess the damage, but she wouldn't allow it. With a whimper, she initiated the kiss again, guiding his hands back to their eager work and reaching for the buttons of his shirt. When a button fell to the floor, it was her turn to pull back in dismay at the mishap.

"J-Julian . . . we seem to be—"

"To hell with it!" He couldn't care less if they ended up shredding each other's clothes into rags, though a faint, practical sliver of his mind did note that without clothes to spare, it might make for an interesting carriage ride back to Shelbrook's.

Breathing hard, they undressed as quickly as they could, and Eve began to smile as the layers melted away without regard. "Do you think we're odd to . . . delight in . . . each other's company the way we do, Julian? Is this . . . unique?"

He clawed merrily at the buttons on his trousers as they strained against his erection. "We are a strange pair, you and I."

Eve peeled off her stockings and stood before him wearing nothing now but the red corset, its ribbons dangling over the curve of her thighs and teasing the swell of her bottom. She instinctively knew it pleased him to see her like that, and her inner thighs clenched with the powerful need to have him there. Her body was already dripping wet in anticipation.

How do I ask him if it's normal for me to want him like this? To ask him if it's strange to think of nothing but the way his body tastes or the way I—

"Eve." The last of his clothes fell away and he stood before her, proud and beautiful, the evidence of his arousal jutting defiantly toward her. His eyes glittered with a ferocious lust and an intensity that took her breath away. "Say it."

"Say what?"

"Say exactly what you were thinking just then."

A jolt of panic whipped through her. "I couldn't possibly—"

"Say it, Eve. It excites me to hear your every carnal thought. To see those red lips of yours giving form to whatever wicked secrets you are contemplating behind those eyes." He pulled her against him, catching her as momentum robbed her of her balance. With one hand at her back, the other slid down between her thighs to part her curls and find the creamy folds he desired. "Say all of it, Eve."

"Truly?"

His fingers paused in their skillful explorations, then caught her wrist to guide her hand onto the unyielding length of his cock. "Oh, yes. Talk to me, Eve. I saw it in your eyes, and now I wish to hear it."

"I'm . . . I'm not sure I can, Julian."

He slid her fingers up and down, scattering her fears as the familiar emptiness between her legs began to ache in a pulsing rhythm that made her knees weak.

She tipped her head back. "If you laugh . . ."

"I swear I will not."

Oh, God, I believe you. One deep breath and what would be the harm?

"I think you've ruined me, Julian. At every turn, even in drafty rooms full of old women or lifeless drawing rooms where I sit against the wall and pray for invisibility, you are all I can think of—just like this. Naked and wanting and . . . mine to touch."

His fingers slipped back between her legs, rubbing her clit and spreading her flesh. "Tell me what you want, Eve."

She lifted her leg to give him more access, her hips instinctively bucking against his hand, while her own fingers began to draw against his shaft. "I want you . . . to take me the way you threatened to . . . in the garden that first night."

"Yes?" The pace of his touch quickened, but he was like a golden lion waiting for the critical moment when she broke cover.

"Standing. Against a wall. With my ass in your hands." She gasped in shock at her own words, then continued, the fire between her legs giving her courage, and the hotter fire in his eyes sending her over the edge. "I want you to . . . finish what you started that night. Please, Julian."

It was all he needed to hear. Before she could blink, he'd retrieved a condom from the tin and returned to lift her without another word, spreading her thighs to wrap around his waist and impale her in one swift move. She screamed at the tight, sweet balance of pain and pleasure as her muscles clenched around him and her clit squeezed against his cock. The room spun only once and she knew he'd carried her across the room toward one of the walls. The crash of a few bric-a-bracs falling from a side table and the portrait of some generic country scene struck the floor as Julian ensured that there was nothing behind her to cause injury.

Then Eve was sure there were no more thoughts of anything. No words. Each thrust was so deep, so strong, so powerful, that there was nothing she could do but cling to him, her legs wrapped around his waist to ride each soul-jarring stroke until she knew a surrender she had never dreamt of.

She cried out, the coil inside her so tight she wasn't sure it was possible to let go without shattering, without irrevocably breaking something inside herself. Tighter and tighter it spiraled inside her. Eve bit his shoulder to fight it, but he wrested the battle from her control by moving his hands over her naked bottom, cupping her to lift her even higher so that he could drop her a few critical inches and add to the invasion of his body into hers.

Eve tasted his blood and gave into the blinding spasms of her release, wave after wave cascading through her until she was past all fear and reckoning.

"Yes! Julian, yes!" She screamed again, the storm too beautiful to master, barely aware of his cries as his own climax chased hers. Eve struggled to catch her breath and keep from fainting.

He cradled her against his chest, the last waves

of her climax still wracking her body, and carried her to the bed. They sank into the soft feather bedding, and Julian gently continued to thrust into her, riding out each spasm until she was completely and truly spent in his arms.

Eve sighed, her eyes closed as she savored the impossible happiness that coalesced around them.

He stroked her hair, unraveling curls and twisting a length around his fingers. "Ah, Miss Reynolds. You do have a way with words."

She smiled and weakly managed to tweak his chest hair before resigning herself to the fleeting peace of the time they had left. *No more talking. Not now. I'm just not ready to let him go—to let this go.*

She felt a surge of fierce possessiveness overtake her, pushing out all speculation and worry. Eve was sure that if she got wind of her uncle taking any action, there would be time enough to send word to Julian. After all, he had Hightower in his sights, and if tomorrow night went the way her uncle envisioned, that distraction might give her another week or two with Julian.

Please God, just a little more time to feel like this—to feel as if I belong in his arms.

"Women are dangerous, Julian." Barnaby leaned forward unsteadily over his cards, and Julian tried not to smile.

"Perhaps, but they don't make for an unpleasant

end." Julian threw down a card to retrieve another for his hand. "I can think of worse ways to die, Lord Shelbrook."

"Can you really?"

Julian's attention sharpened at the strange shift in Barnaby's mood. His question had no hint of a jest but instead the heavy weight of a man attempting to resolve a painful issue. *Oh, not now! If ever I needed to not have another jealous husband on my hands . . .* "What's on your mind, old friend?"

"You're still young, Julian. I know you think I'm a bit of a duff, but I wasn't always an idiot." He shook his head sadly. "I was quite the man once."

"You still are." Julian set his cards down. Whatever Barnaby intended, it wasn't the time for games.

"No, not anymore. But I was! When I married Beatrice, I was so sure I had it all in hand. Little did I know that I had, in fact, just handed over the reins like some drunken sorrel horse too blind to see the road."

Julian shifted in his chair. Drunken confessions always made him uncomfortable, but he felt honor-bound to hear the man out. "Wives do have a way of managing things, from what I understand of it."

Barnaby chuckled. "Oh, yes! Management. It's a skill I think they learn along with embroidery." Barnaby refilled his glass from the decanter at hand, his expression growing more grim. "I won't ask if you're using the house on Bell Street with some Covent Garden dove. I like to think you are. Hell, I still occasionally like to think I might again one day!"

"You should." *God, man, get ten mistresses! Your wife is certainly adept at finding her own entertainments. Why the hell shouldn't you?* Julian pushed his glass forward to join his host's, though he had no plans to keep pace with Barnaby's consumption.

Lord Shelbrook shook his head. "It's been six years, Julian. Six years since I bought that house for the sweetest dove to ever grace this world. She was a plump little thing, but oh, my, I loved the way she laughed, and no matter what I seemed to say, she was always so pleased and happy to listen. I'd ramble for hours and she would just sit like a cheerful bird, so attentive. Can you imagine it? A woman who listens?"

"I'm trying to picture it in my head." Julian sipped his brandy. "Really, Barnaby, this is—"

"Six years! Six wretched years since I set her aside at Beatrice's bidding, since I broke that sweet girl's heart and turned her out—and I'm still in the ice house! I shouldn't have let Polly go, Julian. If I'd known the torture was never going to end, I might as well have been happy."

Julian couldn't think of a response. What did you say to a man who had sacrificed his "sweetest dove" for nothing?

Barnaby went on, a slight slur detracting nothing from the wisdom of his words. "If you have any chance at happiness, Julian, you must take it. If you see it—that slim, marvelous opportunity—no matter what it costs, you cannot sit idly by! Whatever else you do in this life, don't be a cowardly idiot and think that there will always be another just like her."

Julian nodded. "I swear I won't."

Barnaby opened his mouth to say more, then closed it abruptly with an audible snap, his eyes darting to the doorway. Julian followed his gaze and realized that Beatrice was there, listening and immobile, her expression neutral and unyielding.

"Are you gentlemen hungry for a late supper, or should I tell the cook to stand down for the night?"

Julian stood and gave Barnaby a half bow. "No, I believe we're done for now. I shall see you in the morning then."

"Good night, Julian." Barnaby waved him off and reached for the decanter again.

"Good night, Lady Shelbrook," Julian said as he walked past her as nonchalantly as he could. *How much did you hear, Beatrice? Let's hope just enough to inspire you to be a little kinder to your husband. But from the look of you, I'd say I'm the one in the ice house now.*

Chapter Seventeen

Lord Westleigh,

I will expect you at my home this afternoon at 2 pm to discuss a matter of extreme importance. Your refusal to come will only confirm the worst of your reputation. I shall hope that you are a man of some honor and await your prompt arrival.

Mr. Warren Reynolds

"What the hell?" Julian stared at the note and reread it again just to be sure. Even on the third pass, it was a high-handed little summons coming from a man he suspected he might hate. Had he been wrong about her all along? Was this the infamous moment where terms of extortion would be laid out?

His instincts told him that this was a new twist. If she had known it was coming, she'd made no indication of it. And there was very little danger of actual blackmail. Public opinion being what it was, Julian felt confident this scandal wouldn't rate two minutes of breath amidst the Ton. Reynolds had more to lose.

Until now, Julian had respected Eve's wishes and given the man a wide berth, but . . . a meeting was inevitable. He'd been looking forward to his next rendezvous with Eve tomorrow, especially after what he'd dubbed in his mind "the red satin afternoon," but this business might change things.

Damn it! If Reynolds is about to step in the way and interfere with my affair with Eve . . . Then again, this meeting is a chance to assess him in private and uncover what he is up to.

Julian grabbed his coat and rang the bell to arrange for a carriage. If nothing else, he suspected this was going to be an interesting outing—especially if Mr. Warren Reynolds survived past three.

Barnett, the butler, showed him in, and Julian noted that while he was typically hard to read, like most men in his position, he looked as if he would rather be elsewhere. The fashionable address didn't disappoint, and the ground floor was ostentatiously appointed with oriental antiques and opulent fabrics. A single staircase to the left led to the upper floors, though it was hard to see much beyond, as the lights were off above stairs. Julian surveyed it with a jaundiced eye, aware that things were not all that they seemed with Mr. Warren Reynolds, wealthy industrialist.

He was led to the library, and there, waiting for him, was none other than the man himself. *Pretentious, aren't you?* "Mr. Reynolds?"

"Lord Westleigh. You came." Reynolds stood and came around the desk to offer his hand, his expression stern but neutral.

Damn, I'm going to enjoy this. Julian looked at Reynolds's hand as if he'd been holding out a hedgehog, then gave him a cold look designed to quell the haughtiest souls—or send a creditor back to his coach in tears. "Your note was at best intriguing and at worst insulting. I suggest you tell me what business it is that gives you the right to summon me in such a way."

The older man bristled but kept himself in check. "I apologize then. But it is an intimate business that demands your discretion."

Julian took the room's most comfortable chair without being asked, stretching out his long legs to relax. "Go on then."

The maneuver gave Warren pause, but he recovered to soldier on. "It relates to my niece, Miss Eve Reynolds."

Julian nodded, giving nothing away. "Yes."

"Sh-she is extremely dear to me, Lord Westleigh." Reynolds clasped his hands behind his back and continued the tale. "My sister-in-law was a delicate woman, and when she died when Eve was very young, I did my best to keep track of Eve and my brother. Naturally, when he fell ill and sent word begging me to take her, I never hesitated."

Julian made no reply. So far, the preamble was familiar ground.

"I have plans to achieve a good match for her. Women can be so impulsive, and Eve is no exception. But she is generally a levelheaded girl, and I rely on her a great deal. I'm not looking forward to letting her go, but I'm willing to part with her for the right man."

Julian decided to play along. "She is a beautiful young woman."

"But I'm afraid you are not that man, Lord Westleigh."

"Pardon?" It was only years of prevarication at gaming tables that kept him from revealing his surprise at this amazing turn in the conversation. He'd been completely prepared for blackmail—not a blacklist.

"A friend tells me that you have shown an interest in her." Reynolds paced, then turned back in a theatrical gesture. "Is this true?"

He doesn't know anything. Is it possible I'm here just to get waved off? "I won't lie and say that your niece has escaped my notice, Mr. Reynolds. She is truly unique, and your friend may be eager to keep your ear by exaggerating a few innocent public exchanges," Julian replied carefully, reining in an amused smile.

Mr. Reynolds read the glimmer of a smile as the best sign. "Well, I am relieved! I don't wish to offend you. I'd spoken to Eve earlier in the Season about the matter, but it came to me that as a gentleman you might appreciate a direct approach. I had to ensure that you knew that your attentions are—undesirable, sir."

"I see. May I ask why?"

"I've been told . . ." Reynolds pulled himself up and took a seat. "Well, let's just say that while I am sure you're a fine fellow, others seem to object to your past indiscretions. And frankly, I'm worried that Eve and I will be viewed differently if your association with her goes too far."

It was like a very bad play. The old fraud was sitting behind a desk and claiming the moral high ground, but from Julian's vantage, there was little he could really say without revealing too much. Still, something about it didn't ring true. Old instincts rose, and Julian decided that if this was a clumsy trap, it was one of the worst he'd ever encountered. What sort of con artist was he? "Perhaps I could see her with a chaperone to keep your 'friend' from getting the wrong impression."

"A kind suggestion, but I'm afraid not." Reynolds leaned forward with a conspiratorial wink. "We both know a determined man can get around a chaperone or two if he wants to. Though you seem most honorable, Lord Westleigh."

"Seem?" Julian stood in one fluid movement, enjoying the fleeting panic on Reynolds's face.

"You radiate honor!" Reynolds stood as well, bowing a little as he came around the desk. "Please forgive my choice of words, Lord Westleigh. I've no gift for diplomacy. But I already feel better about our conversation, don't you? I would ask you to stay to dine, but we are going to a private dinner at an old friend's tonight, a Mr. Daniel Hightower. He has a lovely home and no less than three carriages here in town."

Julian stared for one fleeting instant at the hand that was extended toward the doorway and absorbed the realization that this little toad of a man was showing him out.

"Hightower?" Julian suppressed a laugh. *Poor Eve. Hightower's a windbag with a talent for whining that can curdle milk.* "Enjoy your evening, then, and please, give Miss Reynolds my regards and let her know I wish her the best." Julian gave him a curt nod and let Reynolds walk him out.

"Yes, yes, of course! No hard feelings!"

On his way out, Julian made light conversation. "Have you found this house a pleasant one? I was looking for another town house and had considered this street."

"Remarkably so! So quiet, despite it being so fashionably situated."

"Not drafty then?"

"Not on the ground floor. My rooms are here and I have found it very comfortable. Eve is on the first floor, and as all women are wont to do, she fusses about every little breeze. But the house is very solid, and I would recommend it to any buyer, Lord Westleigh."

"Thank you, Mr. Reynolds. You are too kind."

Julian walked out and climbed back into the carriage, where he signaled the driver to hurry. The daring plan came together before he reached Shelbrook's doorstep. Julian decided that he would spend a leisurely afternoon at his club. Once it was well after dark and Warren was out with his niece, he would go back to their town house. It wouldn't be his first attempt at house burglary, and technically, he wouldn't be stealing. But he had a few lingering questions, and Julian wasn't in the mood to wait for answers. Nothing about the interview made sense, and he was starting to doubt every assumption he'd made about Eve and her uncle. And if he'd been wrong . . .

It was unthinkable.

* * *

Even as an amateur, Julian acknowledged that the break-in was going remarkably well. The servant's entrance was easily breached, and he didn't see a soul. He'd been prepared to duck if he had to avoid a servant or even Barnett, but no one appeared. *Did Reynolds give the entire staff the night off?*

It gave him a moment's pause, but it didn't change his course of action. The house was dark—none of the lights had been left on—so Julian was forced to locate a small handheld lamp before he could continue. In the library, he found Mr. Reynolds's accounting ledger in a bottom drawer of his secretary next to a bundle of unopened letters addressed to Eve. Julian recognized the handwriting as distinctly feminine and wondered who Miss Jane Kingsley of Warring Cross, England, was that her correspondence needed to be intercepted.

Still, it was the ledger that he retrieved and studied. He scanned the numbers, unsure of the meaning of the codes next to most of the entries. They looked like initials, but they were interspersed with roman numerals and a few odd pet names. Ignoring the puzzle for now, Julian realized the numbers probably told more of the tale in any case.

Apparently, he's a better gambler than Andrews thought—or Eve is. There was well over twenty thousand pounds in the running tally. Julian shook his head in disbelief before carefully closing it and returning it to its place in Warren's desk.

What the hell am I looking for? Proof that the pair of them are in London to win their fortunes? Hardly. I want proof of this trap Reynolds is clumsily dancing around. I want proof that her hands aren't in it too deeply—that this game she is playing with me won't make me the world's greatest fool.

He left the library and skirted past the man's private rooms to head up the stairs. Within seconds, he was sure he'd entered another world. As soon as he was out of sight of the landing, every luxury disappeared. There wasn't even a runner on the floor, and Julian slowed his steps to quiet them. No antiques graced tables here, and not one painting or plant decorated the hall. In awe, and forgetting for a moment the need for stealth, he tried the gaslights and electric switches only to confirm that they didn't work. *Who the hell doesn't have lights in this modern day and age? Cheap bastard! There were lights aplenty downstairs when I was here earlier today. He's cut the service to the top floors . . .* Not that it was the worst the man could do, but Julian was irrationally irritated at the discovery. What was that he'd said? Something about women complaining about every draft?

The search proceeded quickly enough, as most of the rooms were empty, with dustcovers over the few pieces of furniture there were. It was eerie to see the chandeliers still wrapped against the dust, white cloths hanging like mute ghosts of the house's once proud owners. Undoubtedly, the house was out to lease to help them retrench their debts or improve their accounts—and Reynolds had made a good bargain of it.

At last Julian found a room at the end of the hallway that must be hers. It was the only one in a state of use, and Julian pursed his lips in distaste as he recalled the man saying her bedroom was on the first floor. But how could this be Eve's room?

His jaw clenched at the sight of the Spartan welcome of it. It was late June, but the room held a chill that defied summer's existence. It was drafty, plain, and frankly miserable looking, in Julian's opinion. He had never bothered with décor in his life, but her bedroom made his chest ache with some unnamed emotion.

No frills. There are no china bits and glass bowls of whatnots I assume every woman can't live without. Damn it, where are the flowers? Where the hell is the rug or lacy bedding or . . .

Her vanity caught his eye, and he walked over to survey its contents. It was as dismal as the room, and while he'd never before appreciated all the nonsense women accumulated, there was something sad about her hairbrush and comb sitting there so neatly. He pulled open the drawers and realized the girl had no real jewelry to speak of.

There was one plain locket, with a scrap of blue ribbon inside, and matching gold earrings, which, if he recalled correctly, he'd seen her wearing on that rainy afternoon. Otherwise, she favored the carved onyx bead on its blue ribbon.

A woman like that should be dripping in diamonds.

There was nothing of her spirit here. He headed for a door that looked like a dressing room, and instead located her water closet and bathroom. Again, it was neat and tidy to the point of feeling sterile. A bar of scented soap drew his eye, and he lifted it to inhale the familiar magic of honeysuckle and orange blossoms. His eyes closed as he remembered the vague sweet smell her skin gave off when she climaxed against him. His eyes opened. He meant to set the soap back as he found it, but it slipped from his hands. Retrieving it, he spotted a change in the grout of two tiles near the floor. Julian's brow furrowed at the subtle difference, and impulsively, he set the lamp down so that he could kneel down and take a closer look. Within seconds, the tiles gave way to his fingers, and he realized there was a bundle of oilcloth tied with ribbon behind them. He set the tiles aside carefully, aware that if he broke one it could spoil his hope of leaving undetected. Pulling the bundle free, he untied the blue ribbon, recognizing it as a match to the tiny bit inside the locket. *What an odd, strangely melancholy thing to do, Lamb!*

Inside were dozens of rag-wrapped smaller treasures, and he unwrapped one or two in wonder to discover diamond earrings, jet brooches, emerald pendants, and all manner of fine jewelry. There were even small pouches of loose stones, rubies like pebbles that gleamed and winked at him in the lamplight. Trinkets of all kinds filled the bundle, and at the bottom, he even found one or two gambling chits and a small, shabby wooden box with a childlike drawing of a bird on its lid.

He expected diamonds inside the little box. Instead he almost dropped it in astonishment when he found a tiny speckled egg, a broken hair comb, two feathers, and a child's gold ring.

Eve Reynolds. At last, Lamb, I think I may know a bit of you after all.

"What are you doing here?"

Chapter Eighteen

He spun around to face her, feeling trapped and stupid. Her treasures were spread beneath his feet, and the look on her face was full of pain and astonishment at his invasion of her privacy. *What in the world did a burglar say at such moments? "Oh, my! You're home early"?* "Your uncle commanded me to meet him this afternoon. I confess I came back to make sure I hadn't missed anything important in our conversation."

"To my rooms?"

He sighed and kept his voice low. "Not my best strategy. I wanted to see if I could uncover the truth. To see if you'd taken souvenirs to show your uncle later or created a diary to prove our affair."

"You . . . you think so little of me?"

"Not—no! Damn it, woman. This is your fault.

You won't tell me anything. Your uncle is up to some clumsy scheme, but you won't tell me what it is. I know just enough to know that I couldn't just stand by any longer. And when your uncle tried to pull on my leash this afternoon, I decided there was no time like the present to ascertain the truth. I deserve to know what I'm up against, Eve."

"You *deserve* for me to start screaming and bring the house down around your ears!" She rushed forward and dropped to her knees, her hands shaking as she gathered her things, rewrapping them as quickly as she could. "You had no right to touch my things! No right!"

"True." He knelt next to her, trying to help, but he wisely stopped when she slapped his hand as he attempted to hand her the wooden box. "An odd place to store your jewelry, Eve. Trouble with the staff pilfering your baubles?"

She shot him a venomous look and finished roughly wrapping everything into the oilcloth, clutching it to her chest as she stood. "As you've seen, Julian, there is nothing of yours here and no *diary* or whatever nonsense you were seeking, so feel free to get out!"

"Not until you tell me what it is between you and your uncle. Not until I understand why the man seems to think he knows so much of me and why—why does he know nothing of us?" He lifted himself from the floor, but only to sit on the edge of the bathtub, not willing to tower over her and play the bully. "Why, Eve, when it would seem the obvious choice for a quick fortune if it is in fact blackmail you intend?"

She froze, her expression a mask he couldn't read. "I suppose I have spent a lifetime earning that. Very well, Lord Westleigh. Not that I envisioned explaining anything to a common housebreaker—"

"It's not my general profession, Miss Reynolds, but I didn't see any other way. Not that it was hard to get in! Your uncle should be more careful."

She knelt down to put the bundle back in its hiding place. "If he'd suspected you'd do such a thing, he probably would have instructed the servants to let you gain the house only so he could catch you red-handed and force you into a payoff to avoid scandal. Not that I expect you to fold so easily, but you're lucky he's in a penny-pinching mood and sent the staff home for the evening. That left only old Barnett on the door, and I'm betting he fell asleep in the pantry listening for the bell."

"And where is your uncle now?"

"He'll be home any minute. He sent me on ahead of him in a hackney, no doubt to linger over brandies and see if he can soften Hightower up for another delightful dinner." She stood again and crossed her arms. "You should go now while you can. I recommend the window."

"Eve, tell me." He held still and waited. "Everything."

For a moment, he was sure she would refuse and start screaming after all. But then the fight drained from her eyes and she sat woodenly on a stool next to the clothes stand. The sight of her looking so defeated lashed at him, and Julian regretted the questions he had asked and now couldn't take back. He wanted to take her in his arms and soothe away whatever pain he'd caused, but it was too late and he needed to know the worst.

She took a deep breath and began her story quietly. "I never had any intention of blackmailing you. I never . . . wanted anything of my life to ever touch what we . . . I selfishly thought I could do as I wished without my uncle's interference—without him ruining it. But I was wrong."

"He hasn't ruined us yet. But I can see why you'd want to keep it from him."

She shrugged. "He isn't much of a villain, but he does have an uncanny way of knowing when to—how did you put it? Oh, yes, 'pull on the leash.' "

"An accurate phrase then?"

"Most insightful of you." She straightened her back, suddenly regal in the unlikely setting of her bathing closet.

"He wants me to steer clear. Not the first male relative to convey that message, but honestly not what I'd expected from Mr. Warren Reynolds, the wealthy industrialist."

"Take it as a compliment. No matter how he blusters about reputations, I'd say it's due to the fact that you are not a manageable mark. I wonder if a part of him realizes that you saw him cheating at the Boar's Head, and that he's really just trying to protect himself. Though truthfully, you're too smart and much too savvy to suit his purposes, Julian."

"Well, that makes me feel better. I take it Hightower is more to his taste."

She nodded grimly. "Exactly."

"How did you get into all of this?" he asked.

"My father played. He was a cheerful gambler, reckless and dishonest. I never realized it, but then I was a child. I adored him. He was murdered in Athens when someone found extra cards in his pockets, and my uncle took me in."

"How old were you?"

"Sixteen." She waved the point away. "It doesn't matter. My uncle took me in, and things changed. I became aware of the criminal flavor of my life, and when I was seventeen, my uncle discovered that I had a gift when it came to the tables. Since then, I have provided my uncle with incomes. Countering him is . . . not as easy as you might think. Uncle

Warren has a knack for getting his own way, and I look at him and . . . struggle not to see my father and wish that things were different."

"And now?" Julian prompted gently.

She held up her hand. "It all ends after this Season. I am collecting these jewels in my games. Quietly and without his knowledge, so that soon I'll have enough to escape the leash once and for all."

"How did you stake the games if your uncle doesn't know?"

"He knows a little, but not about the jewelry. No woman throws out a piece of jewelry unless there is a shiny something to be gained. I stole a cache of gems from a certain countess in France. Not my proudest moment, but she . . . Francesca and my uncle were very close, and any woman who takes pleasure in the suffering of others can stand to lose a few colored stones, in my opinion."

"And the plan?"

"Once I have enough, enough that even the cheapest fence won't be able to keep me from it, I'm going to run away. I'm on English soil at last, Julian! Years and years, I've dreamt of . . ." She dropped her eyes briefly, and he could tell she was trying to decide how much to tell him. Finally, she raised her eyes, and they shone with a luminous hope that took his breath away. "I will find a home of my own somewhere in the countryside. If I have enough, I will buy it! A small country cottage where there are trees and a little garden where I can grow roses and hollyhocks or whatever I want, or I'll find I can't grow a thing and water the poor things to death . . ." She smiled. "Something all my own, and a simple life where no one can find me and where I can put all of *this* behind me. I know how it must sound to you, but I'll walk through green grass that stains my skirts and touches my fingertips, I'll learn to make pies, and he'll never use me again for his own gain. No one will."

She faced him, a proud and unbroken warrior queen, braced for his farewell and prepared to offer to help push him out the window so that he could make his retreat. *God, woman, you do make me want to punish your uncle. I think I may do it just for the sheer pleasure of guaranteeing you the peace you dream of. Later.*

"Tell me how you do it. Is it sleight of hand? Are you marking the cards?"

"I don't cheat, Lord Westleigh. I never have."

"I see."

"Do you?"

Julian abandoned the topic, unwilling to disrupt the conversation. "I'm surprised that with all his pretensions of respectability he hasn't insisted on a chaperone for you, Eve."

"Chaperones present more problems than they solve. It's too difficult to find one who can be trusted and who won't realize the potential for blackmail, since he's a perpetual impostor. The risk is too great. Trust me, my uncle keeps a close watch and chooses our venues with care. Besides—" She cut herself off.

"Come now, don't stop now, Eve."

"Any man who tries to trespass may be viewed by my uncle as a potential candidate for additional profit. I . . . I don't want to talk about it."

"I don't care. Tell me."

"Surely you can guess the rest."

"I don't like guessing games."

"He sets them up to catch them trying to . . . express their ardor. They generally pay to avoid a scandal."

"Interesting."

"It isn't interesting at all, Julian!" She took a deep breath. "I don't want you to think that I—I've never allowed anyone to . . . get this close to me before. I wasn't with you as part of some greater scheme."

"I believe you. But Eve, unless I'm misinformed on practical matters, you weren't a virgin when you came to me."

"Does it matter?"

"I don't know. Does it?"

"I was nineteen. I was stupid. I thought I'd met the man of my dreams while we were in Venice, and that he would take me away and give me a new life. It's an old tale, but he promised to marry me."

Her look was unapologetic. "It was . . . disastrous. Uncle Warren took me back and forgave me, but he's never allowed me to forget my greatest folly."

Julian reached out to gently stroke her face, wishing he could think of some clever or comforting line to ease the awkward pain in her eyes at the memory. She leaned her cheek into the warm well of his palm, and he smiled.

She looked up at him through the black veil of her lashes, a mischievous glint coming into her eyes. "Care to share the harrowing tale of your first time, Lord Westleigh?"

"Never!"

"In any case, after that first misstep, I decided I was ill suited to passion." She made a face of distaste.

"Venice, eh? I might have to find that man and kill him."

She left her stool and crossed from him to hide the tears that threatened to overtake her. Before he could even rise to follow, she turned, a woman once more in control. "That's the worst of it, Julian. You'd already guessed his secrets—the cheating, the lies about his situation, the sordid schemes. And now you know mine. You can walk away now unscathed, and he'll be none the wiser."

Julian tilted his head, considering the implications of everything she'd told him. He could hardly believe it. His lack of money aside, he was the embodiment of the perfect pigeon. Who the hell would have blamed her for not instantly alerting her uncle to the possibilities? He'd been blind with lust from the first moment he'd met her and had vastly deserved to be sitting at the wrong end of a scheme or two. Her uncle might have discovered that it was impossible to extort a man who enjoys a good scandal and has empty pockets, but Eve hadn't known that. *Perhaps "losing" might not be so bad after all. And if ever there was a damsel in distress . . .* He stood slowly and buttoned his coat. "I would like to propose a different ending to our affair, Miss Reynolds."

"Pardon?"

"A business proposition."

"Business?" She crossed her arms again, wary but attentive.

"Strictly business." He took a deep breath, then sighed. "Without your luck, I am a bit light in the pockets myself these days. Fortune hasn't been kind, and a man can't live on his title, good looks, and charm forever. So, here is my proposition. I will help you escape your uncle—for a price."

"A price?" she asked him in a shocked whisper.

"You wouldn't trust me if I didn't look out for my interests as well."

"Go on."

"For a percentage of your stashed winnings, I'll arrange for your departure. I will effectively 'steal you away' to one of my family's country holdings and hand over the deed to a smallish house I own. It's not much, but Devon is generally considered very pretty."

Her mouth fell open, but she recovered quickly. "You'll just hand it over? A house?"

"For some of those baubles, recall. Nothing is free, Miss Reynolds."

"How many? What percentage did you have in mind?"

He shrugged. "Does it matter?" He shifted, watching her closely. "Come, Miss Reynolds. This is a one-time, fleeting offer. In one swift exchange, you secure your freedom and, frankly, mine, if you agree to my terms. What say you?"

"I say"—she took a single step toward him—"I need time to complete what I've started with the ladies."

"It's dangerous to linger, Eve."

"I know. But I have to live the rest of my life on what I take with me, Julian. I've sworn to stop playing after this Season."

"How long do you need?"

She calculated it quickly. "One week."

"Very well. We leave in one week. In the meantime, we'll continue as we have. It's too dangerous to meet at Bell Street anymore, but I'll do what I can to find you."

"Tomorrow . . . I need to see you, Julian."

He read the misgivings on her face. "I don't think it's safe. I'll see you at Lord Andrews's party on Saturday at the very latest, though I make no promises to behave myself."

He meant to just kiss her and go. But after everything that had passed between them he lost his place at the first brush of her lips against his. He lost every tether he had to logic and reason and the sensibilities of a man who prided himself on detachment. It was a kiss like their first, surprising him with the overwhelming heat and sweet fire of it. *I swear I could spend a lifetime just doing this . . . not that I would!*

She was his, holding nothing back from him, and he savored the wave of sensations her surrender evoked. In complete quiet, the embrace went beyond a simple kiss, and he lost track of where he ended and she began. The room echoed every breath, and he held her tightly, unwilling to be the first to let go.

Finally, she pushed against him, panting and flushed. "Julian, go." He agreed, not trusting his voice to argue. Her uncle could be home any moment, and it would spoil everything if he caught them now. With one last smile, he climbed out the window onto the terrace and made his way down the outside of the house. *Not a bad bit of climbing for an amateur. A man could get used to playing the hero.*

* * *

She was left to sit in a stupor, a fog clouding her thoughts as she checked again to make sure that her hidden alcove was invisible to any casual inspection. *What an unbelievable twist of fate!* She'd trusted him, almost from the first, and now her life was almost entirely in his hands. She waited for fear to settle in, but it never came. She felt numb. There were a hundred potential outcomes, most of them dreadful. The next few days would decide her fate.

He could still simply walk away.

He could betray her to her uncle after taking his percentage.

He could hurt her in more ways than she ever thought possible. *Because I trust him like no one else. Because I've let him in. Because I told him about country cottages with gardens and silly dreams of walking in green grass.*

Because I've fallen in love with him.

The truth hit her hard, and she sank to the floor, her skirts pooling around her. *Truth, at last. I'm the world's fool and desperately in love with a professed, unrepentant rogue—a gambler, no less! How is that for a reliable, stable bid for happiness?*

Now, no matter what happens, I cannot win. I will line my pockets with other people's gold and jewelry and escape my uncle and I will lose because ultimately I've lost my heart.

There was nothing left for it. Eve lowered her face to her hands and cried scalding-hot tears until she couldn't weep any more.

Survival seemed like a petty goal in light of this new revelation, but there was no going back now. She'd allowed for every outcome but one. Now she would take what she could, in every sense of the word, pray that he would hold to their agreement, and follow her original plan.

And when it comes time to say good-bye?

She knew she would have to play it like the most important game of her life and never let him know what it would cost her to let him go.

Chapter Nineteen

The Tuesday gathering was a bit larger this time. Eve felt almost cheered at the sight of all of them, mingling over cucumber sandwiches, pastries, petit fours, and Lady Morrington's best sherry. Their quiet game had grown popular as money followed money. It was her last time to join the group, and the knowledge made her nostalgic. The ladies had been kind, and she'd always enjoyed these games, despite the pressure from her uncle and the tension behind all her aims. As it had played out, though, the higher the stakes, the more the women had seemed to glory in their wicked hobby. The talk had been potent. "Why, we are as naughty as our husbands, are we not?" Mrs. Seward had remarked, and they'd happily agreed, increasing their bets with relish. *Rebellion and sin are a powerful mixture when enjoyed in good company.*

"Would you care to deal, Miss Reynolds?"

"Oh." Eve brought her focus back to the game at hand. They'd broken off into pairs for a bit of whist, and she reminded herself that this was her final opportunity to pray for a bit of luck. "No, Lady Shelbrook. I confess I am all thumbs today, and you are so much faster at it."

"Am I?" Lady Shelbrook arched one perfect eyebrow before reshuffling the cards and setting the game into motion. "I find your play is . . . quite skilled for one so young."

Eve gave a genuine laugh. "I think you are too young yourself to say such sage things!"

"Am I?"

Eve's smile faded at the caustic echo in the question, and she was suddenly unsure whether Lady Shelbrook was friend or foe. *Not your friend. None of them are, and it was stupid of me to forget that. Careful.* Eve studied the beautiful woman across from her, this aristocratic creature with ice blue eyes in a couture concoction of pale yellow and white lace. *Every player has a weakness. Is yours vanity?* "I spoke sincerely and without thinking, Lady Shelbrook. I think you are lovely, and I forgot myself."

Beatrice shrugged off her words and, from a deep pocket in her skirts, withdrew a diamond brooch. She tossed it carelessly on the table between them. "Here. How is that for an ante?"

Eve's breath caught in her throat. There was no mistaking the expensive gleam of those stones. It was a phenomenal trinket and far too valuable to consider. She looked up at Lady Shelbrook, warier at this reckless bet than ever before. She had no choice but to proceed delicately. There was something else happening, but Eve couldn't quite see it. "That looks like a sentimental piece. Perhaps you'd prefer not to—"

"It means nothing to me." The blonde leaned over conspiratorially. "May I confess something to you, my dear? There is nothing sweeter in this world than taking a little slice of revenge."

"Oh." Eve wasn't sure what to say. The other women were too far away across the room to hear them, and she was grateful. No matter where this led, she didn't need an audience.

"My husband is a fool. So I lose his gifts. It's the least I can do to the poor man, and it does pass the time!"

"But that's . . . creative of you."

Something must have shown on her face, for Lady Morrington crossed the room to join the pair. "I'm so glad you two are becoming friends! Why, Beatrice, you must be sure to tell us all how you've enjoyed having a house guest all Season!"

She gave Eve a merry look of mischief, and before Eve could think to wonder why, Lady Shelbrook provided all the answers as her hand subtly hid the brooch on the table from Lady Morrington's gaze.

"The Earl of Westleigh has been a joy!" Her look was smug, and suddenly Eve remembered the first time she'd seen Julian Clay.

"You told Lady Morrington he was a perfect gentleman," she echoed softly, then realized she'd spoken aloud as the distant memory swept over her—the forgotten snippet of a conversation she'd hardly been paying attention to at the time. The dear matchmaker had no idea of the implications, and Eve was trapped in her chair.

He'd been shot by a jealous husband and the ladies were surprised, and made light of it when they spoke of him. Even her uncle had noted his penchant for married women. *How could I be so stupid not to have recalled it? Not to remember where he was spending the rest of his nights . . . oh, God.*

"I did, but even if he were not, what woman could complain about such a beautiful man?" Beatrice teased, and the other ladies began to titter at the scandalous edge to Lady Shelbrook's wit. "Don't you agree, Miss Reynolds?"

It's a game. Don't let her rattle you.

"Indeed. I remember Mrs. Cuthbert saying that

any woman would be quite taken with him." An innocent enough deflection, but Lady Shelbrook's expression gained a light layer of frost.

"And are you?"

"Am I what, your ladyship?" Eve asked.

"Taken with him?"

Eve struggled to look completely indifferent, but Lady Morrington laughed, still oblivious to the venom being spit across the table. "Of course she is! Dear little thing! And he with her, if I have the right of it!"

"Another hand, Lady Shelbrook?" Eve offered, gathering the cards. Lady Morrington cheerfully returned to the group she'd temporarily abandoned, and the pair was left alone again to finish the game.

"Well?" Lady Shelbrook moved her hand to reveal the brooch again.

"I have nothing to match that." Eve began to set her cards facedown to fold, but Beatrice reached across the table to seize her wrist. Her delicate-looking hands belied her strength, and Eve did her best not to wince at the sharp pain Lady Shelbrook's fingers inflicted as they pressed into her skin, then folded the brooch against her palm.

"I think you do, Miss Reynolds."

"No, I assure you I d—"

"I'll give it to you if you vow to never see him again."

It was like a nightmare, except Eve was fairly sure that in a true nightmare, she'd have forgotten to dress. "I'm not sure you—"

"It's priceless. Think about this carefully, girl. You won't see another like it in your lifetime."

The fingers on Eve's free hand clenched reflexively around the jewelry, its weight hypnotic. *The income I need, right here in the palm of my hand.* Eve forced her hands to relax, her fingers trembling as she released it to fall back onto the table. "He's not mine to wager, Lady Shelbrook, as much as I might wish it were otherwise. And I suspect he isn't yours to keep either." Lady Shelbrook released her wrist in disgust, and Eve gathered her winnings, then stood from the table as gracefully as she could. Even without the diamond brooch, it had been an incredibly profitable day. "Thank you for a lovely afternoon." In horror, she was forced to rush from the party with barely a word of farewell to the sweet ladies who had given her the opportunity she'd needed to try for a life of her own.

She told herself she would send notes later—to all of them, but especially to dear Lady Morrington, who had wanted the best for her—but for now, there was nothing more pressing than reaching the safety of the carriage and getting away from Julian's vengeful lover. Eve rushed down the steps, and for one impulsive moment she considered telling the driver to take her to Bell Street. *He won't be there. He said it wasn't safe.*

She suspected she now knew why—Lady Shelbrook. Eve climbed into the carriage and sat down with a sigh. But before they could pull away, there was a hard knock on the door, and Eve almost gave a startled cry when it was thrown open.

Lady Shelbrook was framed in the opening, an icy fury radiating from her that made Eve's eyes water. The woman was formidable, and Eve had a split second to decide how to play it.

Lady Shelbrook hissed, "You're one of those grifters, aren't you? Cheating at cards and taking anything you can get your filthy hands on. Well, I know what you are, Miss Reynolds, and I intend to call the authorities."

"I have never cheated at a single game, Lady Shelbrook, but you have the power to malign me at will and I know better than to try to dissuade you. Most people will happily take your word over mine. But this isn't really about cards, is it? Please"—she took a deep breath, her eyes filling with tears—"he . . . he broke it off last Tuesday."

Lady Shelbrook's fury froze, and her eyes took on a calculating look. "Really?"

"Lady Morrington has been such an advocate. I couldn't bear letting her know that I never really had his affections."

"You're lying! I know you met him at Bell Street!"

"H-he said he would teach me how to improve at the tables. I wanted to win enough money to—" Eve blew her nose. "My uncle doesn't approve of artists! I wanted to win enough money to return to Italy and study painting and I would have, but now . . . I have gotten better at playing, that's all! Ask Lady Morrington!" She began to cry. "I kept the lessons a secret, and I shouldn't have! But then after our last meeting, he . . ."

"He? He what?"

"He tried to *kiss* me!" she confessed in a disgusted whisper, then recovered to go on, "And when I wouldn't, he said I was a cold fish and that he missed y—" She put a hand over her mouth in a show of shame, cutting off her words, allowing Beatrice to assume that a declaration of Julian's desire would have followed. "I'm not a cheat! Please, Lady Shelbrook! Please—"

The woman held up a hand in disgust. "Dear God, you're too stupid to even realize what was happening! And to think of all the time I've wasted worrying about you and imagining that you were some kind of match . . ." She laughed, a bitter, dry sound that made Eve genuinely cringe. "Painting? It's too ridiculous to even think of! Go on, then. And here!" Beatrice held out the diamond brooch.

"Buy watercolors and brushes and rot happily in Italy."

"I can't take it! It's far too valuable for you to throw it away like this!"

"It's worth it to me to have you gone, you little idiot!" She pressed it into Eve's gloved hand, then stepped back to slam the carriage door shut in her face. "Bon voyage, Miss Reynolds!"

Bon voyage, Lady Shelbrook.

Chapter Twenty

Who does this? Who waits for a woman who isn't coming? Hell, I told her not to come here, so what am I doing? Julian paced the house, a caged tiger moving from room to room driven by a restless energy he couldn't name. *No one does this. No one but me—which may sadly confirm that I've lost more than my bank accounts over the years. This is ridiculous!*

This was supposed to have been his Season to regain his footing, reunite with Lady Luck, and reestablish himself after so many lackluster years. But rather than spending the last few weeks courting other players and exploring London's seamier side, Julian knew he'd gotten a little "sidetracked." *Hell, I didn't do a damn thing except spend every waking moment in pursuit of Eve. I think Barnaby won more money this last month!* Even more disturbing, it struck him that every time he'd bedded her, instead of feeling satiated and ready for the next conquest, he'd only wanted more of her.

He abandoned the bedroom and moved back toward the sitting room to pour himself a whiskey. *A few more days, we get through Andrews's party, and then we're off!*

Andrews was no small obstacle to overcome. The man was a veritable gremlin when it came to potential chaos, relishing it like someone else might look forward to a horse race. Elton was probably the least of his worries, but also the only one he could actively manage, so a wise choice to—

"You said you wouldn't be here. You said it was too dangerous."

He wheeled around, too pleased to see her to chide her for the risk. "Did I?" He crossed the room and swept her into his arms, the speed making her laugh as her feet briefly left the floor. His lips captured hers in a searing and possessive kiss. "It appears I've become sentimental in my old age."

He would have kissed her again, but she put her fingers up against his mouth. "Julian—I'm out of time."

"What happened?" he said as he released her, a surge of concern making it easier to relinquish the contact of her body against his. "Tell me everything."

She related the afternoon's events in entirety and didn't bat an eyelash when describing Lady Shelbrook's threats or what the woman had implied. "She gave me this to fund my excursion."

He recognized it instantly but said nothing to her before placing it back into her reticule. "Anything else?"

She shook her head. "That wasn't enough of a disaster?"

He smiled but took a few moments to consider their options. At last he spoke. "Painting? You really said painting?"

The tension was broken, and she began to laugh as the anxiety bled from the room. "I . . . I thought it sounded . . . plausible."

His look was pure sin. "Well, I'm not going to applaud that bit about making it sound as if I am still interested in that woman."

"It's what she wanted to hear, Julian." A guilty flush came over her cheeks, and he could almost read her thoughts. It's what Eve most wanted to hear, he guessed, but she went on before he could reassure her. "So see to it that you don't give her the cold shoulder until I'm safely away! That is . . . if you still want to help."

He caught her and pulled her close, one hand cradling the back of her head as he swept his lips over hers, this time in a teasing touch she couldn't escape until she sighed and leant into him. "I've never kidnapped anyone before. I think I'm looking forward to it."

"You are a well-practiced woman snatcher, Lord Westleigh. Have you forgotten that you kidnapped me from Lady Morrington's when you bribed my driver? Besides, this is not actually a kidnapping, Julian. I'm fairly sure it doesn't qualify if the woman has packed a bag."

"Hmmm. I'll have to consider that one for a while."

"Please," she moaned, and pushed away from him. "I can't think when you're touching me like that."

"I'll keep it in mind for later then. It may prove a useful tactic someday."

"Uncle Warren may not expect me home this early, but we need to go. If we wait until tonight . . ."

"It doesn't leave much time. Can you get your things without him stopping you?"

"Yes." Her face flushed, she looked away from him, and he could see her distress.

"I should come with you. Even if I wait in the carriage, at least I could be there in case things go badly."

"No. If someone sees you, it could ruin you, Julian. I know you're reckless when it comes to your reputation, but even you have to see reason this time. You must."

"I thought that word was forbidden?"

"Only when you say it, Julian. I can handle my uncle well enough if it comes to it."

He kissed her yet again, inwardly noting that every time he touched her, the contact seemed more intense. "Very well. But if you're not back here before dark, I'll storm your uncle's house and make quite a scene. Agreed?"

"Agreed."

Eve quickly put the last item inside her trim leather bag. She'd been mentally packing and making lists ever since she'd accepted Julian's business proposition. It had been all too easy to decide what to take from the closet full of things she would happily leave behind. Even so, her hands shook as she made one last pass with her hands over her precious winnings to make sure they were safely tucked underneath the bag's false bottom. The buttons were secured, and she straightened to survey the room one last time. The bedroom had never reflected her, and she'd made no effort to change that. They moved too often to bother with décor, and she'd never wanted to grieve over simple possessions.

But now there would be a little home and curtains to buy and a garden to tend. The thought of it gave her a flare of hope and warmth, and Eve relished it as she turned her back on her past and gathered up her small suitcase.

She crept down the stairs, hugging the wall and doing her best not to make even a single board creak and betray her presence. Eve reached the bottom of the stairs and nearly screamed when her uncle called out to Barnett from the library, "Has Miss Reynolds returned yet?"

It was only then that she realized Barnett was there, standing in the central hall near the library door, a sentinel with eyes that even now tracked her every move.

"Barnett!" he yelled again, more impatiently this time.

There was nothing she could do. She was frozen on the last step, robbed of the ability to move. The door was less than twenty steps away, but Eve felt a wash of suffocating and paralyzing fear she couldn't shake. *Oh, God. This is so obvious it's laughable—suitcase in hand, I must look like some vaudeville print of a moral tale gone wrong. There's no disguising this as a quick trip out to go shopping.*

"No, Mr. Reynolds. Shall I hold dinner for her?"

"No! She'll have eaten. But inform me the instant her carriage pulls around."

"Yes, Mr. Reynolds." Barnett gave her a wink, then pulled the edge of a familiar brown packet from his pocket. Eve almost fainted with relief when she recognized the medicine she'd gotten him from the apothecary.

Here was an ally she'd never known she had.

Fear doesn't guarantee loyalty, Uncle Warren. Whatever percentage Julian takes, it will be worth it. I swear I'll hand over every gem if it really means I never have to see you again.

The moment was upon her, and there was a shiver of real fear as she opened the front door. She'd be leaving her only relative, poor dear Uncle Warren, with his endless schemes and greedy hands. Who would look out for him now? But Eve knew that she could drown in a river of cards and wagers and never save him, no matter how much she longed to. The future loomed, unknown and foreboding, but nothing was worse than the devil she knew. So she made the leap . . . and prayed that she would land on her feet.

Chapter Twenty-one

The kidnapping was trickier than he'd anticipated. He'd dismissed his driver for the night and decided to take the reins himself, if only to avoid having a witness for his first foray into stealing young women. Leaving London was the simplest leg of the journey, but driving along country lanes at nighttime at breakneck speed was a feat even Julian had to admit was foolhardy on his part. Still, time was the enemy, and he didn't want to leave anything to chance. As soon as she'd left to retrieve her bags, he'd made some frenzied last-minute arrangements. It had been a harrowing business, but he could only hope he hadn't forgotten anything critical. But then, he'd reminded himself wryly, life was a gamble, and what was a gamble without a touch of risk?

Beatrice's interference stung his conscience like nettles. *It was stupid to think she would be satisfied to just pout after I set her aside. But damn it, it's not as if I'd sworn my undying affection or offered to poison Barnaby. How could I be so blind? Hell, you try to oblige a woman and be a good house guest and this is the thanks you get!*

He suspected now that it was Beatrice who had alerted Reynolds of the affair and put Eve's plans to escape her uncle's custody at risk. It still rankled him that he couldn't just confront the man, but there was still time.

Reynolds's weakness was his dependence on Eve, and by taking her tonight and depriving him of his future income, he'd already struck the first blow. Julian knew for a fact that Eve had done her best to leave him a sizable savings before running away, but men like Warren Reynolds weren't likely to be grateful for the gesture.

Julian would have left him a purse full of rocks if he'd had the final say, but Eve's feelings had prevailed. She'd become more precious to him than he'd wanted to admit to her. She still surprised him. Any other woman would have asked about his relationship with Beatrice and demanded the truth, yet she hadn't pressed him—not because it didn't hurt her to think of him with Lady Shelbrook but because, he suspected, she knew it didn't matter anymore.

She was so young and so emotionally strong. Years of greed and graft hadn't touched her, not really. Her years under Warren Reynolds's thumb hadn't reduced her spirit or diminished her capacity to love. He was pained to admit that he hadn't emerged as unscathed from his own self-imposed vices. He'd wasted more time in useless vengeful pursuits and worthless pastimes than most men, and he couldn't remember anymore how he'd been wronged in the first place.

After a lifetime of risk, Julian realized that he'd never really experienced fear. Not once. But he felt it now. For her. Nothing else mattered in the world but getting Eve to safety and then making sure that she was never in a position to feel vulnerable to men like Warren Reynolds again.

Nothing else mattered.

The decision to take care of her and remove her from harm's way had been effortless. There could be a firestorm to face in London when he returned, but a part of him welcomed it. He'd earned his share of hell, and it seemed only fitting that he receive his portion in full measure. It made no sense, but he wanted to walk through fire.

For her.

He drew on the reins, his hands aching from the strain, and leaned forward in the seat as he navigated a harrowing turn. Julian growled at the darkness and urged the horses to speed on. *Hell, why walk through fire when a man can run?*

When they arrived, it was pitch black. He found her asleep on the seat, curled up against the cushions clutching her leather satchel. In the carriage's lamplight, she was a vision of vulnerable beauty and alluring feminine textures. He lifted her effortlessly, rumpled and drowsy, from the carriage, then carried her up the stone path to the house. His sense of chivalry almost evaporated as her hands slipped inside his coat and her lips nuzzled his neck, where she mumbled something about the way he smelled.

"What was that, dearest?"

"Smoke and sandalwood."

He didn't bother with the lamps, recalling the layout of the rooms before carrying her upstairs into the master bedroom. He carefully removed her shoes and began to do what he could to make her comfortable.

"Julian?" she asked softly.

"None other, Lamb." He smiled in the dark.

"Are we there?"

"Yes. You're home, Eve." Julian gently released the buttons of her traveling coat. "Rest, Lamb, and tomorrow you can start to settle in. I sent an express to Mrs. Connor, and she'll come in to see that you're fed and looked after."

"Hmm."

He shook his head, fully aware that he might have just lost her to the ether. *Oh, well. Mrs. Connor is a kind and practical creature if I remember her rightly, and I'm sure she'll manage her own introductions.*

He leaned over to kiss her before leaving, only to discover that Miss Reynolds hadn't entirely lost consciousness. His gentlemanly kiss became a slow exploration of the sensual friction of her mouth beneath his.

"Julian, come to bed." The invitation was accompanied by her warm hands finding the gaps in his shirt, tugging at him and drawing him downward into the luxurious, if slightly musty, depths of the feather bedding. "Please."

Stupid man. I should be racing back to London, not—oh, no . . . I don't think I could race through this if I wanted to, Lamb. Oh, well. Let's let the cards turn up as they will, shall we?

He surveyed her, a starving man who didn't know if he had the strength to abandon such a feast, no matter what the consequences might be. Moonlight alone touched her body, and he felt a fierce, possessive urge to hide her even from the moon, she was so beautiful to him.

Oh, Lamb, now is when a good man would leave. And even acknowledging that, I cannot do it.

Undressing her without disturbing her was an

exercise in languorous torment, but Julian reveled in every instant as if it was the last. *As it well could be . . .* He was sure it was the first time in his life he'd attempted such a thing, so he took his time unbuttoning, untying, and removing each layer as it presented itself. Memory served when the light wasn't adequate, making him smile as he recalled her telling him that the dark gave her courage.

Finally, she was naked but for her chemise and a single layered petticoat, and Julian leaned back to congratulate his efforts. She was lush and ripe, all curves and long lines. There was nothing pert or childish about her figure. His Eve was all woman, and the moonlight carved her in alabaster and ebony, a feast for the eyes in cream and contrasts. Her nipples were shadows through the ivory of her chemise, begging a man to taste and suckle until he was nourished and replete. Her hip bones invited his hands to grip them, or plane his fingers across the rise and fall of her body there, the swell of her belly above the triangle of black curls he could see through the sheer cotton of her underskirt.

Julian let his hands skim where his eyes led him, too lightly to disturb her as she drowsed, but enough . . . enough to bring a flush of warmth to the skin that met his hands. Enough to make her breasts swell and lift under his palms, enough to watch her transformed as if in a dream to become a woman he couldn't deny—an enchantress with a fan of black silken curls beneath her: his gypsy queen.

Eve sighed, stretching out in his arms like a cat and giving herself over body and soul to the sleepy magic of his slow hands across her skin. Goose bumps appeared at the feathery stroke of his hands, but she didn't feel chilled. It was a drowsy exercise that soothed her body and warmed her blood.

He covered her with his naked body, and she felt safe at last in the harbor of him, his weight hovering above her as he balanced on his elbows to kiss her. Each kiss was like a link in a sensual chain, each kiss complete and whole but invariably leading to another and another until there was no beginning or end . . .

It was a dream. He was so tender, so careful with her, as if she'd been a woman of silk and glass instead of flesh and blood. She felt like she was drifting on tiny waves of ecstasy evoked by his touch, lost in a fog that comforted and sustained her. He didn't hurry his hands, and her impatience was a phantom without substance, since he seemed to anticipate the demands of her body, was there before she was forced to wake enough to ask. His hands were everywhere, without a hint of rushing, magically intertwining with her body to find every inch of her he desired.

Her thighs parted without effort, her hips lifting to the pressure of his stiffening cock against her wet core. Her nether lips tingled at the familiar intrusion, the hot, ripe head of his erection stretching her entrance as he encroached ever so carefully, waiting for her body to adjust before he pressed any further. With each breath, her body accepted another fraction of his length until, with a sigh, he was buried inside her up to the hilt of his shaft. The kisses that flowed between them changed tenor, but they remained unhurried, the pace steady and redolent with smoldering tension.

He rocked into her, not really withdrawing, but simply adding the weight of his hips behind his cock, then lifting that weight so that an erotic illusion overtook her. The friction was almost nonexistent; instead, the sensation was like melting into him as her inner muscles spasmed to keep him inside her, gently fighting to hold his cock against the most sensitive inner curves of her body.

Without effort, she gave in to the gentle pull of her desires, wrapping her arms around his neck and clinging to the solid, muscular warmth of the body that fit so seamlessly into the soft curves of her frame.

Never leave me, Julian.

It was as if he'd heard her heart's cry, and he held her without retreating, each taut inch serenely pressing into her and caressing every luxuriously aroused part of her until she was sure he meant to indolently make love to her for the rest of her life.

She arched against him as the first slender thread of an orgasm began to unravel to overtake the dream. Instead of an explosion, it unwound deep inside her, as if to kiss the flesh that joined hers and coax him to fall with her into the slow-moving river of euphoria that was carrying her away. "Julian," she sighed, and shuddered at the lull and rise of each new wave that came.

"I know, my beauty. I know," he murmured as he kissed her hair, simply holding her and ensuring that she be free to find her pleasure at her own drowsy pace. "Just let it happen."

It was easy to obey, exhaustion lending each release a long, delirious hold that bled into the next until she was too weak to attempt to control them. Finally, they faded, and sleep threatened to overtake her.

"It's so quiet," she murmured, stifling a yawn. "Thank you, Julian."

"You wished for quiet, Lamb. Sleep now and know that you are safely away."

"Will I see you again soon? When . . . when are you coming back, Julian?"

"Sleep, beautiful, willful girl. Just sleep now." His lips were hot against her forehead, this kiss so different that even on the edge of dreams, she recognized it for what it was. *Good-bye.*

Chapter Twenty-two

Eve awoke slowly, the unfamiliar sounds of cheerful songbirds so dreamlike that she feared it was all a fantasy—the escape and her arrival at a house he'd sworn to gift her with. *Not a gift, he said, but I doubt he profited from the exchange . . .*

She cracked open one eye to peek at the room, then abandoned the technique in a surprised and sputtering gasp. She sat up almost too quickly, pale green chintz and sumptuous furnishings swimming before her astonished gaze. The room was charming, with an aging country elegance that mocked her dreams of a rough little dwelling of her own. Awash in jade greens, with pale pink-accented silk ties and crystal sconces, she felt like a princess as she took in the lily-carved bedposts and bright, inviting décor. Multipaned windows beckoned, and Eve took in a view that brought tears to her eyes.

It was the garden of her dreams. Even in its overgrown and unattended state, she could see the remnants of an intricate knot work of low hedges, herbs, and flowers. A crushed gravel path wound through it. Beyond it all, she caught a glimpse of a shaded walk along a stream. Beyond the once civilized patch inside the walls, a wild countryside beckoned, and she knew she would never see its match. Between her impressions of the room and the riot of color spread out beyond her window, Eve knew that no matter what Julian had said of his "smallish house," she was well and truly in love with her new dwelling.

As she turned back to the room, her eyes lit on a formal packet of paperwork resting on the bedside table. She knew without breaking the red wax seal that it was the deed to the property, just as he'd promised. Arms wide, Eve fell back into the bed with a squeal of delight as she landed amidst the feather-soft bedding. "I'm home!"

A knock at the door startled her from her euphoric celebration. "Miss? Are you up then?"

Eve clutched at the bedding in panic to cover her undressed state. "I'm . . . yes, thank you."

The door opened, and in swept a woman in a crisp white apron. Her plain broad face was alight with friendly cheer. "Good morning, Miss Reynolds! I'm Mrs. Connor, dearie. Lord Westleigh said you'd need a hand, and wasn't I thrilled that Mary's had her lying in and I could come at a moment's notice! Such a to-do, and it'll be days before we get the dust off the credenza and all the little shelves and curios, but a lovely young lady can't live in such a state. Gentlemen just don't see these things and think to send better warning, but I'll have it shining! You'll see!"

"Oh!" Eve was positively speechless as the woman bustled about and drew the curtains.

"I have breakfast on a tray for you outside the door. I'm no fancy Frenchie chef, but mind you, it's good food I can make and pretty enough for company when you have it. Mrs. Morgan is always trying to wrangle my recipes away, but it's a house secret's my reply. Lord Westleigh says he never eats as well as when he comes here and sits to my cooking. He's fairly starved all these years, and no one can tell me otherwise! Poor thing! I'd send pies to tide him over, but what a handsome gypsy he is! Well, I'm to fatten you up, and that's the man's orders! Preserves, miss?"

"Preserves?" Eve had the feeling it would take a while before she was accustomed to the whirlwind that was Mrs. Connor.

"For the bread. I made the preserves myself, not that Mrs. Morgan would—"

"Yes, thank you." Eve shifted to the side of the

bed, modestly looking about for her gown. "I think I'll get dressed and just . . . come down for breakfast, if that's all right."

"I'll have it waiting for you in the little dining room. Lovely light there of a morning, and you can watch the birds in the garden—and that mischievous squirrel that keeps stealing the silverware. I think there's at least two full service sets out there under the lilacs if we dug for them, but he's too cute a moxie to hang as a thief. There's dresses in the wardrobe arrived from London for you, miss, but he said you had your own things and might prefer them. Shall I unpack your bags and brush something out for you to wear, Miss Reynolds?"

"No." Eve felt a stab of concern that the woman would see her jewels and little else and good impressions might be lost. "I prefer to put things away myself. But thank you."

"Of course, dearie, of course. Easier to find things later, I always say." She bobbed a rough curtsy and headed back toward the door.

"Mrs. Connor?"

"Yes, dearie?"

"Lord Westleigh . . . hired you. Did he . . . say anything of . . ." She suddenly realized she didn't know what to ask, or even if she wanted to know the answers to the dozens of painful questions floating through her mind.

"I'm to tell you I come with the house, he said.

No worries, dearie. I'm to take care of you and keep out from underfoot if you wish, but he said that you're not to go wanting. So the pantry's to be stocked and the dust cleared off, and whatever you need, well, you just ring a bell or call for me and I'll come as quickly as I can. Naturally, you can hire other hands, but I'm hoping to prove myself before you do so. Was that what you were asking, miss?"

She nodded, completely stunned at this stranger's warmth. "Yes, thank you."

She waited until she heard Mrs. Connor's steps retreating down the hall before making a search for her satchel. At the foot of the bed, she knelt to open it with nervous hands. She pulled back the bag's false bottom and retrieved her sack of jewelry. Within seconds she had unwrapped its contents and spread them out across the floor around her. The rushed inventory's results made her slow down and look yet again.

"Did you take nothing, Julian?" she whispered.

Finally, the truth couldn't be denied. He'd taken almost nothing of her hard-won treasures. One or two of the notable pieces she'd acquired, but what took her breath away was the fact that he'd mostly taken her personal jewelry. They'd been sentimental, nothing in value compared to the others—her onyx bead necklace on the dark blue ribbon, a foolish charm bracelet she hadn't worn because of its broken clasp, and her locket with the scrap of her mother's dress inside.

Eve had no choice but to hide away her stash, but she couldn't explain her wicked lover's designs.

Was that the percentage? Surely not. He won't get two pounds for the lot, and no sober man would sell his house for a scrap of ribbon.

He would send word of his price. He would have to. If not, what was he up to? Just as Mrs. Connor had said, there were already dresses in the wardrobe against the wall, and Eve recognized each one from the prints in Madame Dellacourt's shop. She remembered how he'd held up the patterns in front of the mirror and touched her until she'd thought she'd go mad. Her fingers trailed over the gowns—every one was a masterpiece, and all in shades of indigo and sapphire.

His generosity was too much to take in. She dressed quickly in one of the new day gowns and left the bedroom to find her way downstairs to the "little dining room." She peeked in every doorway, and with every step Eve became more and more astonished at what she was seeing.

Each room was charming. Even through the dust cloths and netting, she could still see the elegant furnishings and wealth proclaimed by every vaulted ceiling and every carved corner. Though neglected and in need of repair, it was a house that proclaimed a proud history. Her dream of a rustic cottage had been replaced by a real country manse—and only Julian could have told her why.

She found her breakfast at last and sat down just as the tears finally overtook her. Eve put her face into her hands and surrendered to illogical, bone-wracking sobs over a plate of fine china fit for a princess.

He's gone. No note, no promise or word of his return, and like an idiot, I didn't ask him to! Whatever business we had is surely completed now, and he's rendered payment in full for my "services" . . . so now what do I do?

"And here I thought you'd like the place . . . ," he sighed from the doorway, his lean frame propped up casually. "You are a hard woman to please, Miss Reynolds."

"Julian!"

She leapt up from the table and raced into his arms, a cascade of relief almost robbing her of speech before he rained kisses onto her cheeks, then found her lips. The nature of the embrace changed, the fire between them instantly sizzling back to life. Eve pressed into him and Julian lifted his head, staring down into her eyes with muted regret. "I can't stay long, Lamb. I have to get back to London, but I couldn't leave you with a bully like Mrs. Connor without at least saying goodbye."

She playfully pinched his arm and stepped away, wishing she could dissuade him from going. But Eve knew better, and his urgent business in London was ensuring that he wasn't accused of her disappearance. "Mrs. Connor is a dear and you know it!"

"You see? You're already joining forces and pitting yourselves against me." He drew her back into his arms, his golden gaze roaming over her face. "Let's take a walk, Eve."

She nodded, barely managing to hold back all her questions until they stepped outside. "Julian, this is not—"

"Not yet." He tucked her hand into the crook of his arm. "The house is . . . as you see. Twelve rooms, a bit of an antiquity, drafty as hell, but it has nice clean lines and a garden, of course. This is one of three, and before you ask, no, this is not by any means the primary estate. That house is a dreary stone affair, too castle-like for most tastes, and when last I was there, infested by bats and a few disgruntled mice. I'd have considered it for our deal, but I can't imagine you clapping your hands in delight when you saw it in broad daylight." He gave her a wry grin. "The mud-filled moat is nice."

"I'm sure it's lovely." She smiled in return, convinced he exaggerated its deterioration. "Do you stay there often?"

He gave her a horrified look, and Eve laughed.

"Julian, it wouldn't be so dreary if you took care of it, or saw to the maintenance. If you have three houses with land, then you have the potential to make them profitable enough without any regard to gambling. Are there tenants?"

"Yes, and this is where I deftly change the subject." He kissed her fingertips and led her down the path toward the stream and wilderness. "I should have left already, and yet here I am, about to debate land use and economy with the most delectable creature I have ever met when I should be carrying you back to bed."

"We can . . . do both, Julian."

He shook his head. "One thing at a time, Lamb." He kissed her again, a slow, searing touch that made her feel branded by the possessive heat of it. His tongue swept across hers, and she instinctively matched his movements to suckle and taste him as if this kiss would be their last. She was dizzy with it, and he lifted her against him, molding her body to his and cradling her in his arms.

Finally, he released her, holding her arms until he was sure that she was steady on her feet. "I have to go, Eve."

She tried not to let her distress at his impending departure show. "Your payment. You at least need to take—"

"I'll come back for it, or send a hired courier if I need to," he cut her off. "Now, I have to get back to London, or there will be hell to pay."

"My uncle will suspect that you helped me, Julian. If he confronts you, just promise me that you won't hurt him. I know he's . . . a bit of a blustering pain, but his bite won't have any teeth—not now."

He nodded solemnly, but his eyes twinkled. "He's not the least of my worries, but no duels, I promise. Don't worry, Eve. I'll do my best to keep him out of harm's way."

"Thank you."

"I don't know how long my business will take, but stay to the house and gardens as much as you can. Mrs. Connor knows not to share your name with the locals, but it's better to be cautious at first. Just wait for news, and then we'll argue about the house if you still want to."

"I don't want to argue about the house, Julian. It's just so much more than—"

"*After* there's news, Eve." He kissed her again, and Eve forgot all her questions and fears. If only for the moment, there was Julian, and she suspected that he didn't have most of the answers she desperately wanted.

And then he was gone.

Julian Clay, the Earl of Westleigh was a man of his word. They'd struck a deal, and he'd fulfilled his end of the bargain flawlessly. *What complaint could I possibly have?*

Except that the declaration she'd secretly longed for had never happened.

And I'll probably never see him again.

Chapter Twenty-three

He'd returned to Shelbrook's exhausted and drained. Now the late afternoon sun was starting to leak through his bedroom curtains, and Julian awoke to realize that there was someone knocking firmly on his door.

He struggled to sit up, wincing at his aching shoulders and back. The knocking persisted, and Julian shook his head to try to clear it. *No future driving a mail coach, old man. It's one thing to do this for pleasure in broad daylight—but I think I'd rather face another loaded pistol than attempt that again.* Still, Eve was safely tucked away in Devon, and that was all that mattered.

"Wait!" He sat up and groggily grabbed his robe just in case Reynolds had already called the authorities. Julian wasn't sure he wanted to face them without his pants on. "Come in."

Beatrice breezed in, pouting slightly at his state of dress, undoubtedly disappointed to have missed the best views. "A late night, Lord Westleigh? You didn't even bother coming in the night before . . ."

"Ah, the hospitality of the Crimson Belle! What time is it?"

"Nearly three in the afternoon," she announced brightly, loud enough to make him wince if he'd had a hangover. Julian obliged her, just to play along and add to the impression that he'd spent the last two nights in town carousing.

"That early?" He tugged on the robe's belt to make sure it was secure. "What brings you to my bedroom at such an ungodly hour, Lady Shelbrook?"

"I just got back from my social calls and apparently there is a bit of news, fresh from Lady Morrington's run-in with a Mr. Warren Reynolds at her home this morning. It was quite the exciting topic of discussion. Miss Eve Reynolds, do you remember her from Whetford's ball, Julian? Well, Miss Reynolds has absconded from her uncle's home and no one knows where."

"Really?" He yawned. "No note? I understood young women were practically driven to leave sniveling notes of farewell and heartfelt explanations whenever they absconded."

He stood, dressing in front of her without a hint of modesty. *Look your fill, you vicious harpy.* "Well, thank you for sharing this 'delightful' gossip. I'm not sure I can repeat it with the same relish you seem to have for the tale, but I'll give it my all."

She drew closer, drawn like a moth to a flame. "Julian . . . you've been so unkind lately. Surely you never meant to—"

He buttoned his pants and pulled on his shirt. "Never meant to what, Beatrice?"

"To hurt me." It was a whisper, but it caught his complete attention.

"Hurt you? That's not possible, madam." He closed the distance between them and seized her upper arms, a quiet fury consuming him. "What do you envision, Beatrice? Are you so bewitching a woman that I would have been happy as your obedient servant, living off your husband's largesse and dining at your table like a lapdog waiting for scraps? Do I strike you as the kind of man to be grateful for the ice-cold crumbs off another man's plate?"

"N-no, but—"

"Were we going to run off in a great scandal and settle in the wilds of Ireland?"

"No! I never thought—"

"No, you never thought of anything except the selfish little quivering meat between your thighs and how delicious it might be to get back at old

Barnaby for an affair he had over six years ago! Damn, woman! How many men have you had pumping between your legs on that tired excuse?"

"You have no right, Julian! I cared for you. I truly did!"

"Truly?" He let go of her, disgusted at the contact. "Such care could suffocate and kill a man, Beatrice. If you'd cared, you would never have interfered. The girl is nothing to me, but I don't doubt you had everything to do with Miss Reynolds's departure, so you'll pardon me if I tell you to take your care and go to hell."

"She said you'd thrown her off! She's a heartbroken fool, and if I urged her to go, it was to ease her—"

Julian held up a hand, cutting her off. He closed his eyes to fight the impulse to strike her, then opened them, unwilling to spare her a glimpse of his rage. "Make no mistake, Beatrice, my *darling*." The endearment was a snarl of contempt. "I am angry with myself for blindly indulging you in the first place, for assuming that you would have the grace to let go when I clearly didn't want you anymore. I'm furious with myself for not realizing how petty and dangerous you could be, madam. But let me rectify one thing while I still can. I shall remove myself from this house, and when anyone asks, I will say nothing but wonderful things about you. However, if I hear one solitary whisper about this . . . *indiscretion*"—he spat out the word—"or even against Miss Reynolds, I will be the first to proclaim you for the heartless whore that you are, Beatrice. And believe me, your reputation will suffer far more than mine."

"You wouldn't dare!"

"Wouldn't I?" He waited, his expression nonchalant. "Test me then, madam. I find I am eager to share stories with my peers over a few drinks at White's."

The color drained from her face. "You're a demon, Julian. And one day, you'll see what it is to be at the wrong end of a rumor. Your turn will come."

"Perhaps, but not this time."

Beatrice turned and left, and for several moments, he held his place, unsure of himself. He'd been cruel. Horribly and unnecessarily cruel—but he had to ensure that whatever wrath she had was aimed at him and not at Eve. If she discovered that he had fallen for Eve or that he had been the one to take her out of London . . .

Hell hath no fury like a woman scorned.

Still, he hoped he'd cut off her means of immediate vengeance. She couldn't expose him without ruining herself, too. In any case, he would get out of the house and head for Lord Andrews, who had offered him a safe harbor.

God, I really am a villain! I used Beatrice without

any regard, and even now I can't seem to dredge up any remorse except to think that Eve deserves better than me, demon that I am, on her doorstep.

Poor Barnaby! I suspect he's going to have a rough few weeks, and not a single clue as to why.

Chapter Twenty-four

Five thousand pounds!" The young rake threw down his cards with a wild look of disbelief in his eyes. "I'm ruined!"

Julian shook his head. "Not ruined. Just dampened a bit, trust me." He left the young buck to lick his wounds and headed back toward the main salon.

Andrews's party was the sort of gala affair he'd normally have relished. All was just as it should be, and in the days since he'd returned from the wilds of Devon, London and Lady Luck had both fallen at his feet. He'd meant only to throw himself briefly into the social scene to divert attention from the "missing Miss Reynolds," but instead he had regained the golden touch that had eluded him for so long. Without precedent, he'd felt invulnerable against his peers at the card tables. He'd gambled like a man possessed in reckless game after reckless game, and he'd won vast sums that even Julian Clay, the notorious rake, had never before envisioned. His fortunes had been righted in one brilliant winning streak, and for the first time in years, he was flush with ready cash, his creditors were paid in full, and not a single solicitor had gone wanting. Even if he tried to lose, he found himself winning. But it was like a strange curse that he wasn't enjoying nearly as much as he'd thought he would.

I keep wishing I could tell Eve.

And his popularity had soared. Andrews had helped him there, fueling the rumors that added to his "heroic and slightly tragic" public persona. The stories made him a more interesting dinner guest, and his presence had instantly become a vaunted feather in every hostess's cap. His breakfast tray now overflowed with invitations to every kind of party and gathering imaginable. According to Elton's version of events, Julian had been jilted, cruelly left by the lovely Miss Reynolds to face alone the public humiliation of a man rejected. It would have been comical to him except that the consequences of her disappearance were very real and extremely personal.

"Of course, I also heard a bizarre tale that she's run off to Italy to study oil paintings and do studies of more than just bowls of fruits . . . Nudes! Can you imagine it? How delightfully entertaining of her!" Elton whispered salaciously.

Julian almost rolled his eyes. Lady Shelbrook would have been the natural source for that last one. Elton had been a little too helpful in repeating the outlandish tale as often as he could, but that he kept adding ridiculous details made Julian marvel at the man's cheekiness. Still, the confusion helped diffuse some of the whispers that once again the Earl of Westleigh was a bit too close to some unknown dangerous and scandalous circumstances and that this time, he might have learned to hide the body a little better.

Julian looked up as Lord Shelbrook and his wife entered the party. "Elton, you do love to invite an interesting collection of people."

"Hmm, what do they call that? Clairvoyance?"

"Sadism."

Lord Andrews laughed before he threw a bit of spice into the stew. "I sent an invitation to Sotherton."

"Too low, Elton."

"No worries. He sent his regrets, as his wife seems to be under the weather. I think she's harboring happy news in the way of an heir, but time will tell. Still, what an evening the Deadly Duke would have made of it. A shame he'll miss it, eh?"

"Even you should know better than to drag

Drake into all of this." Julian shook his head and caught sight of the man he'd been waiting for.

Mr. Warren Reynolds made his appearance in the doorway. His eyes grew wild when he spotted Julian with their host. He crossed the room, and Julian noted the room's general interest in his aggressive speed. *Hell, it's what they were all probably hoping for. Nothing like a delicious scandal after dinner!*

"Mr. Reynolds," Julian said as he stood with smooth grace, smiling. "A pleasure to see you again."

Warren pushed him without preamble, a bulldog squaring off against a very large and dangerous cat. "Where is she, Westleigh? What have you done with her?"

"Done? Are you mad?" Julian asked him quietly, and the room froze in fascinated silence as the scene unfolded.

"Y-you . . . have her!"

"Do I?" Julian's eyes never wavered in their glittering challenge, and Reynolds's bravado began to falter as the Earl of Westleigh lifted an eyebrow to mock the veracity of his claim.

"I have it on—good account that you do, Lord Westleigh!" He looked around the room, but no one stepped forward in support of his attack on one of their own. But Julian noted that it was dear Beatrice who Reynolds looked to, and he caught the imperceptible nod of her blond head that egged the poor man on. "He trifled with my niece! And stole her from my home! And who knows what he's done to her to avoid his responsibilities!" Warren looked back at Julian, his bluster strengthening again. "You are a cad, Lord Westleigh!"

Gasps and outraged rumblings circled the room, and Julian simply waited. A public accusation and insult ensured that this was no laughing matter, but Julian stayed focused on his endgame. All eyes were on them, wondering what he would do in response. *God, he's a bit of a buffoon . . . but one wrong step, and I could easily be on the bad end of things.*

"You're entitled to your opinion, Mr. Reynolds. But since the lady in question isn't here—"

Warren had to restrain himself from spitting on the floor in anger. "I am well within my rights to call you out, villain!"

Julian closed his eyes for a moment, then looked at Reynolds as if a new idea had just occurred to him. "I would be an odd villain to come here tonight, knowing that you were on the guest list. You could call me out if you honestly believe that I'm guilty of wronging Miss Reynolds." He tilted his head to one side, as if studying a spider on a windowpane. "I take it you have proof of my involvement in her disappearance then?"

"Not as such, but—my instincts tell me it was you. We spoke and I forbade you to pursue the relationship . . . you must have . . . although Eve was . . ." Once again his accusations faltered in the face of Julian's unruffled demeanor and the scathing looks from the party guests.

"Eve is an independent young woman, and I will confess that I admire that quality in her above all things." Julian took a deep breath. "So, I'll tell you what I'll do, Mr. Reynolds." Julian made sure he spoke clearly enough for every guest to hear him without raising his voice. "Let us set aside for one moment your own prejudices about my dreadful character, wicked past, and the myriad of reasons why I am not the best choice for your niece." He took a step closer to Reynolds. "I am, as is very well known, a gambling man. So I propose that we play a brief game, you and I. I'm willing to wager all the holdings, possessions, and accounts in my name, essentially everything I legally own and one thing I don't—your niece, Eve Reynolds—on the turn of a single card. If I lose, I lose everything but my name—which may not keep me from the streets for long."

The room held its collective breath as Mr. Reynolds's gaze narrowed, clearly enticed by this unprecedented offer. "And if I lose?"

"If I win, I win her and you agree to a dowry of twenty thousand pounds. You'll relinquish all claims to Miss Eve Reynolds and leave England on the first ship that sails."

"On the turn of a single card?" he asked in astonishment.

Julian nodded. "We'll let our host shuffle the deck, and we can draw from the top."

Julian waited, watching the turn and twists of Reynolds's thoughts as he weighed out each outcome and the potential for such an immense gain. All the holdings in the Earl of Westleigh's name against one girl who had already fled the house; it wasn't as if he had the means to retrieve her, and this would be his one chance to turn loss into victory. Julian could almost see the moment when the decision was made, the color of Warren Reynolds's eyes darkening with determination and the thrill of a good wager. "I want it in writing."

"As you wish." Julian nodded to Lord Andrews. "Draw it up, Elton, and be quick about it."

"Agreed then!" Reynolds held out his hand, and the men shook hands briefly. The flurry of excitement and buzz in the room was like a warm wave washing over the men as they moved to take over a table in the center of the salon. The wagering contract was signed, and Andrews put it away with shaking hands. Guests shifted to find a good spot from which to view the exchange, eager as they were to witness this once-in-a-lifetime gamble. One woman fainted at the tension but recovered enough to refuse to be carried off. No one was willing to leave the room.

Julian looked up, and his eyes rested briefly on Beatrice. Her color was high on her cheeks, and her eyes shone with malevolent interest in the proceedings. *There's a woman who's not going to offer to kiss me for luck.*

Andrews shuffled the cards and placed them facedown in the center. The silence was renewed as the men stood on opposite sides of the table. "Y-you're sure about this, Lord Westleigh?"

"Never more so, Elton." Julian gave Reynolds a dazzling smile, as if they'd been sharing port and a cigar and not about to decide who would be ruined with the draw of a single card. "Mr. Reynolds, you may go first."

The older man's hands shook as he reached for the card on the top of the deck and laid it down for all to see. His look was pure triumph. The queen of spades winked up at them and the room rippled in reaction.

Julian reached out and touched the top card, letting his fingers linger there as if resolving himself to his fate.

Courage, Lamb.

It was the king of hearts.

The roar of approval was deafening. Cheers went round spontaneously, and a few ladies fainted in earnest. Under the cover of the noise and commotion, Julian leaned forward and said, "You are a fraud and a cheat, Mr. Reynolds, and I encourage you to leave London as quickly as your horse can manage it. Keep the money and consider it a parting gift from me and from your niece. You're a lucky man, Mr. Warren Reynolds."

Warren's look was pure confusion. "Twenty thousand pounds? You're not going to collect it?"

"No," Julian said as he stood from the table. Warren reached across to catch his arm.

"But that's a fortune! I don't understand. You won and yet you're going to just give me that kind of money?"

Julian had to swallow hard to get rid of the lump in his throat before he could answer. "My God, you're a small man, Reynolds. You just bet your niece and lost her to the likes of me, and all you can think about is a stupid pile of notes." He shook his head. "I never understood her urgency to escape you—not really. But I see it now. You never appreciated how incredible she is and how singular a spirit she has, and I'll be damned if you ever get close enough to her again to find out."

"You—you can't keep a man from his only dear niece!" Reynolds protested.

"Can't I?" Julian held his ground. "You have nothing she needs."

"But I have something she wants!" Reynolds stepped closer, his voice quietly laced with desperation. "Letters!"

Julian rolled his eyes. "Thank you for reminding me, Mr. Reynolds. I'd almost forgotten Miss Kingsley and those letters to Eve in your desk. See that you send the bundle to me before you go, or I'm afraid I'm going to renege on my offer of that twenty thousand pounds."

"Y-you wouldn't!" Reynolds's eyes widened as he finally realized what Julian had confessed. "But how? My desk—"

"Elton, would you kindly see that Mr. Reynolds is shown out?"

Lord Andrews made a quick signal to the footmen, and poor Warren Reynolds, the renowned industrialist, was tumbled to the floor by several men when he began to struggle and kick like a wild animal, howling with fury and frustration at the arms that held him to the floor.

Julian shook his head in amusement as the commotion finally died down, then realized the guests were frozen into a strange tableau. He surveyed the room anxiously. "Is everyone all right?"

Lord Andrews shook his head. "Oh, dear! I'm afraid my Marie's favorite portrait of her pug has taken a bit of a tumble during the altercation." Then he winked and added quietly, "No great loss! I shall send the man a thank-you note."

Julian bowed and tried to withdraw—if only to consider his next step and how exactly he could excuse himself to go "claim his prize." Andrews touched his arm and handed over the contract. "Just tell me this, old friend. Why would you enter such a mad wager? If you'd lost, was she truly worth everything you own?"

Julian smiled, unwilling to give Elton the satisfaction. "We'll see. Apparently, I have some letters to deliver."

"Not in Italy?" Lady Shelbrook asked from behind them, her tone hollow with shock. She stepped forward and clutched at Julian's arm, her color gone. "She's not in Italy?"

Andrews shrugged. "So much for that rumor. I cannot imagine what dolt helped that one along."

Her eyes searched Julian's, frantic and furious beyond reason. "No?"

"Beatrice, please. If for no other reason than I love this girl, just let it go and—" He held his breath, suddenly aware that Beatrice had lost her hold on self-control. Here was a battle he'd have preferred to avoid in public. There was nothing he could do to stop her from speaking, and he steeled himself for the worst.

"My brooch! Eve Reynolds is a thief! Someone call the authorities immediately! That little *slut* stole my great-grandmother's diamond brooch, and I want her charged with it! You'll find it on her! She has it! That whore has it and I won't stand by while you—"

"Beatrice—" Julian began.

"No! It's priceless and that whore pilfered it! Lord Westleigh, I demand you to tell them where she is and—"

"Beatrice!" He raised his voice and the room took yet another shaky, albeit collective, breath in anticipation as the curtain went up on a new surprise fourth act in the evening's entertainment. "She doesn't have your brooch. I'm afraid you left it in my room when you came for me that night."

Her eyes widened with horror as she realized what he was saying.

Julian went on relentlessly. "I found you in my room, remember? You were in my bed, waiting for me. And when I ordered you to leave, you neglected to retrieve it along with your clothes and other items."

"I . . . oh!" She was frozen and helpless, and Julian felt no pity for her as he continued with the coup de grâce. "I put it at the back of the drawer in the nightstand by the bed for safekeeping, and I regret I forgot to mention it to you when I left the very next morning."

"Y-you're lying!" Her protest was weak and far too late to make a difference. Every eye was on her as Barnaby came to her elbow.

The men looked at each other, and an unspoken understanding passed between them. *He'll punish her by not defending her, letting everyone know that she isn't worth a fight. And since the brooch is exactly where I said it is, he knows it's over for his lovely harpy. Her talons will never be as sharp, and Barnaby knows it, too.*

Lord Shelbrook took her arm. "Come, my dear. Let's go home and get your bauble."

"No, no, no." She whispered her denials over and over in heartbroken humiliation, the murmurs and comments in her wake breaking against her like waves on the shore—relentless and powerful. Lady Shelbrook sagged against her husband, a pitiful caricature of an aristocratic woman of a certain age who preyed on handsome guests in her home and seemed to have lost her way.

Julian shook his head. It wasn't fair, but once she'd proclaimed Eve a thief and a whore, he'd hardly cared anymore about what might have been fair. *All is fair in love and war. I'd never have betrayed you, Beatrice, but I had a feeling you wouldn't look at it the same way. It's one of the reasons I made a point of racing back to London—to make sure I got back into my bedroom to return that hideous brooch.*

"My God, Julian! You are the best house guest I have ever had!" Elton put a hand on his shoulder. "You are welcome at my home any time."

"I'd say I've given you enough stories and excitement in trade to last a lifetime, Elton."

"Oh, I hope not. If you've settled down and turned into some lovesick bull, I shall be heartily disappointed, Lord Westleigh."

"Sadly, you are not the person I am concerned about disappointing, old friend. Good night."

Julian left quickly, a new urgency surging through him. He ignored the guests who stared at his retreat, oblivious to their whispers.

It's late, but if I hurry and manage not to run over anything too deadly, I could be there tomorrow morning—and then we'll see if this gamble has paid off.

Chapter Twenty-five

Eve in the garden!" She turned with a laugh at the sound of his voice, her heart skipping a beat at the thrill of seeing him coming toward her through the arch the willows formed. "The only question is, am I Adam in this scenario—or the snake?"

"You are very tempting, in either regard." Eve forced herself not to skip like a child, determined to hold herself in check just in case he'd come to pay his final compliments or request a true percentage. "Though to hear Mrs. Connor tell the tale, you are neither!"

"And who would dear Mrs. Connor have you think I am?" Dappled sunlight made him look like a golden lion slipping through the trees.

"Apparently you are frozen in time, a sweet, if

mischievous, boy of approximately eleven years of age. I'm sure she's seen you in long pants, Lord Westleigh, but I won't be surprised if she's making a tray of sugared biscuits and cakes for you even now."

He smiled, drawing closer to lessen the gap between them. "I wouldn't wager against it." He stopped a few feet from her, a polite distance that made her wonder what he was up to.

"You left without . . . I wasn't sure if you were planning on returning, Julian."

"Sorry about that," he offered soberly. "I wasn't sure myself. There was business in London I had to finish, and I didn't know how long it would take." He drew closer, his expression difficult to read. "So, do you like the garden and the house? I know you spoke of a forest, but I seem to recall a fair number of trees on the property."

"I love it. It would be impossible not to, but it's too much, Julian. I cannot accept it. It's nothing less than a country estate! You said it was a smallish cottage. I imagined something with a thatched, leaking roof and dirt floors."

"I think the dining room is prone to leaks in the spring."

"That's not what I meant, and you are deliberately trying to distract me."

"There's a potting shed around behind the greenhouse, if you'd prefer." He sighed dramatically, as if extremely put out by her words. "Really, Eve, if you'd really wanted one of those, I wish you'd been more firm about it when we spoke last. I'd have saved myself a lot of hard riding. Hell, I think there was a damp storeroom behind the Bell Street house I could have let from Lord Shelbrook for mere shillings."

She tried not to laugh and approached him to playfully push against his chest, but he caught her hand to hold it against the steady thrum of his heartbeat. "You know what I meant, Julian. I can't take all this in exchange for a few worthless beads and ribbon."

"Oh." He smiled. "Well, it's a good thing, since I'm returning your personal jewelry. I took them to London with me to have them reset and repaired. They seemed to be your favorites, and I couldn't resist. So I'll just pick a different jewel or two then, all right?"

"If you took every jewel and trinket I have, it wouldn't be a fair trade for . . . this."

"And what would be a fair trade?"

"I'm not . . ." Eve held very still, unsure of the value of dreams. "I don't think I have enough to—"

"Shall I set a price then?" His fingers covered hers, then he reached out to sweep back a stray curl that threatened to fall into her eyes. "What if . . ." His fingers traced the curve of her cheek as he spoke. "What if you loved me? What if you adored every troublesome habit and announced that you couldn't live without my wicked wit and charms?"

"I . . . I do. I—"

He cut off her declaration by ruthlessly stepping back. "No! Wait, Eve. This is no light supposition. I shouldn't have—you wouldn't know what you are saying. You would be professing to love a monster. I don't think there is a tale amidst the Ton that isn't horribly flawed and wrong when it comes to my character. Perhaps they have a hint of my past taste for corrupting other men's wives, but I imagine it would be just a hint of the truth."

"There may have been . . . whispers," she conceded quietly.

"If you doubt them, you can always ask the Duke of Sussex about his first wife, Lily. You can ask Drake Sotherton what sort of man I was, what I was capable of once. Even if I repented it a thousand times, I'm not sure I deserve to be forgiven anymore for my part in Lily's tragic end."

"I don't care."

"Do you not? Where others stumble in scandal and rumor, I've played that game like no other, with remarkable success and ease. I've slipped in and out of bedrooms I had no right to trespass in and never given a whit for the consequences. Worse, if I could take vengeance by bedding the wife of a man who'd bested me at cards or dared to think himself above me, I never hesitated. I don't even know how much ruin I've left in my path because I never bothered to look back." He took a deep breath. "What kind of man does such things?"

"I don't know. Perhaps it's a man who couldn't see how to lose gracefully because he was afraid he'd already lost too much—of himself?"

"A graceful loser . . . that I have never been," he agreed. "I am a better gambler than I am a man."

"I disagree, Julian. And"—she stepped toward him, framing his face with her long, cool fingers—"once you've apologized for interrupting a lady during her most ardent declarations, I'm fairly sure we can settle this between us."

"Do you . . . love me, Eve?"

"Yes." She ignored the flush of heat in her cheeks and held his gaze. "I love you and every troublesome habit. But I still cannot take this house. Not for— I would love you no matter what, Julian Clay, but I think house keys in exchange for declarations are going to muddy the waters."

Silence spun out between them, and she thought he might argue—as if she couldn't love him without a ridiculous bribe or two. But then something in his gaze flared and shifted from defiance to the sweet fire of pure victory and relief.

When he dropped to one knee before her, she was sure that the world had suddenly decided to turn in a completely new direction. "Julian!" she sputtered.

"What if you married me, Eve Reynolds? And before you say yes, consider it carefully. Consider the terrible price I'm imposing for this smallish cottage and ramshackle garden." He held out his arms, as if to prove he was unarmed and at her mercy. "My past aside, you'll be agreeing to put up with me for all the days to come—and as you may have surmised, I might be imperfect."

"Might be?" She couldn't resist teasing him.

He shrugged, then took her hands into his. "Hush, woman! You're spoiling my romantic gesture."

"Go on then."

His eyes darkened as he sobered a little and stood to face her. "I mean it, Eve. I find myself wretchedly addicted to you and unable to think of much else. You have clearly ruined me for life when it comes to other women. But beyond fidelity, what else can I offer you? Not sobriety, economy, or any virtue that men are encouraged to embrace like monks these days. I am not going to reform."

He released her hands and turned his back on her as he continued. "As I've already told you, I am a terrible person by most measurements. I'm impulsive and reckless. I enjoy gambling for the sheer thrill of it, and I can't remember regretting many of the mistakes I've made." He paced a bit, then faced her squarely. "I like a good cigar, a good spirit in my glass and a good hand of cards. And I don't see that changing—ever!"

"As you say."

"I suppose it's possible—I may want to alter my behavior someday. But I cannot promise it with any honesty. I am a man of my word. But that's not much to build on. An honest despot is not anyone's ideal husband, Eve." He crossed his arms defensively. "Well?"

"You're not just asking me to marry you in order to shock Lady Morrington or infuriate my uncle, are you?"

"Lady Morrington is the least of my worries. I think she's already decided our match is the ultimate feather in her bonnet, and as for your uncle, he can hardly protest, since I've already publicly won you."

"Pardon? I'm 'publicly won'?"

"A quick wager at Lord Andrews's party. Your uncle lost a bet and agreed to give you over to me—with a small dowry."

She shook her head in astonishment. "And . . . what did *you* wager that he would risk such a thing?"

"That I would relinquish you, naturally, to him."

"You can't wager another human being, Julian. I can't believe the bet was so simple." She crossed her arms. "What else was there?"

"If he won, there was a minor matter of giving him all the property in my name. But no fear, your smallish cottage was already deeded over, so I knew you would never have had the man as a landlord."

"Y-you . . ." She felt as if all the air had vanished from the garden, and an odd, dreamlike wash came over her. Julian led her gently over to a nearby bench, and she sat down, grateful for the support. "*All* the property in your name?"

"I'd still have had a title." He shrugged. "I'm sure someone would have offered me a warm bed to sleep in."

"Oh, my goodness!" She put a hand to her chest, still trying to absorb his cavalier words and fathom the risk he'd taken. "And you won?"

"Of course I won. And he won't be bothering you ever again—even if you deny my petition to wed." Julian turned her palm over to trace the lines there, a whisper-light touch that soothed and grounded her. "It is what they call a win-win for you, I think."

"A win-win . . ." She took a deep breath. "And are you sure you now desire a warden?"

"It was stupid of me to think that loving someone meant I would be . . . imprisoned."

"No. I love you, Julian. And I would always wish you to be free . . . to let you go if even that would make you happier."

"And if I never wish to be without you? If the only freedom I wish is to please you and worship every inch of you for the rest of my life?"

"Then"—she tilted her head to one side, a devilish smile lighting up her features—"please me, Julian."

He pulled her into his arms, sealing the contract between them for all time with a kiss that left no room for games. Eve felt as if every bone in her body had melted away, and she clung to him, unwilling to relinquish the fiery contact of his mouth to hers. But then her thoughts wouldn't stop churning, and the reality of all he'd risked hit her again. She pushed away from him with a smile. "I cannot believe you wagered everything you owned!" Another idea came to her. "Did you really? Or are you simply having me on, Lord Westleigh?"

"No, and there were witnesses to keep us both honest, as well as a scrap of paper with signatures! You may ask Lord Andrews for an account, and I'm sure he'll glory in recounting the entire dramatic event that led to your independence and Mr. Warren Reynolds's public humiliation."

"You've lost your senses, Julian."

"Perhaps, but that's no excuse not to marry me, Eve." He lifted her fingers to kiss and suckle on each tip, teasing her until she was breathless. "Tell me, my beloved fiancée, did you happen to look at the paperwork I left you?"

"Not really. I confess I just tucked them away in my vanity drawer for safekeeping." She gasped as his teeth grazed the tender flesh on the inside of her fingers. "Why?"

"You should study them more closely one day. Reading legal documents is never very exciting, but I won't have you later accusing me of not admitting to the truth of what happened when I took that wager with your uncle."

"I don't understand."

"I took the liberty of deeding all my property to you, and so there was technically nothing in my name to lose when I gambled with your uncle. I knew that you were safe, and I'd decided that I would rather risk everything with you than your villain of an uncle. But now that you've agreed to marry me, wretch that I am, it's all worked out for the best."

"When? When did you do all this?" Eve's mind reeled with this news. There'd hardly been time to pack a bag after she'd told him about her dreams and before Lady Shelbrook had sent her running.

"I must have initiated things after that afternoon at Madame Dellacourt's. It seemed like a heroic gesture, a way to give you the upper hand over your uncle without too much fuss—and hell, I was in danger of losing it all anyway. Why not hand it over to someone I knew would appreciate it? And I did hope you would say yes to a match at some point in time."

"And how did you know that I would? Why wouldn't you think I'd take this fortune and send you packing, Julian?"

"Because I trust you, Eve. I always have . . . and as you said, you would never cheat me. Not at cards, and certainly not out of the happiness I think we'll have, you and I. Am I correct?"

"You are impossible!"

"But more important, I did it because I wanted you to trust me." He took her hand. "Do you trust me, Eve? With your life, and your heart?"

"I do. But you realize that you're insane?"

"I am that, and ridiculously rich at the moment after another lovely run of luck while I was waiting for your uncle to make his scene. So no accusations of fortune hunting on either side, see? A win-win." He held out the bundle of letters he'd retrieved before leaving London. "And these are for you, my love."

She recognized the handwriting instantly. "Jane! How?"

"There, you see? Burglary does have its uses." His look was pure mischief, and astonishment turned to pure joy as Eve realized that her beloved was sure to be a rogue to the very end of his days.

Declare your tricks!"

It was a dreary, rainy morning, and a fire in the grate gave the room a warm glow as the Earl of Westleigh and his bride were still abed. With sheets pooled around their waists, jewels and trinkets strewn everywhere between them to shine in the lamplight, they were decadently indulging in a naked game of piquet.

"Carte blanche!" He cavalierly threw down a diamond necklace and a long rope of pearls to sweeten the wager.

"You're cheating! You cannot possibly have carte blanche!"

"Can't I?"

"No, Julian. I'm looking at my cards, and I'm afraid it's impossible."

"Impossible?" He attempted to look contrite. "May I see them to make sure?"

"You cad! No, you cannot see my cards! It is a terrible ploy on your part, and if you're not careful, I shall take all your jewels in forfeit."

"Well, that doesn't seem right. I am accused of cheating, and when I try to gather the facts that I need to defend myself, I am forced to forfeit." He licked his lips. "You are a master at work, Lady Westleigh."

A ripple of desire at the sight of his tongue across his lips made her gasp. He was incorrigible, and she loved him for it. "If I am, then how is it that I cannot master you?"

"Do you want to?" He dropped his cards onto the bed and leaned forward, his golden eyes locked onto hers as he drew closer and closer. "Do you?"

She shook her head, her reply a whisper against the warmth of his lips. "Never."

"Then how is it I seem to be so completely enslaved?"

"Are you?" she asked, a note of awe creeping into her voice. "Whatever will I do with such a handsome man to do my bidding?"

His hands swept down over her breasts, lifting them slightly, the weight of them heavy against his palms as they swelled with his touch. Her nipples hardened, and he lightly teased each one with a kiss before he looked up. "If you command me to stop,

I'll spank you until that delectable bottom of yours is bright red."

She threw her head back, arching to give him better access to each sensitive peak. "That wasn't the command that came to mind, Julian."

"Thank goodness." He began to move his hands, the soft drag of his fingers against her skin sending arcs of sizzling white heat down her body to pool between her hips.

"Julian," she murmured as she gently pushed against him. "I just remembered something!"

"Unless it's how much you wish I'd hurry . . ."

"Julian, I . . . I swore I would never play cards again after I escaped my uncle."

He stopped what he was doing, and she braced herself a little for him to mock the irrational turns of his bride's mind. Instead, his expression sobered, and he shifted to pull her gently onto his lap. "Truly?"

She nodded.

"But it's not as if you are gambling in earnest, Lamb. After all, the jewels will go back into your little bag when we finish. It's hardly a risk."

"I know. It's just I'm . . . so happy with you, and all my dreams came true, Julian. What if I'm tempting fate or something?"

He rocked her in his arms for a minute as he contemplated the challenge of oaths and the contrary whims of Lady Luck. "No cards?"

"No cards."

Another few moments of silence passed, until her handsome husband began to smile, a sinful grin that melted away the last of her superstitious fears.

"Julian," she asked softly, "what are you thinking?"

"I'm thinking"—his golden eyes flashed—"that I have dice in a coat pocket somewhere."

She tilted her head to one side, sure that no woman had ever been happier.

"All or nothing then?" she offered, deliberately looking at him through her lashes in a way guaranteed to please him.

He laughed and laughed, and Eve joined him, reveling in her husband's wickedness and the sweet gift of a game she would play for the rest of her life—and never lose.

Acknowledgments

I have so many people to thank that I'm sure I'm in trouble. I just can't imagine life without my fabulous editor, Maggie Crawford, and for her efforts to keep me on track, I'm beyond grateful. And I want to thank my agent, Meredith Bernstein, for all her support and guidance. I aspire to have that woman's energy one day.

I don't think "thank you" covers it, Laura and Janet. With a toddler on my hands, you intervened and let me do what I needed to do, and kept the Elf smiling so that I could avoid "mom guilt" for spending all my time with my computer recently.

I want to thank Lee Jackson. What a treasure trove of Victorian expertise . . . like a guardian angel, the man has saved me more than once! Also, a special thanks to Laurel Letherby at Mystic

Castle for making my website look fantastic and for putting up with my anti-technology issues. (It's not that I don't love technology, friends. It's just that it apparently doesn't return the sentiment and has decided to "get me" whenever it can.)

To all my writer friends who put up with me . . . I owe you more than thanks.

And finally, to all of the readers who have sent gracious notes and emails, it astonishes me every time. Thank you for picking up the stories and for being so kind.

Madame's Deception

RENEE BERNARD

Turn the page to read an excerpt from Renee Bernard's dazzlingly daring and sensual earlier novel in her Mistress trilogy. . . .

Welcome, sir." The butler opened the carved doors to the fashionably situated house on the edge of an upper-class neighborhood in London. The discreet appearance of the Crimson Belle contributed to its success, and the tolerance of her neighbors was a credit to the Belle's management and craft. He knew of a few similar houses, but none had the Belle's reputation for elegance.

The last time he had crossed the threshold, the hour had been unfashionably early. Alex had never seen the house lit and fully occupied. At the time, he'd been at leisure to note the artwork and admire the owner's tastes. Now there was a great deal more to catch a man's eye.

Brightly lit candelabras added to the ambience, though only to augment the beautiful gaslit fixtures throughout the rooms. The foyer was warm and welcoming, and a uniformed attendant was instantly at his elbow to take his coat and hat. "Is the gentleman expected, or shall I make arrangements?"

"I have come impulsively without an appointment." He heard music and muffled male laughter coming from one of the adjoining rooms, and questioned the wisdom of his decision. "And would prefer to avoid . . ."

"Of course, sir." The man instantly ushered him into a smaller salon off the foyer, unoccupied and separated from the livelier part of the house. "This room is entirely private, m'lord. You wish to make an arrangement for the evening?"

"I wish to see Madame DeBourcier."

The man's expression became more guarded. "Madame DeBourcier does not receive guests this evening. Is there something else we can do for you? Several of the ladies are available, if you care to—"

"No," Alex cut him off, unwilling to hear him recite some kind of illicit menu. "If she isn't available this evening, then I will make arrangements to come another time."

"If you'll excuse me, sir." The man made a brief bow and exited the room, leaving Alex to wonder if he'd just met with success or failure. The answer wasn't long in coming. He recognized Madame DeBourcier's manservant in the doorway and ignored the surge of resentment at the sight of him. In all his privileged life, Ramis was the only one who had ever "shown him the back door."

Ramis bowed respectfully before greeting him. "You have returned, sir."

"Yes. I wish to speak directly to Madame DeBourcier."

"Madame DeBourcier is not receiving guests this evening."

Alex took one deep breath to try to calm his fury. "She would prefer another evening?"

"No offense is meant, but I think not, sir. The house is not closed to you, but Madame DeBourcier is not receiving guests. It is rare for her to do so and I have my instructions." If the man's tone was apologetic, his expression was implacable.

He has his instructions? What the hell does that mean?

"No offense is taken." He reached inside his waistcoat pocket for his card. "If you will be so kind as to give her my card. Ask her again if she'll make an exception. I will wait."

Ramis eyed the card before accepting it reluctantly. "As you wish."

He nodded, confidently waiting until the man bowed and left to deliver the card as ordered. *At least I'll exit through the front door this time if the woman sends me packing.*

He certainly had no intention of allowing history to repeat itself, but he accepted that if he pointed out to her manservant that there were any number of respectable establishments that would be glad of his card, his coin, and his company, his chance at an interview with the elusive mistress of the house would undoubtedly evaporate.

No woman is worth this aggravation.

Begging for a damn conversation with a reclusive Madame wasn't a likely method for satisfaction, he told himself.

Of course, if a man was honest with himself, Alex conceded, it would take more than a conversation to relieve the heat that coursed through his body. Since that morning when he'd chased her ghost, he'd composed a hundred speeches to reintroduce himself to the beautiful vixen of the Belle. The hours of waiting had put his nerves on edge and fueled an unmistakable desire for more than Madame DeBourcier's witty repartee. There was no logic to it, and for a man of reason, the irrational pull of memory was difficult to accept.

He turned away from the window, the wait grinding against his nerves.

"He sends his card," Ramis noted as he extended the object in question toward her. "And insists on waiting below for your response."

"I see." Jocelyn accepted the thick ivory card and carefully considered the elegant script. "And I honestly thought never to see him again."

Lord Colwick, the Hon. Alex Randall.

She hadn't known his name until this moment. It had been months and somehow she'd never forgotten him. Her first thought when she'd seen him had been that she'd somehow magically conjured up the man from her schoolroom daydreams of romance and first dances and heady courtship. He'd stood in her house, a striking man in elegant clothes, tall with broad shoulders and an impossibly handsome face and figure—lithe and athletic but not menacing. She'd guessed at his good breeding, but was more impressed by his lack of arrogance—at least at first. His hair had been unfashionably wild with dusky caramel curls and she remembered how warm his brown eyes had looked, blazing with sincere concern and curiosity. He'd come seeking information, no doubt with a bribe tucked into one of his well-tailored pockets, and Jocelyn remembered the telling moment when her handsome visitor had hesitated to give his name. She'd refused to help him and had angered him beyond measure after she'd signaled Ramis to show him the back door. Since then, he had featured in countless daydreams of opportunities lost and sensuous interludes found.

And now he'd left his card and was insisting on an appointment.

Why? Perhaps he has another question I won't be able to answer.

Ramis cleared his throat. "He will be turned away."

"No." Jocelyn tucked the card into a deep pocket in her skirts. "I'll see him."

"But . . ." His protest trailed away. "As you wish."

An odd flutter of nerves made her smile. "I wish it. Now stop worrying and please make sure that the Sauterne is chilled properly for Mr. Everton and remind Moira to keep her feet bare. The gentleman wishes to see her toes."

"I will do so and then return to ensure that this man does not—"

"No!" Jocelyn cut him off, surprising them both. "I do not need a chaperone, Ramis. Not tonight."

He touched his forehead briefly and bowed before leaving to carry out her orders.

She retrieved the card to study it again. Ramis was being protective in his role as the head of security and her trusted adviser. Her sudden decision to alter her own habits was hard to explain. After all, she'd been reclusive originally to hide her age and inexperience. Then, in an attempt to scare away clientele, Marsh had spread rumors of her being a diseased and disfigured hag, and in doing so he inadvertently gave her a great gift. Jocelyn had decided to play along, turning the tales to her advantage. Few guests had ever seen her face, though they enjoyed the rare conversation with a masked, elegant hostess. The mystery served its own purposes. It added to the allure of the Belle and gave her an interesting vantage point from which to manage her business. Rather than getting tangled in petty politics, she gave her edicts from the shadows—that way they carried more weight and met with little resistance.

Besides, the Belle's wealthy clients respected a desire for anonymity.

But months ago she'd met with Lord Colwick face-to-face on a whim. She'd been in another odd mood to break her own rules that day.

Like the mood I'm in now.

The ghost of an idea coalesced, and her fingers trembled as she made her way to her desk. Marsh's threats and news of murder had unsettled her, but somehow a simple vellum card offered calm.

This is foolish. It's just a calling card and he is just a man.

Jocelyn sat carefully at her vanity to ensure she'd not wilted entirely from the long day. She smoothed a long red curl that had escaped the loose twist atop her head. She quickly selected a carved ebony hair comb to secure what she could and to accent the riot of gleaming copper tendrils. Jocelyn added a small touch of rouge to her lips, a defiant and mischievous light coming into her eyes. She'd had a taste in their last meeting of his sensibilities. With a flourish, she pinched her cheeks and decided she'd better change her clothes and head downstairs before she changed her mind and the impulse evaporated. "Let us see what you're up to this time, my lord."

* * *

Alex refused to look at his pocket watch to count the minutes he'd been left to cool his heels. He'd studied every object and evaluated the art, and his mood had hardly improved. Alex began to consider that the only thing worse than being refused an appointment with the elusive Madame DeBourcier was having to wait for that refusal.

"To hell with this!" he muttered, only to hear the door open. He turned, expecting Ramis to haunt him like a dark demon, but instead an angel in peacock hues breezed in to steal his composure.

She was just as he remembered, but even more impossibly lovely. Patrician features were softened by a mischievous smile, and her jade-green eyes sparkled as if she were receiving an old friend or welcome acquaintance. His anger evaporated and his heartbeat increased as he took in more of her appearance. Over an iris-colored dress, she'd draped an Oriental embroidered shawl with green beads that shimmered in the lamplight across her ivory shoulders. Petite in stature, her figure was lush and balanced, the sight of her narrow waist making his hands itch to span it and draw her close. Her hair was an artful tangle of curls secured by an ornate comb of black lacquer, and he marveled again at the color of molten copper that beckoned a man's touch. There was simply nothing understated or muted about Madame DeBourcier.

"I'm sorry to have kept you waiting, Lord Colwick," she said, offering her hand.

He bent over her fingers, his breath alone grazing her warm fingertips to savor the connection between them. "I understood it was a woman's prerogative to make a man wait." He straightened, unconsciously keeping a soft hold on her hand.

"Nonsense!" She laughed. "It's rude no matter what a person's gender, and judging from your expression when I came in, you had quite a lecture composed and ready, sir."

"Perhaps just a line or two," he conceded. Her humor made it impossible for a man to keep his balance, and Alex began to experience the same delicious sense of play that he recalled from his last encounter with her and that had kept her so fresh in his mind.

"Lord Colwick?"

"Yes."

"As a hostess, I would normally offer you a drink"—she lowered her voice as if they were friendly conspirators—"but I'm afraid I'll need my hand back."

"Of course." He released her fingers, wondering at his own lapse.

"Come, sit!" She gestured toward the settee he'd been circling earlier, taking a place near a side tray. "Something to drink, then?"

He took the seat she'd offered, nodding. "Whatever you are having."

With graceful hands, she poured them each a small glass of tawny port before settling in. She tucked her feet up into her skirts and faced him like an exotic house cat content on silk cushions. "I rarely meet visitors, sir. But for some unknown reason, here we are again."

"I'm glad you've made an exception for me, Madame."

"Did you wish me to guess again why you've come to the Belle?"

"You've a talent for it, Madame DeBourcier." God's truth, he recalled she had an uncanny talent for it.

She straightened, alert for the game. She took a moment to study him, an open assessment that did nothing to slow his heart rate. Alex couldn't recall the last time he'd volunteered for a woman's scrutiny, but with the lovely young Madame it was an experience he had no desire to forgo. She completely bemused him as she even went so far as to lean over to carefully note his shoes before sitting back to begin her queries. "Well, if you've come to do battle again, it's clear you're trying a new strategy. You've certainly come at a different hour this time, though Ramis advises me that you discreetly used a hired coach, so you aren't entirely comfortable with your own coachman knowing your destination."

He nodded, conceding the point reluctantly.

"It seems you haven't come for a simple evening's entertainment," she continued. "Or you'd have accepted any number of the ladies' company when offered. I assume it was offered?"

"It was." He took a sip of the port, beginning to enjoy the game.

"Instead you asked for me." She shifted slightly, pausing to enjoy a taste of the amber liquid before going on. "And gave your card, probably to make up for being so difficult on your last visit."

"I wasn't difficult. I was unprepared."

"There's a difference?" she asked him playfully.

"Absolutely."

She shrugged, merrily dismissing the past. "You asked for me, and since you are not a client and have not accepted an offer to become a guest of one of the ladies . . ."

He held his breath.

"It's a puzzle, my lord." She set her glass down, then smoothed out her skirts to retuck them around her feet. "Perhaps you wished to speak to me before making a request for the Belle's services because you have a unique need that you aren't sure we can satisfy. Something you feel is forbidden or unspeakable?"

He sat up abruptly, unable to hide his dismay at this unanticipated turn in her thoughts. "No! I can assure you that my needs are not unique."

She smiled apologetically. "I meant no offense. I admit there are tastes we do not serve. Younger girls, for example. Or boys, for that matter. I would have to direct you elsewhere."

"Damn it, I didn't come here to ask for—"

"Of course not." She waved away the notion,

apparently unruffled at the prospect. "And since you're not here for the business of this house, I'm left with only one conclusion."

"And that would be?"

"You're on another mission."

He let her guess linger, beginning to question his own sanity. How does a man come to this place without any logical cause and expect to apply reason? She sat there, an irresistibly pert siren challenging him with each glance, and Alex considered that no man should fight every temptation placed in his path. "In a way, yes."

"You'll simply have to confess then, sir."

"I wanted to see you again." Alex took a deep breath, determined to navigate the next few moments without losing any ground.

Her expression conveyed surprise. "To see me again? Your mission was to see me again?"

"Why does that shock you?"

She recovered her glass from the tray and he recognized it for the defensive gesture it was. His curiosity was aroused as he realized the lovely young Madame DeBourcier was actually nervous in his presence.

"It seems an odd mission . . . after all this time."

He nodded. "Perhaps. But time did nothing to diminish your memory and I could wait no longer."

"I wasn't aware that I'd made an impression on you, Lord Colwick." The color on her cheeks heightened by another delicate shade. "At least, not a favorable one that you'd wish to sample again."

"Not at all," he countered. "I fear I was the one who made an unfavorable impression, remember?"

"Did you come to apologize?" She shook her head. "You needn't have troubled yourself. I understood you were under a good deal of stress and worried about your friend. I've harbored no ill will."

"Your manservant has a different view, I suspect."

"Ramis is protective and slower to forgive." She smiled, and Alex's breath caught in his throat at the sweet beauty of it and the small jolt of jealousy he felt as she spoke fondly of another man.

"Madame," he began again. "I have no gift for intrigue and, as my friends are fond of telling me, no talent at all for deception. Not that the art of flirtation necessarily involves either one—"

"Not always!" she chimed in merrily. "Pardon the interruption, Lord Colwick. Do go on."

"So," he continued calmly. "I thought you would respect a more direct approach."

"A direct approach to . . . ?" The question trailed off, and one slippered foot peeked out from beneath her skirts as she shifted forward.

"I want my own decadent Season."

"P-pardon?" It was a breathless whisper, and Alex suddenly didn't care how much aggravation or how many challenges this woman presented. He would have her. She was everything he shouldn't desire, but there was nothing he wanted more.

"You helped a particular friend of mine to enjoy a single decadent Season. And I don't see why you couldn't help me as well."

"You . . . came for lessons?" Her confusion was transparent, and both feet now emerged as she moved to find her footing. "I generally only counsel women on the art of seduction. Perhaps another tutor would suit you better."

"I am not here for lessons, Madame." He took another sip of the port, savoring the flavor before he went on. "I am normally not a man who . . . looks beyond his circle and I don't have a reputation for reckless indulgences. In fact, I have a decidedly stern reputation for following the rules of polite society. But since I met you, I can't seem to stop wishing that things were otherwise."

She held her place and Alex decided it was all the encouragement he could expect at this point.

"I have always put duty and responsibility first, and it occurs to me that there hasn't been much time for pleasure. Or more precisely, that I haven't made much time. I've decided to remedy that mistake."

She shook her head slowly. "There is nothing to stop you, Lord Colwick."

"I'm glad you think so." He let out one slow breath, savoring the moment before he continued. "And that brings us back to the matter at hand."

She smoothed her skirts. "And how is it exactly that I can assist you?"

"I want you."

"Oh, my!" She held still for a moment before replying. "I'm flattered, sir, but I'm sure I've made it clear that—"

"You do not take appointments, yes, it was made clear, Madame." Alex studied her over the rim of his glass, appreciating each curve and line that comprised her beauty. "I'm not asking for an appointment."

"As you say, but . . ." Her argument seemed to falter and fade before she gave voice to it as her eyes met his. "What are you asking?"

"You are the object of my desire and I wish to spend time with you while I'm in London."

"How much time?"

"Time enough to discover why you have haunted my thoughts these past few months." He stood, determined to end the negotiation. "I will naturally expect to pay for the privilege."

She stood as well, her hands at her hips, her eyes bright with anger. "And do you *naturally* just expect me to agree to this?"

She took a ragged breath and he knew she was about to vent pure fire to ward off his bold request. But this was no wide-eyed innocent debutante, and Alex's temper flared to match hers. Before she could speak, frustration and desire pushed him into action.